I0654943

The Emerald

by Bob Nailor

Book One in the Shiyula Realm series

Dedicated to my writer friends, especially
Dave Kish and Garry Ward who gave me
Insight, Perspective, and Inspiration.
A special thanks to Joette Rozanski who
read and suffered through the original.

Book cover by Sheri McGathy and Bob Nailor
Visit Sheri: http://coverdesign.sherimcgathy.com

This page left blank.

© Copyright 2019 Bob Nailor

ISBN: 978-1-61877-168-1

The Emerald

All rights reserved. No part of this book may be reproduced in any form or by any means: electronic, mechanical or otherwise, now known or hereinafter invented, including xerography, photocopying and recording, or by any known informational storage and retrieval system, is forbidden without the written permission from the author.

Discover other titles by Bob Nailor at

www.bobnailor.com

This novel is a work of fiction. Names, characters, places and events are either the product of the author's imagination or are used fictitiously, and any resemblance to actual persons, living or dead, events or locales is entirely coincidental.

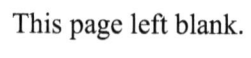
This page left blank.

Table of Contents

This page left blank.

CHAPTER ONE
The Prisoner

Jewyl shivered, a chill curling down her spine. The massive oaken doors before her were closed, yet she could hear the mumblings of voices, and the sound of music from the other side. She glanced once more at the clothing she'd been forced to wear: light brown with three large emeralds, and a smattering of other gems. She loathed the implication it indicated. If the fabric had been pure white, and the three main jewels rubies, the servants who dressed her would now be dead. In no way would she wear a wedding or betrothal gown, especially as a prisoner. Jewyl inhaled deeply, and waited, the chains which bound her, heavy and silent.

"Bring her in!"

Jewyl cringed, yet tried not to show it. She despised the man and now, his bellowing voice demanded her attendance in the Grand Hall.

The heavy doors glided open on their bronze hinges allowing the music and babbling voices to gain clarity and volume. She hesitated, and was quickly urged by spear point to move forward. Jewyl strutted into the chamber, her head held high, ignoring the chains on her wrists and the shackles that bound her feet. The room's torchlight glinted off the gold threads of her gem studded garment. Her green eyes flashed, taking in every aspect of the chamber, including its occupants who now huddled in whispering clusters as she moved toward the throne where Lord Azre sat. She despised his leering at her.

Attending guards loomed over her on each side, holding the ends of her wrist chains securely in their strong hands. Their grunts kept tempo with their lumbering strides. Their heavy leather boots pounded on the marble floor in complete contrast to the long, rattling chains Jewyl dragged behind her sandaled feet.

Lord Azre sat sprawled on his throne, slightly turned. He

studied her from atop the dais.

"Jewyl, your very being exudes your namesake." His deep voice resonated throughout the hall. He waved his hand to dismiss the guards, his bare-chested muscles rippling in the action. The guards immediately dropped the chains, the metal links clattered to the polished floor. They stepped away from their prisoner.

"You flatter me, Lord Azre," Jewyl replied softly, and pushed a stray lock of red hair behind her ear. The chain attached to her wrist pulled closer. A large gaudy earring glistened in the torchlight as she bumped it with a chain link.

She stood proudly in the center of the chamber and continued to nonchalantly examine the assembly: a cluster of women in the right corner, gathered nobles to left of the dais, plus other assorted members of the court who huddled near the walls to view her. She silently counted the number of guards she could see: one near the throne, another at each corner of the dais, another couple at the side entrances and although she couldn't see them, the two who had escorted her had to be behind her somewhere, perhaps no less than a mere ten feet away, plus two more who had opened the massive doors which she was sure were now closed.

"My dear, you are a vision." Lord Azre straightened on the throne then leaned forward, placing his chin to rest in his uplifted hand. "Truly a rare beauty to behold." He slowly stroked his chin, massaging the short-cropped beard as he took in her loveliness. "I see you come to me wearing three jewels. Are you offering me your mind, your heart and your soul in a contract of marriage?"

"What you see is nothing more than what you requested of your handmaidens." Jewyl lifted her arms, dragging the attached chains which sprawled across the floor just a little closer to her. *Cold metal whirling in the air is a weapon*, she thought. She covertly assessed the chains. "Your servants put these garments on me at your request." She shrugged. "I had nothing to do with my appearance. I am nothing more than a canvas for your handmaidens to paint upon." She cocked her head to the side then slowly bowed. "I come offering you nothing, most assuredly not my mind, my heart or my soul in ceremonial marriage apparel." She dropped her hands to her sides in a complete bow. "I am but your humble prisoner."

Once more she lifted her head and stood before him, glaring defiantly, her whole body tightly set, ready to spring into action at any point. A plan of escape hadn't fully developed, but escape was the goal.

Sweat beaded on Lord Azre's brow below the simple band of royalty. He slowly tugged at his beard then shifted in his chair, throwing his fur robe to the side to reveal even more of his muscled upper torso. He leaned back in a sprawl on the throne and swiped his hand across his forehead, wiping the sweat away. Lord Azre turned to glare at the young servant girl who slowly swayed the large feathered fan above him. A well-timed cock of his eyebrow with a narrowing of his eyes, the maiden immediately increased her endeavor to cool him.

Lord Azre turned his attention once more to Jewyl. "What would you have me do?"

"I told you, I am your prisoner." She shrugged. "What do you wish of me?"

"I offer you freedom." Azre threw his hands into the air.

"Freedom?" Jewyl queried.

"You continue to refuse my marriage proposal — to become my queen. Would that not be freedom?"

"I wouldn't call your offer a means of freedom," Jewyl replied. "Marriage? For me, that would be a living death. Is that your idea of freedom?" She shook her head. "I shall pick my own husband, if and when I find him. I am not a prize to be won or captured." She threw back her head, and the jeweled comb fell from atop her head. Set free, her long, red locks cascaded down her back. "I am Jewyl, the Princess of Shiyula." She took a deep breath. "I have no regard for your purported authority."

"Shiyula?" Lord Azre eyes widened. "There is no Shiyula. It is a land of legends. It doesn't exist. I am the ruler of Dianiya. I am the Dragon God Incarnate." A curl of the lips attempted a smile. "Tell me, Jewyl. If you are truly the Princess of Shiyula, where is your sword of authority? Where is the Sword of Shiyula?" He leaned toward her. "I see no proof."

"Dianiya was a regency, a mere monarchy." Jewyl stamped her foot on the floor, the chains clinking loudly to emphasize her action. "Dianiya, Abriela, and Meisa all paid homage and tribute to Shiyula and to its ruler, my grandfather, King Asthral. Your father's father paid obeisance to the King of Shiyula. In the battle, when the three lords betrayed my grandfather, the Sword of Shiyula was lost."

3

"How old can you be, Jewyl?" Lord Azre examined his prisoner. "Younger than me, for sure, and I don't remember Shiyula. There was no Shiyula in my childhood; it was but a word never to be spoken on the threat of death."

Jewyl fumed in silence. How could she explain what her mother had taught her of the treachery? Of how the sub-lords of Dianiya, Abriela and Meisa, together raised up against her grandfather, killing him? Vaela, her grandmother, pregnant with her father escaped the castle before the siege. She went into hiding, living with a friend in the distant village of Eichla.

"I am who I say I am," Jewyl finally replied. "I am the rightful heir, the Princess of Shiyula. Why would I wish to marry you?"

"It is your inner quality, your fire that excites my heart." Once more Azre leered at her, his lip curling at the corner in a secretive smile.

"You are only excited because you can't have me," Jewyl sneered. "I loathe you, and everything you represent." She pulled at the thin fabric draping from her belt, barely hiding her thigh and legs. "You dress me in jewel-trimmed frills. My inner qualities? You jest." She laughed aloud before folding her arms before her and defiantly glaring at him.

"Those frills are merely garments to enhance your outer beauty, my dear Jewyl." Lord Azre's voice deepened, becoming husky. "Do you not like being desirable?"

Jewyl glared at Azre. She lifted a chained hand to the emerald gleaming from the gold circlet in her hair. "This is my mind?" She pointed to the emerald at her breasts. "This is my heart?" She gestured to the emerald in the belt hugging her hips. "And this my soul?" She laughed.

"I prefer my swords and knives." She narrowed her eyes at Azre. "There is comfort in their cold metal, especially if my hand were to be sliding a dagger across your neck."

A ruckus in the corner caught everyone's attention. The music stopped for only mere moments before it once again began. Jewyl watched the women huddle and scurry in their attempt to cover what appeared to be a mistake. One tall, slim woman with a strange gait caught Jewyl's eye, and she watched the woman move away from the group. This woman carried a tray with a small

4

amount of meat. What caught Jewyl's eye were the two small daggers, standing from the meat, while on each side of the meat, barely staying on the tray, lay swords.

"Again, I ask you—" Azre stomped his foot to gain her attention. "Will you be my wife?"

Jewyl turned back to Azre, once more crossing her arms and staring at him. Something niggled at her mind. She frowned.

The woman moved toward her and danced between Jewyl and Azre, bowing deeply to the man on the throne, all the while keeping tempo to the music. She held the platter up for all to see and continued in a small circle around Jewyl. The woman's movements were far from graceful, but quite agile considering the awkwardness of the item she carried.

Jewyl's hopes lifted, and then dashed when she recognized the swords and daggers: one set was hers; the others belonged to her companion, Chardo who was currently in the dungeon.

Only a self-serving fool like Azre would dare to have the enemy's weapons so proudly displayed before them, Jewyl thought. *There has to be a way to make this work for me. With a quick flick of my wrist, I can wrap a chain about the woman's neck and have my sword.*

"Be ready," the husky voice of the woman whispered as she leaned in, yet continued to dance about Jewyl.

Jewyl's brows knitted in a momentary frown. She smiled. The scarf covered the head and a veil hid most of the face, but Jewyl recognized the voice of the man hidden within the female facade. It was Chardo, her companion. What in the name of Hagontha was he thinking? The goddess had best be smiling today on his crazy plot.

"What do you find amusing, my dear?" Azre's face was strangely complacent, and he seemed not to be concerned. "Care to let me in on the secret?"

"Marry you? Would you be man enough to bed me and be a husband? Could you close your eyes? Could you sleep comfortably knowing I lie beside you — awake?"

Azre scowled.

"Don't get him too mad," Chardo whispered. "A guard comes on your right side."

"Or would my hands be bound?" She lifted her wrists with the chains up toward Azre. "Treated, no doubt, lesser than a chamber

5

maid or whore?"

"I told you — not too angry," Chardo muttered and attempted a leap.

Azre jumped to his feet.

"Your insolence is dangerously close to treason." He pointed at Jewyl. "They claim The Emerald is a female with flaming red hair, and eyes of the deepest green. Are you she?" He glanced at Chardo. "Who is that clumsy woman dancing with the meat tray?"

"The Emerald? Treason?" Jewyl yelled with a quick glance at the guard coming toward her. "Has that person ever been arrested or held prisoner? How can I be accused of treason? I am your prisoner! Are not prisoners already treasonous? If I were The Emerald, my dagger's blade would be in your heart where you now stand!"

"Jewyl!" Azre stepped down from the throne, enraged. "You dare to threaten me in my own castle?"

"Now!" Jewyl turned quickly to swoop the sword from the tray and retrieve her dagger from the charred flesh holding it.

"Finally!" Chardo dropped the tray, grabbing his sword and dagger as the platter fell to the floor where he pushed it away with his foot. The tray skittered toward the wall as the meat rolled away, greasing the floor. Chardo yanked away his veil and head scarf.

Jewyl twirled, slicing left to remove the head of the guard who came up behind her. She quickly turned her attentions to the man on the dais.

"What are you thinking? Any plan?" Chardo asked.

"Attack them," Azre screamed from his throne.

"You looked much better under the veil, Chardo." She watched three guards moving toward them. "Be ready on your back," she added. "Three."

"Two right behind you, Jewyl." Chardo twirled.

Jewyl dropped to a stoop, pivoted, reaching out and slicing with her dagger at the ankle of one guard. He roared in pain, but continued the attack. Both guards had their swords up for a downward slice, Jewyl held her sword above her head to ward off the strike. The ring of metal sang as the blades hit and slid along the length of her sword's blade. Taken by surprise, the second guard faltered. Jewyl lunged upward with her dagger into the guard's stomach. The blade's point held a brief second before the oncoming momentum of the man pushed it inward and upward to his heart. She pulled the bloody blade out. In a sigh of agony, the guard crumbled to the floor. Jewyl forced her dagger between ribs of the guard she'd lamed. He pulled away, nearly ripping the blade from her hand. The guard held his hand over the wound, stumbled backward, slipped on the meat grease, and finally fell to the floor. He wasn't dead, but disabled too much to fight. He crawled away to safety.

Blood and meat grease now combined to inhibit easy movement on the floor. Jewyl glanced at Chardo who had already dispatched two of the guards and was in an intense sword fight with the remaining guard. Jewyl could see another guard coming up on Chardo's backside. She reached down and grabbed a double bladed dagger from the dead guard's sash. In a flash it headed at the new assailant. He never knew what hit him as the blade plunged into his stomach.

Jewyl twirled around at the commotion behind her. Two more guards charged forward to attack, but a third guard who had lingered in the shadows now impaled them with spears, stopping the two guards in their tracks.

"I'm Chardo's friend," the guard said while moving to Jewyl's side.

"He's okay," Chardo yelled while removing his sword from the dying guard he had been fighting. "He's not really a part of Azre's guards."

Jewyl ignored the newcomer and turned her attentions once more to the dais. Azre was gone. The throne area was clear, the room now empty except the guards they fought. All the nobles had escaped.

Chardo was at her side. "Well, m'dear," he said. "What do we do next?" He reached over and patted the guard on the shoulder. "By the way, this is Jopab."

Jewyl scrutinized the newcomer. "How did we gain him?"

"He was another of Azre's toys in the dungeon," Chardo replied with a smile then shrugged. "Another prisoner."

"And like the good guy you are, you sprung him?" Jewyl smiled before cocking an eye at him. "For your own purposes? Am I correct?"

Chardo grinned. "One never knows."

Jopab frowned then shrugged. "Perhaps we should get out of here? The guards aren't going to wait forever. Reinforcements will be quick in coming."

"I'm not going to run around with any amount of stealth wearing these cuffs and shackles." Jewyl held up her hands with the dangling chains. She pointed at her feet. "Any idea of how to get these off and get us out of here?"

Chardo held up a small wire. "This should work." He knelt and quickly wiggled the wire into the key mechanism. The cuffs fell from Jewyl's wrists. Chardo began work on the shackles.

"We don't have time. Follow me." Jopab pointed at the new guards running toward them, and darted across the room in long strides. He headed for the dais.

Chardo glanced about the room and stood. "I don't think these are coming off right now." He noted the guards coming at them from the side entrances. "Run the best you can with them."

"This way," Jopab shouted. "Quick!"

Without questioning, Jewyl followed Jopab with Chardo quick on her heels, trying not to step on the dragging chains. Jopab slammed his hand on the wall, a door slid open, and before Jewyl realized what was happening, she was scurrying down a dark passageway behind Jopab.

So this is how Azre was able to disappear so quickly, Jewyl thought.

Jopab stopped and slammed a clenched fist onto the wall. "There," he said. "That should stop them." The last glimmer of light disappeared.

"Unless they know how to open the door." Chardo leaned against the wall, catching his breath. "Which I'm sure they do."

"This escape is not known by very many," Jopab retorted. "I doubt even Lord Azre knows of its existence. He fled out the side entrance and nearly knocked me down."

Jewyl suddenly felt awkward. *Who is this man?* Her mind raced. *How does he know so much about secret tunnels within this castle?*

"It's dark in here," Chardo whispered in jest. "Oooooh."

"Knock it off," Jewyl jabbed an elbow, making contact with Chardo's chest. "My eyes can see some things, so it isn't totally dark." She scrutinized the walls. "Is that a glow?"

"Yes, and fortunately it isn't that strong so we are safe. Follow me," Jopab whispered. "We need to get moving. This was a

8

secret passageway, but since they saw us go in, they will figure it out sooner or later."

Jewyl's brows knitted together. She was reluctant to allow another to take charge, but relented. "Okay, lead on. Still, what I want to know is how we're going to get out of the city once we get out of the castle?"

"I agree," Chardo chimed in. "You're dressed as a guard, Jopab, but we're going to stick out as terribly obvious. I'm a man in a woman's dress and Jewyl is practically dressed for marriage."

"Enough!" Jewyl's voice echoed in the passageway. "The garment is not white, and the gems are not rubies."

"Lower your voices. There is more to this passageway than meets the eye," Jopab replied as he slowed and his fingers played on the wall.

"What's going on?" Chardo asked, bumping into Jewyl.

"Ah, there it is," Jopab replied, and stooped down.

"What is?" Jewyl asked before tumbling over Jopab in the darkness as Chardo pushed forward. "By Rorc's ass!"

"Profanity is unbecoming of you, Jewyl." Chardo gazed at Jewyl and Jopab on the floor. "What are you two doing down there? I don't think we really have the time for that."

"It was your buddy's fault," Jewyl replied. "Trust me, I'm not interested."

"I had to read the instructions to know where the release mechanism was located. It is here on the floor." Jopab scrambled about, his hands playing across the stone floor. "I had it just before she fell over me. Ah, here it is."

The sound of a stone being moved grated loudly in the darkness.

"Help me," Jopab said. "Push against the wall."

The wall moved and light glowed around the section.

"Another good push!"

Chardo and Jewyl grunted as they pushed. Jopab peeked around the edge of the hidden door.

"Good, the room is empty," he said.

"Where are we?" Jewyl asked.

"This is what they call an Exchange Room." Jopab strolled into the room, picked up the candle on the table, and held it to the flame of the dimly lighted lantern above them.

Jewyl and Chardo followed Jopab into the room.

"Would you mind? We need to put the door back into place." Jopab nodded at the gaping hole.

Jopab and Chardo leaned against the large stone door. The section grated back into place, moving much easier than when opening.

"That doorway hasn't been used in a long time." Jopab shook his head. "At least, now we can rest here and not be bothered." Jopab leaned closer to the hidden doorway and placed his ear against the stone. "This should confuse anyone who is lucky enough to follow us."

Jewyl quickly surveyed the room: a table with the candle, four chairs, an overhead lantern, a shelf with a couple of jugs, some wrapped packages, and an array of mugs.

Chardo knelt before Jewyl and fiddled with the metal anklets she wore. "I should have these off in less than—" The metal fell to the floor. "Picking locks isn't really all that hard."

"Why are you helping us?" Jewyl stared at Jopab.

"Please," Jopab whispered while placing an index finger to his lips. "Keep your voice low so we may hear if we're being followed." He reached and pulled a jug and three mugs from the shelf. "Drink?" He poured wine into three mugs. "Why am I helping you?" Jopab reiterated, his voice barely a whisper. "First, Chardo helped me get out of that dungeon. Of course, the main reason is simple. I've been searching for you, Jewyl."

Chardo raised an eyebrow.

"You're searching for me?" Jewyl repeated. "Why?"

Jopab smiled then sipped from his mug, watching. "Did you not say that you are Jewyl of Shiyula? The princess? Let me put it this way – the Princess of Shiyula?"

Jewyl sat in a chair and sipped her wine, coyly watching him. She placed the cup on the table and idly traced her index finger around the lip of it. "I can't deny my heritage." She lifted the mug to her lips.

Jopab lifted the small loaf of bread as a question to the group if they wanted some. "Are you not also known as The Emerald?"

She choked, sputtered, almost dropped the cup and stared at Jopab.

"You dare to call me, a princess of Shiyula, an assassin?"

Jewyl stood up and grabbed the sword against her hip.

"Hush," Jopab said. He again lifted a finger to his lips. "You must learn to keep your voice down. All walls have ears in this castle. I only repeat that which I've learned. If you are truly The Emerald, then my search is over."

"What need do you have of an assassin?" Chardo asked, coming between them. "What do you offer?" He glared at Jewyl. "Business first, m'dear. Pleasure later. Now, put the sword away."

Chardo pulled a chair out and seated himself, stretching out to put his feet onto the table top.

Jopab suddenly raised one hand and placed an index finger to his lips. He cocked his head toward the hidden door they'd come through.

"I can hear them," Jewyl replied. "They're certainly noisy."

"Where does the passageway end?" Chardo asked.

Jopab smiled, his eyes sparkled. "No place. There is about another twenty or thirty feet beyond this entrance. It is a dead-end passageway if you don't know where to find the trips to open the doors." He pulled the bread apart and offered a piece to Jewyl.

"They figured out how to open the first door." Jewyl took a sip of her wine before continuing. "I'm sure they'll figure out how to find the entrance to this room." She bit into the bread expecting it to be old and hard. "This is pretty fresh."

Jopab nodded. "The bread is probably from yesterday, perhaps today." He pointed to the stone doorway. "Since each tripping location is different in appearance and location, maybe they'll figure it out, maybe not." He held up his hand as a muffled sound issued from the passageway. "They've come back, a wise decision."

The three sat quietly in the hidden chamber listening to the guards stumble back toward the original opening.

"A wise decision?" Chardo queried.

"The doors don't remain open forever." Jopab nibbled on the bread. "They close automatically, some sooner than others."

"Who thought this whole thing up?" Jewyl whispered. "There seems to be no pattern to this plan."

Jopab sat down and solemnly placed his hands on the table, palms up in meditation. He inhaled deeply, exhaled slowly then stared at them for a few seconds.

"The Elder Priests built this structure before Dianiya existed." Jopab spread his fingers on the table top as he spoke. He glanced at Jewyl. "This place existed before Shiyula came to be." Jopab closed his eyes and took a deep breath. "This originally was a temple to She Who Cannot Be Seen." He smiled slyly. "In the fulfillment of time, She Who Cannot Be Seen fell from favor and Shiyula came into existence. With it came Chaos and chaos must be upheld."

"Hagontha?" Jewyl whispered, her eyes wide with surprise. "The Goddess of Chaos?" She paused. "This place was built before the goddess Hagontha existed?"

Jopab eyed the two, calculating, then with a small nod, acknowledged Jewyl's question.

"With the loss of She Who Cannot Be Seen, the priests at the temples moved forward in the acceptance and adoration of chaos. Now the followers are many," Jopab said. "We must go to Bashiwa for all to be revealed."

"Are you saying the priests of Hagontha want to hire an assassin?" Chardo leaned over the table to scrutinize Jopab.

"I can say no more," Jopab replied. "The answers are in Bashiwa."

Jewyl stood up. "I don't like this, Chardo." She began pacing the room. "He tells us a little, but never what we ask. We want to know who you are and who wants to hire an assassin."

"Ah," Jopab replied. "You won't even admit to your identity, yet you want me to gush forth with my information." He held his arms apart and his hands open, palms up to them as if performing a benediction.

"You wanted assassins?" Jewyl held up the dagger and quickly moved it to beneath his chin. "You've got them."

"I am Jopab, a priest of Hagontha," he said. "We must leave quickly for Bashiwa."

"Do you think the passageway is safe?" Chardo asked.

"It matters not." Jopab offered a sly smile. "Do you prefer water or land travel?"

Chardo looked to Jewyl and shrugged. "Your call."

"Water," Jewyl replied. "At least from here at first. Water surfaces make it a tad difficult to track, and may help to keep us hidden from them for a few days. At least, that is, if we make the river without being noticed."

Jopab nodded his head ever so slightly. "No problem."

Chardo stood and headed for the wall with the hidden door they'd come through.

CHAPTER TWO
The Escape

Chardo knelt on the floor and scrutinized the seam between floor and wall. *There has to be a mechanism of some sort to open this door,* he thought. *I'm not a thief worth my weight if I can't find it.* He glanced nervously at Jewyl and Jopab to see if they were watching before allowing his fingers to softly trace a path along the seam, wandering a little above it onto the wall and straying an inch or so onto the floor. He inspected each fault and pebble.

"It has to be here," Chardo mumbled.

"Let me know if you find it, my friend." Jopab grinned. "But don't trip it. We need to do a few things first before we leave. Plus we'll need to move this table." He offered a sly smile at Jewyl.

She watched him and waited. Jopab, she felt, was enjoying being in control. She didn't like situations where she was at someone else's beck and call.

Jopab placed the mugs back on the shelf along with the jug of wine and the partial loaf of bread. He took a copper coin from his belt and placed it on the shelf before removing two wrapped packages.

"Where does all this come from?" Jewyl waved her hand to encompass the shelf. "Somebody has to keep the oil going, replace the candle, the wine. Who does it?"

"An assigned priest of Hagontha." Jopab placed the packets on the table. "I know not who he is. It is his duty to check the Exchange Rooms and make sure everything is always ready."

"Rooms," Jewyl repeated. "There is more than one? Why do you call them Exchange Rooms?"

Jopab ripped the wrappings away from the first one, ignoring her question. "Ah, we have some bread and dried meat." He pulled the wrap from the other package. "And some clothing. Very good."

"Clothing?" Chardo turned to glance at the contents strewn on the table's top. "Almost anything would be better than this silly dress I'm wearing. Jewyl? Would you like it? After all, it will cover more than that half-ass wedding regalia does."

"If I must," she replied. "Although I would prefer leggings, tunic and a pair of solid leather boots." She pulled the garments out to review what the package hid. "This I could wear." Jewyl held up a long, woolen tunic. "A belt around the waist and I'm set."

"I'll take the vest and pants." Chardo snatched the items from the pile. "I guess we'll stay in our sandals." He gave the shelf a glance. "Don't see any boots."

"What do you two think," Jopab queried. "Do I stay in the guard's clothes or change to match your apparel?"

Chardo removed the dress, and stood naked looking at his companions. "What?" He put the breeches on.

"Your modesty, as usual, is overwhelming." Jewyl rolled her eyes at him before slipping the long tunic over her head. Her hands moved beneath the fabric and the belted harness fell to the floor.

Jopab's face reddened. "Perhaps it would be best I remain a guard."

"They will be looking for a guard." Jewyl looked up and saw Jopab's awkward stare. "You should probably change to match us." She pulled the jeweled top out the sleeve and played with the intricate thin gold filigree attached to the front of the garment. "These gold wires and gems could serve us." She threw it at Chardo. "Here, dig out the jewels so we can use them and not have to carry that damned thing around."

Jopab looked at the remaining garments: another long tunic but with a hood, another vest, and a long skirt. He wrinkled his nose.

"I guess I will be wearing the hooded tunic." Jopab sighed and began to remove the heavy breastplate and the other accessories. He stood there in the red tunic of the guard's uniform.

"Put on the vest." Chardo nodded at the garment. "Wear it over your tunic and nobody will realize the tunic was a part of a guard's uniform." He paused. "At least, not without a more thorough investigation of the fabric."

Jopab smiled, as relief washed over him for not having to strip before them.

"Of course..." Chardo narrowed his eyes and gave a sly grin. "To see you change into the other tunic could have been interesting." He leered at Jopab and snapped another gem from the garment.

"Chardo!" Jewyl scolded. "Leave him alone.

Jopab scowled and knitted his eyebrows in thought. A smile slowly curled the ends of his lips. "A simple tunic and that—" He pointed at Jewyl's forehead. "That gold circlet and huge emerald is a perfect accent."

Jewyl grabbed the fine gold crown and yanked it from her head. "More gold and another gem." She casually tossed it to Chardo.

"I saw you leave a coin." Jewyl gazed at Jopab and nodded toward the shelf. "We will leave a few of the stones to assist your goddess and the priest who takes care of this place."

"Your kindness will not go unrewarded." Jopab slipped into the vest which covered the top of his tunic. "We should finish." He suddenly looked around nervously.

Jewyl noticed the sudden change. "What is the problem?"

"We need to get about our business," Jopab said. "Even though the oil indicates we have time, we may have dallied too long and the priest may come to check on this room."

"That would be a bad thing?" Chardo asked. "The priest can't see us?"

"You forget, this is a sacred room of Hagontha," Jopab said. "Chaos must be maintained. If the priest discovers us, we must either kill him, or he must kill us. So, let's be on our way."

"Why must that be the action?" Jewyl frowned at Jopab.

"Only the Holy Father knows who the priests are to freshen the Exchange Rooms. They remain anonymous to protect them." Jopab looked at the two who stared back at him. "These rooms are used for purposes of stealth. If the priest were to discover us, his tongue may slip and reveal our actions. By killing us, none will learn of us for he cares not who we are. If we kill him, none will learn of us, for the next priest to come will not know who killed him." He paused. "And he can't mention the dead priest, not even to the Holy Father."

Jewyl considered Jopab's words before nodding in agreement. "We must go."

Chardo gathered the gems he'd removed from the garments and ripped a square of fabric from his old dress to make a pouch. Jewyl gathered the remaining garments and piled them on the shelf for the coming priest to use along with a few jewels to add to their treasury. Jewyl assisted Jopab in making sure everything was ready.

"Now, we must move the chair," Jopab said.

Chardo started to pull the chair across the floor.

"No!" Jopab yanked the chair from Chardo's hand. "There is a pattern in the chaos that must be maintained in this room. He pulled the table back to its proper place. He moved a chair to one side near the table, taking the time to align it properly, then reached under the table, his fingers fumbling, exploring.

Chardo leaned down and watched Jopab search for the mechanism. He saw it and moved Jopab's fingers to it. Jopab pushed it. Chardo heard the click of the tripped devices in the legs' feet.

"Very interesting." Chardo stood and appraised the situation. "Exactly what does that do?"

Jopab lifted the table, tilting it on an invisible hinge to lean on the chair he had so carefully aligned earlier.

"Ah-ha!" Chardo said. "Ingenious, actually quite devious."

Jopab smiled. "You think so? There is just enough stickiness on the edge of the table so when the table returns, the chair will follow and be leaning on the table when the floor is closed again. If you were stumble upon the scene, would you look for a trap door under the table?"

"All well and good," Jewyl replied and nodded toward the gaping hole. "Where does this lead us?"

"To the river." Jopab reached up and took a gem from the shelf. "Listen." He dropped the jewel into the hole. There was a slight hesitation then the sound of splashing water echoed up the tunnel. Jopab smiled. "It is an underground stream which leads to the river."

Chardo frowned. "I know of no such thing. A river under the castle? I'm sure the Thieves Guild would have known of that."

"Chaos," Jopab replied with a smile. "There is a method to every madness. Thieves don't know all the secrets. Praise be to the goddess."

"You make me want to be a believer of Hagontha." Chardo slapped Jopab on the shoulder and winked. "Always a chance."

"Let's get out of here." Jewyl leaned over the hole to inspect. "Ah, a ladder."

"And a boat at the bottom, secured with a rope to keep it from floating away," Jopab said. "Let me go first and I will make sure you can step into it. Follow me" He slipped into the hole and started down. "Chardo, carefully pull the table back over us, making sure the chair remains attached. When it closes, we'll be in the dark but we will be able to see a little." He paused. "There will be a small green glow."

Jewyl followed Jopab.

"Remember, Chardo," Jopab called from the depths of the hole. "Pull gently so as not to disturb the chair."

"Why?" Chardo asked. "Do you think the guards will find the room?"

"No, but the priest needs to know we left by the river and replace the boat below us."

"Would he not realize that when he sees we've taken the clothes?" Jewyl asked.

"I stated that it is an Exchange Room." Jopab continued down the tunnel. "Simply stated, there is more than one way to leave. Remember, I asked you which way you would like to leave the city."

"More than one way out of the room?" Jewyl repeated.

"There were two more ways out, not including this one and the way we came in." Jopab continued down the ladder.

Jewyl couldn't see his face in the semi-darkness, but she knew Jopab was smiling, proud of this escape. "Jopab." Jewyl looked below but saw nothing but a dark blob moving in the low glow. "I didn't see any torches. Don't you think that would be a good idea to have them available in the Exchange Room, or at least in this tunnel? This is very dark and the passageways were, too." Suddenly she heard splashing water and once again looked down. A brighter glow allowed her to see a detailed outline of Jopab.

"I'll suggest it," Jopab replied. "Now watch your step and I'll guide you onto the boat."

His hands were firm in their grip, yet modest in their touch as they slowly crept up her leg to assist. She felt a sudden flush which confused her, and she inhaled deeply. Jewyl felt the boat under her foot and slowly allowed her weight to be steered by Jopab's strong hands.

"Is something wrong?" Jopab asked. "Have I offended?"

"No," Jewyl lied. "I'm fine." She gazed about in the eerie green glow of the walls and found a place to sit in the boat. The waters lapped at the boat's sides as it rocked on the surface of the river. In different locations, the river had glowing green lights to cast eerie shadows.

"Hey, none of that without me," Chardo bellowed.

"Quiet, Chardo!" Jopab grabbed Chardo's right foot. "Let me guide your foot to the boat."

"Oooh, I like that." Chardo smiled as the priest's hands steadied his leg to the boat. Chardo placed one hand on Jopab's back and let go of the rung. "This could be interesting."

"Later," Jewyl said.

Chardo frowned; he was not accustomed to hearing Jewyl's voice sounding so cold. He wished he could see her face better so he could read what the problem was. In the glow, he couldn't tell her mood.

Jopab stood up and nudged Chardo who had turned around and bent over to find a seat.

"No!" Chardo lurched forward, flailing his arms in the air before falling over the edge of the boat. The sound reverberated in the tunnel.

"Do you see what your foolery has done?" Jewyl chastised.

In the green glowing shadows, Chardo stood in chest-high waters. Jopab and Jewyl grabbed Chardo's arms and hoisted him back into the boat.

"Sit here," Jopab said. "In a few minutes we will be out of this runnel and in the light."

Chardo did as he was told and huddled in the bow of the skiff, his body and clothes dripping water. "The water is cold, just in case anyone was interested."

Jewyl giggled. "I would have assumed so." She turned her attention to Jopab. "You called this a runnel. Why is that?"

"A runnel is a water run channel," the priest replied. "Water has secreted through these rocks over thousands of years creating small channels or tunnels. Most of them are very small and not useful, but a few have been discovered and served us well over time. This particular runnel is the largest and will take us out at the base of the castle, just beyond the village."

"Interesting," Chardo said. "Where are the oars?"

"We don't need them," Jopab replied. "The current is carrying us out to the river."

"Fine." Chardo shrugged. "But what happens when we get out on the river?"

"You will see, we are almost there." Jopab nodded toward the direction they were headed. "We will go around this stone wall and through the vines and be on the river in full daylight." He paused. "Then your wet clothing will have a chance to dry properly."

"On a river without any oars?" Jewyl asked. "This should prove interesting."

The boat hesitated and the bow pressed against the massive tangle of vines. Dotted light pierced through the overhang.

"Do you see anyone out there?" Jopab whispered as he maneuvered the boat to float against the growth. "Chardo?"

Chardo fingered into the vines, creating a viewable peephole and checked the river for activity. "You'd think the guards would be patrolling, looking for the escaped prisoners."

"Is there anyone out there?" Jewyl asked.

"No," Chardo whispered. "It's all clear."

"Fine." Jopab pushed against the stone wall, once more angling the bow of the boat into the tangled weave of green growth.

The boat pierced the twisted veil of greenery and eased onto the river. The three of them squinted in the sudden brightness of the sunlight. The boat glided into the middle of the river and floated with the current, twisting and turning. Jopab manipulated the wooden rudder and the boat straightened and gracefully floated with the flow.

"I know this river. It flows to Bashiwa. Do you think we can make it there before dark?" Jewyl asked. "I have a friend there where we can stay."

"We can easily make Bashiwa," Jopab replied. "Remember, it is there that all will be revealed."

"Please tell me you aren't thinking of Hvar's," Chardo said. He smiled nervously, remembering the last visit to the old man's tavern.

"You have a problem with that?" Jewyl gave Chardo a questioning look.

"No." Chardo replied and wiped his hand across his lips. "Hvar does a great dish of venison."

"His son is cute, too," Jewyl said. "Right?"

Chardo grinned at the memory of Vico. "Contrary to what

you think, nothing ever happened." Chardo placed a hand to his chest. "May Rorc rip out my heart."

"Let's hope it doesn't come to that." Jewyl leaned over and let her index finger play on the water's surface. "Hvar might not like seeing you again."

"Perhaps Vico has moved on." Chardo sighed and shrugged his shoulder. "He didn't want to be an inn keeper."

"Why do you insist on calling on Rorc?" Jopab maneuvered the boat through a small rapid. "Is not Mother Hagontha worthy of your praise and curses?"

"Rorc listens to the pleas of thieves," Chardo replied. "He watches over those who—"

"To the shore on my right," Jopab whispered. "A group of the king's guard."

Jewyl and Chardo slowly shifted their gaze to the shore and found the group of three guards lazing under the clump of trees. They sat on their horses, idling watching the boat float by.

"You three in the boat," the lead guard shouted. "Where are you bound and your business?"

"Performers," Jopab yelled in response. "We head to Bashiwa."

"For what purpose," the guard asked.

"We have been commissioned by the Temple of Hagontha to perform during the Celebration of Chaos tomorrow's night."

"We are?" Chardo whispered.

"Hush," Jewyl responded.

The guard held up his hand and Jopab waved back.

"That was close," Jopab whispered. "Praise Hagontha and her chaos." He nodded back at the three guards. "That one guard was a follower."

"He was?" Chardo asked. "How do you know that? Most military are followers of Rorc since he fortifies their strength."

Jopab silently scrutinized Chardo a few seconds, the only noise being the lapping of water against the boat.

"He gave me the secret sign of the priesthood," Jopab said. "Does he know we are the prisoners? I have no idea but, at the current time, we have safe passage."

"Why would he know the secret sign?" Her eyes widened. "Hold on," Jewyl cried. "Here are the rapids."

21

"This is the reason why there is no water trade between Bashiwa and Dianiya." Jopab maneuvered the boat. "The water flows to Bashiwa, but isn't deep enough to come back to Dianiya."

Chardo glared at Jewyl as the boat entered the rushing waters. "Why did you decide on this mode of travel?" He held a cupped hand over his mouth as the boat danced in the water. "Oh, my stomach."

"It is only a small set of rapids, Chardo," Jopab said. "Praise chaos and Hagontha in her mystery."

"Relax, Chardo, dear." Jewyl leaned over her companion as he held his head beyond the boat and lost his stomach. She softly rubbed and soothed his back. "Just think of the inn. Think of Vico's smiling face."

Once more Chardo heaved. "It's not helping," he muttered, and splashed cool river water on his pallid face as another bout wracked his body.

CHAPTER THREE
Inn at Bashiwa

The inn keeper glanced at the three people standing in the shadows of his doorway. *Mother Hagontha's curse. Trouble, I'm sure.* He grimaced, his heavy eyebrows almost knitting together. He shrugged and replaced the scowl with a fake smile framed by his heavy mustache. *Still, three silver decas is three more than I had before*, he thought and flipped the cleaning towel over his shoulder. Hvar grabbed his apron and dried his hands in preparation to greet them.

"Hvar," Jewyl called out. "Have you room for us?"

"I should know you?" Hvar stopped to scrutinize the visitors as he idly stroked the thick mustache. The late day sunlight behind them hid their faces in shadows. He approached cautiously. "By the gods! Jewyl!" Hvar stepped closer and grabbed Jewyl's hands in his. "What brings you to the Red Horse Inn?"

"Travelers," Jewyl replied. "Just simple travelers seeking accommodations for three."

"Oh!" Hvar looked directly at Chardo. "I see you have him with you." The man cocked a furry eyebrow at the thief, but there was no hiding the distaste in his voice as the word 'him' slurred snidely.

"Glad to see you, too," Chardo said. "What is your problem?"

"How many rooms do you seek?" Hvar ignored Chardo and spoke directly to Jewyl.

"Two." Jopab moved forward. "One for her and another for the two of us. If that is amiable to all?"

Hvar reared back and silently looked at Jopab then to Chardo. "So, you two are friends?" He nodded his head and waggled a pointing finger between them.

"We travel together and if it will save us a silver deca or two..." Jopab surveyed the interior of the inn. "Is that a problem?"

Jewyl leaned in, touching Hvar on the bare arm. "We have no

23

coins, Hvar. Perhaps one of these will suffice to pay our bill?" She dropped three jewels into his hand. "Can you get them exchanged without problems?" She paused. "No reason to awaken a dragon..." She smiled conspiratorially. "If you understand my meaning."

"The ruby will more than suffice for your stay." He lifted the gem to check its purity. "Let Hagontha have her way with the dragon. How many days will you need?"

"Tonight and tomorrow." Jewyl smiled. "Beyond that I am not sure."

"We will only need to stay possibly through tomorrow," Jopab added. "The Celebration of Chaos is tomorrow night."

"Hagontha?" Hvar stared at Jewyl. "I didn't realize you followed in her steps."

"Please, Hvar." Jewyl once more placed a hand on the big man's strong arm. "Let us get our rooms and let me rest. I will explain all later, if that is well with you." She smiled at the man. "We have much to discuss."

"Britha," Hvar yelled. "Please show our guests to their rooms."

"Yes, father." A dark-haired, young girl placed a tray of food on a table and headed for the staircase. "Your rooms are up here."

Jewyl watched the lass rush across the room. "How long has it been since I was last here?" Jewyl asked, grabbing Hvar's arm. "This is little Britha? Why Hvar, she has grown up to be quite a fetching maiden. She was just beginning her teens when last I saw her."

"I do what I can," Hvar mumbled. "I don't really want her working here, but things have changed."

"Keep all the stones, Hvar," Jewyl whispered. "Need I mention we are not here?" She gazed out those who sat at the tables. "Especially if Azre's guards come asking."

"Of course," he replied. "You are like a daughter to me." Hvar leaned in conspiratorially. "But, who is your friend?" He cast a glance at Chardo. "His?"

"Right now, let's just say a friend. Later?" Jewyl paused before dashing across the room to join Britha and the two men who had already started up the stairs.

Hvar absently rolled the three gems in the palm of his hand, his thick thumb fumbling over them. *A ruby, an emerald and a sapphire, he thought. Three gems, three visitors, three problems. The last time they were here I lost Vico. What will I lose this time?* He sighed.

# # #

"Father!" Breathless from rushing down the staircase, Britha practically knocked Hvar over in her haste. "Is that truly Jewyl?"

Hvar quickly surveyed the room and found they were alone except for a couple of the regulars he knew to be safe. He then realized he had made a mistake of calling Jewyl by name when she first arrived and he tried to remember who was in the room at that time.

"Hush, daughter." Hvar nodded. "Yes, she is the one who I have spoken of. It was her father who befriended me when I was a young man."

"She must live an exciting life." Britha sat on a chair and propped her head with both hands as the elbows hit the table. She took a deep breath and then exhaled in a rush. "Not something as boring as an innkeeper's daughter."

Hvar glanced at his daughter and could see the wanderlust in her eyes. He wondered what he would lose, and wasn't happy at the answer coming so quickly. He and his wife had scrounged a meager living with the inn until her death. Vico had helped until he left. Now Britha assisted, but if she left and he had to hire yet another to help, he wasn't sure he could continue. He pulled the cloth towel from his shoulder and started to clean tables. "Enough day-dreaming, daughter. Now get about your tasks."

"Hvar?" Chardo called from the landing. "May we speak?"

"Of course," Hvar replied and motioned for him to join him. "Would you like an ale?"

"Please," Chardo replied.

Hvar nodded to Britha and then pointed to a table in the corner. "We can talk over there."

Hvar plopped into the chair, sighed heavily, then aimlessly started to wipe the table.

Chardo dropped into the chair next to him then leaned close. "My friend, Hvar, have I offended you?"

"Here you are." Britha placed the foaming mug of ale in front

25

of Chardo. She flashed a smile at the dashing man.

"Thank you, Britha," Chardo said, and smiled at her. "I will make sure you receive a shiny copper for your service."

Britha curtsied and Hvar waved his hand to dismiss her. "Clean the tables, daughter." He noticed two more regulars walk in and take their customary seats.

Chardo lifted the mug and slugged it down, gulping deeply to drain it. "Another one, please?"

Britha looked to Hvar and he nodded.

"What do you want, Chardo?" Hvar breathed deeply and strummed his thick fingers on the table. "I am a busy man and have no time to idle away uselessly. Speak your wishes."

"You acted very annoyed and angry at me when you saw me." Chardo wiped his chin. "Obviously I have offended you."

"Your ale," Britha said.

Hvar glared at Britha. "Leave us, Britha" he growled and then glared at Chardo, tightening his grip on the twisted cloth in his hand. "Vico," he spat.

"What about Vico?" Chardo's expression of total ignorance confused Hvar.

"You have no idea what you did that night? No shame?" Hvar looked away.

Chardo gulped the ale, finishing almost half. "What night?" His eyes blurred for a few seconds and the room swayed slightly. "You, my man, have the best ale in all the kingdoms."

Hvar threw the cloth onto the table. "Your last night here, you called Vico to your room." A tear welled up in Hvar's eye then cascaded down his cheek. "I bring you into my home, introduce you to my family and you do that to me."

"What did I do?" Chardo asked. "Vico came to my room and we talked."

"You seduced my only son." Hvar leaned in closer to Chardo's face. "You. Had. No. Right."

"I did what?" Chardo sat upright in his chair. He grabbed the table for support as the room swayed about him. "I have never gotten drunk so quickly." He closed his eyes, but it served no purpose other than to intensify the feeling. "Perhaps I should have eaten first." Chardo tried to remember the last he had ate, and the secret chamber was a long time back.

"I am showing Jewyl a kindness by allowing you to stay at this inn again." Hvar leaned back in his chair. "But, you dare to bring your latest conquest? Your lover?"

"Conquest?" Chardo held onto the table and tried to focus his eyes. "Lover?"

"Perhaps you are his conquest." Hvar glared at Chardo. "Nonetheless, you stole my son when you were last here."

"I never touched your son," Chardo slurred.

"Innkeeper!" The command came from the doorway.

"Oh, by the gods," Chardo muttered and his head leaned forward before he passed out, his head slamming to the table.

"Here," Hvar replied and stood. "What is your need?" He glanced at Chardo, and then shook his head in disgust.

Four guards strode across the room, their armor clanging loudly as they approached the table where Chardo and Hvar were.

"You have three guests," the lead guard said.

"I have more than that." Hvar spread his arms out. "Is there a problem?"

"Three guests just arrived at The Red Horse Inn." The guard gave Hvar a look of total disdain. "Where are they?"

"Well, yes, there were three." Hvar frowned as if attempting to remember. "Ah, yes, a female and two men."

"Those are the ones." The guard gazed about the empty room. "Are they here? Where are their rooms?"

"I'm not sure I understand," Hvar said. "There were three, but they weren't together. The female is in her own room and the two men are sharing the last room I had."

"Fine and well. Where are they?" The guard grimaced. "Speak quickly, innkeeper." His hand moved to the hilt of his sword.

"Well, the female is the daughter of my friend," Hvar started. "She is here for the celebration tomorrow. One of the men, I believe, is a traveling priest of Rorc and the third one, his companion, is here, drunk." He nodded at Chardo. "He was my son's first lover, and now, unfortunately, he is of no use to anyone right now. He just found out my son has another lover."

"Those we seek claimed to be performers for the Celebration of Chaos." The guard scrutinized the area and the three other patrons. "They are escaped prisoners."

"Trust me," Hvar said with as innocent of a smile as he could muster. "These three are not performers. Do you have any descriptions so I may recognize them if they were to show?"

"The female is a redhead, the two men I am not sure about." The guard's words came hesitantly.

"I see," Hvar said and guided the guard away from Chardo. "My friend's daughter is a redhead and I can understand the confusion. Obviously you were misinformed about the group being together. Perhaps those you are searching have taken shelter elsewhere." Hvar stretched to his full height, legs slightly apart and hands on his hips. "I'm not the only place to sleep in Bashiwa."

"Hold your tongue, innkeeper. The woman we seek calls herself Jewyl." The guard stopped. He glared at Hvar then glanced once more around the open room. "She claims to be Jewyl, Princess of Shiyula."

"A princess?" Hvar echoed, his eyes wide in mock surprise. "In this place? Oh my. Perhaps I should tidy up a bit." He grabbed the towel and started to wipe.

"None of your sarcasm, innkeeper," the guard said. "She is to wed Lord Azre. You have a redhead staying here, and I won't be put off. Now, either you take me to her room, or I and my attachment will find her ourselves."

Hvar frowned. "Did you not say they are escaped prisoners and one is to wed the Dragon Lord? This doesn't make sense to me."

"Are you looking for me?"

The men turned and stared at the cloaked woman on the staircase.

"Are you Princess Jewyl?" the guard asked. "Remove your hood so I may see your face."

"My name is Britha. I have come here to my father's friend, Hvar and to participate in the Celebration of Hagontha." She paused and smiled. "I am not a performer, nor am I an entertainer of men. I am on a holy journey to understand the chaos of Hagontha."

"What are you doing, Britha?" Hvar whispered. His voice quivered and he didn't move as he stared at his daughter.

"You seek a red haired female?" Britha pulled red locks forward from under the woolen hood. "Am I who you seek?"

The guard pulled his sword, moved toward Britha and gazed into her eyes. "Your eyes are not green." He reached forward to pull back the hood.

Britha pulled back, holding tightly to the edges of the hood. She stared at the guard, not backing down. "My eyes are brown. Is that a problem?"

The guard bent down. "Lift the hem of the robe. Your ankles will tell me if you are truly the person I seek or not." He kept an eye on Britha for any sign of action, holding his sword at ready.

"Allow me." Britha pushed the cloak behind her shoulders, making sure the hood remained on her head, then daintily lifted the heavy hem of the skirt to reveal her ankles and a small portion of her legs. "As you can easily see, I hide no weapons, if that is what you sought."

The three guards behind the main guard stretched and leered at Britha's legs.

"The ankle is clear," the lead guard said. "There have been no irons on these lovelies." He slowly eased his cupped hand up the back of her leg, gently caressing the skin.

"Sir." Britha frowned at the guard. "If you'd please." She dropped the hem and stepped back on the small landing.

"I'd be more than pleased," the guard said and winked at her. "What is your name again?"

"Britha," she replied. "And I am betrothed, and as I stated earlier, on a holy pilgrimage." She stepped down the final three treads and away from the guard and into the protective arm of her father.

The guard sheathed his sword and turned back to his companions. "This was a fool's run." He stomped over to Chardo, grabbed a scuff of hair in his fist and lifted Chardo's head. "Bah, just a drunken lovelorn sod. Such a waste. This much sorrow over another man. I'll never understand it." He released Chardo's hair. Chardo's head hit the table with a resounding thud.

"Innkeeper," the guard called turning to Hvar. "You'd best be watching for three travelers. If they come here, inform me immediately."

"I will, sir." Hvar nodded and offered a small bow. "Immediately."

The guards stomped out of the room, their swords clanging loudly when they hit the sides of the doorway.

"What in the names of the gods were you thinking, child?" Hvar grabbed Britha's arm and turned her to face his wrath.

Britha tossed back her hood to reveal her dark chestnut hair pulled back and fastened with a bow. Locks of red were tied to the sides and fluffed to a fullness.

"Would you have preferred those oafs went upstairs?"

"No," Hvar replied. He stroked a finger down the attached locks. "Where did you find red hair? You didn't cut Jewyl's hair?"

Britha fingered the long red lock and smiled. "Let's just say the red mare's tail is not as full as it was earlier today."

Hvar stared at his daughter a few seconds before realizing what she meant. His laughter was full, true, and rumbled from deep inside Hvar's body. She enjoyed watching him wipe the tears from his eyes. He hadn't laughed that heartily in many years — not since the death of her mother three years ago. She felt a flush of satisfaction.

Chardo moaned.

"The poor boy," Britha said while softly cupping her hand to his forehead. "That had to hurt."

"It did," Chardo replied. "Do you know how difficult it was to remain in a stupor when you're not? That bastard just about yanked my hair out! Then to let my head hit the table, I was almost knocked out cold!"

Hvar slapped Chardo on the back. "At least you are alive and free."

"Yes," Chardo replied. "That is true. Now about Vico. Tell me where has he taken residence since he is no longer here?"

Hvar stopped smiling and glared at Chardo. "In all this excitement, I'd almost forgotten how much I despise you. My son now lives in the south part of the city. Last I knew, he was at the inn called Dancing Dragons."

"Vico?" Britha exclaimed. "There?"

"She didn't know?" Chardo watched Britha step back in shock.

"Not Vico!" Britha knitted her brows in concern. "My brother would never work there. He's... he's not that way."

"He lives there, that much I know." Hvar folded his large arms before him defiantly. "Perhaps he works there. That, I don't know." He raised his hands into the air, turned away and headed for the counter. "I only know Vico no longer lives or works here."

"Hvar, trust me. I did nothing with your son." Chardo stood, weaving slightly. "I will go find him, talk to him and discover what has happened."

"It's obvious," Britha sneered. "You are what happened." She twirled, the cape flaring out in the move. She hastily crossed the room to disappear up the staircase.

CHAPTER FOUR
Plots

Jewyl awoke with a start. Was it the clamor of the inn's patrons? She took a deep breath. The scent of fresh baked bread and roasting venison made her mouth water. Her stomach growled. How long had it been since she eaten? She stretched and gathered her thoughts before moving from the too-soft litter she slept on. A lighted candle on the table caught her eye. She froze. The candle had been unlit when she had fallen asleep. Someone had entered her room. Jewyl slowly scanned the area. She was sure she'd bolted the door. She reached for the dagger under the pillow and glanced to the door. The latch was secured. Concerned even more, she once more surveyed her surroundings more closely, all the while keeping a tight grip on the dagger. On a chair next to the table was a garment, a deep green with leather accents. She was intrigued and let loose of the weapon.

Approaching the table, Jewyl saw the note by the candle, picked up the paper and read:

> *The dragon has spoken.*
> *These garments should hide.*
> *Anointment is needed*
> *To conceal the bride.*
> *Father H. Vaela*

Jewyl knitted her eyebrows in a frown then re-read the cryptic poem. She reached down and touched the garment, it wasn't a rich fabric but a sturdy one that would wear well. Startled by movement from the corner of her eye, she noticed the reflected image of herself moving in the mirror just beyond the table. Jewyl nervously laughed at her silliness.

Vaela? Jewyl thought. *That was my grandmother's first name. Why? Who is Father H Vaela?* Jewyl laid the note down. *H?*

32

Father? Father H? Of course, Hvar. She again glanced at the note. "The dragon has spoken," she whispered. *A dragon? I'm to hide from a dragon? Spoken? The only dragon I can think of which can talk is Lord Azre, Dragon God Incarnate. Azre? Doubtful, but it could be his men.* She shrugged.

"Anointment," she muttered and picked up the small bottle near the candle. The label on it declared the contents to be "Wizard's Brown" which meant nothing to her. She opened the bottle and carefully sniffed at the contents. "Mint?" She poured a small amount onto her finger. It was a deep brown, almost black, and very viscous. *Anointment*, she thought. *That would be something placed on the head.* She rubbed the mixture between her thumb and forefinger then pulled a lock of her hair through the thick substance on her fingers. Jewyl's hair changed. It became a deep, dark chestnut, but there was still a hint of red.

She smiled in the mirror, making a crucial choice. Jewyl grabbed her knife and pulled a long lock of her hair out and cut it so it was no longer shoulder length. She finished by working the Wizard's Brown into her hair. She was no longer a long-haired red-head. A few strokes on the eyebrows and the transformation was complete. She gazed at the assorted makeup items on the table's top. She placed a dab of redness to her cheeks and lips. She hesitated before adding the light shade of brown to her eyelids. Jewyl stared at the slightly familiar stranger in the reflection then grabbed the dress to change. The sounds from below called to her, as did the food scents. She was famished. Jewyl also wanted to question Hvar on how he was able to enter her room and still leave the latch hooked. She smiled knowing Hvar was more than what met the eye.

# # #

Jewyl stood near the top of the stairs, taking a few seconds to survey the scene below her. The evening candles cast a welcoming, soft light. The heavy oaken trestles, joists and woodwork glowed warmly in the low light, and the murmur of patrons filled the air.

"Ah, Vaela!" Hvar called as she descended the stairs. "Join us. Please." He stood up and Jewyl could see Chardo and Jopab were with him.

Other patrons took a quick notice of her and then continued

on with their business.

None seemed concerned, except the hooded person sitting at the table in the shadowed corner. He was intently watching her. Jewyl couldn't actually see the person's eyes, but she could feel their embrace on her body. A shiver coursed down her back.

Chardo pulled back a chair and Jewyl joined the men at the table.

"Why the new look, Jewyl?" Chardo asked.

"Vaela!" Hvar hissed in a low growling voice.

"Vaela?" Jopab whispered. "What did you do to your hair?"

"My grandmother's name," Jewyl replied quietly. "Obviously somebody is looking for me... or at least a long-haired red-head. This shorter hair and makeup should confuse them."

"A truth within your words." Chardo nodded his head. "Jopab just arrived and hasn't been informed of today's events."

"Neither have I," Jewyl replied. "I guess this is what happens when you sleep too long."

"Britha!" Hvar motioned to his daughter. "Bring dinners for our guests." He paused. "And ales for the table."

Jewyl nonchalantly scanned the area again. The hooded stranger was not to be seen.

"He's left," Hvar whispered. "As you took your seat, he stood and left."

"Who was he?" Jewyl asked.

"He's not staying here," Hvar replied. "Although, I do believe he was here when you first arrived. Other than that, I don't know who he is, but I'm sure we should keep a watchful eye."

"Your hair! Is the garment adequate?" Britha placed the three plates on the table. "Father had me buy it for you."

The heady spices of the roast venison and mixed vegetables assailed their noses.

"Let me at it," Jopab said. He grabbed a dish and immediately started to eat. "Excellent," he mumbled between bites.

"This dress is more than adequate," Jewyl replied and slid a smoothing hand down the side of her dress to the waist. "Almost a perfect fit." She placed a hand to her hair, smiled and winked. "A small change."

"I thought you'd like the leather." Britha swelled with pride in her accomplishment. "I wasn't sure of your favorite color or style, but I hoped you'd like this one. I know I do."

Jewyl smiled at the younger girl. "This is exactly what I would have picked."

"You'd best be about your duties, girl." Hvar waved her away.

"I'll be back with drinks." Britha scurried across the room.

"Show as much attention to my table, lass," a man shouted. "And I'll please you with a shiny copper, or more."

Laughter broke out in the room. Britha's face flushed crimson.

"That is my daughter," Hvar yelled. "Share a copper if you wish, but there will be no pleasing. Understood?"

The room suddenly quieted.

Hvar stood, grabbed the butcher knife from his side where it hung and scowled at the patrons. "The whole lot of you." He turned slowly with the knife held in the air. "When she serves your table, you'd best be showing her only a coin for the meal or ale she brings you."

The room once again broke into a ruckus of laughter.

"A copper coin it is, innkeeper," a voice called out.

"One must keep these rogues under control," Hvar muttered as he sat while hooking the knife's handle to his apron. "Now, about this afternoon."

"Here are your drinks," Britha said breathlessly. The tankards clanked on the table.

Hvar looked at his daughter. "If one of these patrons is less than honorable with you, immediately let me know." He raised his voice. "This inn is a reputable place."

"Yes, father." Britha turned and hustled away.

"Jopab," Chardo began. "I think you were asleep upstairs, as was Jew- uh, Vaela."

"We had Azre's guards looking for three travelers," Hvar added. "I was attempting to put them off, yet they were insistent on searching the rooms above."

"I'd been talking with Hvar," Chardo added.

"He was a drunken sot," Hvar replied. "Can't hold his drink on an empty stomach. Still, the guards were insistent and that's when Britha came down the stairs. They wanted a redhead and Britha gave them one."

"But she's not." Jopab looked up from his plate and glanced at Britha to reassure himself he was correct.

"It was perfect," Chardo chimed in. "Britha pulled out her red locks and the guards were assured she wasn't the one who they sought." Chardo brought his hands into the air and pinched the thumbs and index fingers together to form an O. "Her plan worked even more smoothly than did mine back at Azre's."

Azre's, Jewyl thought. *So distant, yet it was only this morning. So much has happened.* Finally the words focused. "Plan?" Jewyl asked. "What plan? Oh, you mean the dancing girl routine? Oh, yes, that was definitely well thought out." Jewyl stifled the laughter, but her grin was more than obvious.

"Very well," Chardo said. "If my plans are so bad, exactly how did you get here?"

"Perhaps I should interject at this moment." Jopab lifted his utensil into the air. "Today I visited my friends at the temple. All should go as planned."

"Everyone making plans," Hvar said. "What is happening?"

Jopab shot a glance at Hvar then a quizzical look to Jewyl.

"He's fine, Jopab," Jewyl replied to his silent question. "He would never betray me."

"You put a lot of trust in him." Jopab nodded at Hvar. "I do not know this man."

Jewyl nonchalantly stretched and scanned the room, nothing caught her attention.

"Hvar was a friend of my father," she whispered. "It was his father who hid my grandmother and helped her escape the attack. Hvar's father wanted to stay and help, but my grandfather was adamant he help protect Vaela. Any man my grandfather would trust, I will trust. It was my life, too, he saved that night. Hvar was born a year after my father. As they grew, he was always at my father's side until his death."

"Fine. Fine." Jopab lifted his hand in the air to stop Jewyl. "So Hvar was your father's servant."

"No!" Jewyl's shout silenced the room. "Hvar was never a servant. They were like brothers and my father allowed him certain liberties. He never bowed to my father."

"My apologies." Jopab nodded to Hvar. "Perhaps you can aid us in our plan."

"Britha! More drinks here," Hvar roared. He scanned his customers as they looked up at his command. "I am the proprietor, mind you, and therefore do have some rights." He laughed heartily and the room laughed with him.

"There were no strange faces in the crowd," Hvar whispered. "Everyone I saw was a person I have known for too many years. I think we are safe." He frowned. "Not even my boarders for the night have appeared."

"First, let me redistribute our jewels." Chardo placed bags on the table. "I have procured three leather bags." He gazed at Jopab and Jewyl. "One each, so we all have the ability to pay..." He paused. "Or, if the bag is lifted, not all our funds are taken." He handed a bag of jewels to each.

Jewyl slipped the strings of the leather bag about her belt, securing it.

"Now exactly what do you want us to do?" Jewyl looked to Jopab.

Jopab quickly glanced about him and then leaned in. The others at the table did likewise. He whispered. "You must kill Hagontha's Holy Father."

Hvar slammed back in his chair as if violently shoved and pressed against a stone wall. He pressed his thumbs to his lips, kissed them, locked his two hands together by the thumbs, lifting the two hands together, he fluttered the fingers into the air. "By Nauwa's wish, on the wings of a butterfly."

Jewyl and Chardo relaxed and attempted to appear casual, not revealing their true feelings as openly as Hvar had. Jewyl slowly cast an eye about the room. She felt a chill, yet nothing had changed, nobody seemed concerned about Hvar's actions.

Chardo reacted.

"You! A priest of Hagontha, and you want the Holy Father assassinated?" Chardo stared absently off into the distance in thought. He nodded his head, his eyes widening in understanding. "Hagontha condones killing; it is part of the chaos. How is this to be done?"

"I was sent to hire an assassin." Jopab hung his head. "I was a priest of Hagontha." His voice muted. "I was defrocked and cast out by my brethren when the choice fell to me. The Holy Father was notified of my status after I had been banished from the priesthood and removed from the temple."

"Wait a minute." Jewyl waved her hand to stop the conversation. "You're not really a priest of Hagontha?"

Jopab picked up his tankard and slugged down the drink, then wiped an arm across his mouth to dry it. He watched his companions, and played a coin on the table.

"Hagontha is the Goddess of Chaos," he began.

"That we already know," Chardo responded, irritation coating his voice.

Jopab lifted his hand and silenced Chardo. "Listen to my tale. Before Hagontha, before there was Chaos, there was The Void, the realm of Yendisa. She fought her brothers and sisters as they tried to create our existence. She existed for only one thing, the continuance of Nothing. To gain our existence, to end the Nothing and become something, that could only be established by including our death. Yendisa required sacrifices. At first it was simple, we gave something of ours that would appease her, yet left us wanting. Then it became more. She wanted blood. Our blood. Our death."

"I've never heard that tale." Hvar sat in awe and sipped his ale.

"The archives of Hagontha in the temple are the only place to still hold the tales of Yendisa." Jopab took a deep breath and slowly exhaled. "At the decree and command of the gods, including Rorc, Hagontha, Diali, Zwa, even Nauwa, all records of her existence was cleansed from human knowledge." He gazed at Jewyl. "Even before the time of Shiyula."

"But..." Jewyl's voice dwindled into silence as Britha returned with a pitcher of ale to refresh the tankards.

"Harmony cannot exist without Chaos," Jopab added. "Therefore Hagontha hid the secrets to keep the records alive."

"So what does that have to do with the Holy Father?" Chardo asked.

"Excuse me." Jopab cocked an eye to Britha, scooped the last of the vegetables from his plate and munched pleasantly while handing the young girl the plate. "Please, give my compliments to the person who cooked this fabulous meal."

"Thank you." Britha blushed as she poured the ale into the mugs. "Our new cook has taught me that if I allow enough time for the meat to properly cook, it will be tender when served." She looked about the room and then to her father. "If business gets much heavier, you will need to hire another person to help serve."

"You'd best get busy then," Hvar said. "No reason to dawdle here." He patted her on the backside. "Now move on."

Britha knitted her eyebrows together in a frown and puckered her lower lip out. "So much intrigue here," she whispered. "Are you sure I can't be a part of it?"

"There is nothing here to concern you, dear daughter." Hvar waggled his fingers at her. "Now, scoot."

Britha smiled, turned and flounced away to serve others in the tavern.

"I've lost two," Hvar muttered. "I'll not lose her." Hvar glared at Chardo.

"I said I will attend to that in the morning." Chardo lifted the mug to drink.

"Enough." Jopab frowned at Chardo then Hvar. "We have more important things at hand."

Jewyl idly played her index finger around the rim of the tankard. "I don't remember saying we would accept this job. I'm not sure about the true outcome of this."

Jopab sat back in his chair and sighed loudly. Chardo rolled his eyes and wiped his forehead. Hvar smiled knowingly

"By Rorc's ass, Jewyl," Chardo cursed. "We will get two hundred gold coins for accomplishing this. Two hundred! Think how long that could last us."

"If we are killed in the process," Jewyl replied. "Exactly how do you plan to spend those pretty coins?"

"Now? You have scruples now?" Chardo jibbed.

"Not scruples," Hvar said. "Caution. Remember the request, Chardo."

"Kill the Holy Father of Hagontha." Chardo muttered, grimaced and shrugged. "Not too complicated or difficult in my book. I'm sure he doesn't wear a sword, and neither do the other priests." He spread his hands out on the table. "I see it as an easy in, slit or stab, and back out. Two hundred coins." He slapped the table. "Easy."

"Do you know who the Holy Father is?" Hvar asked.

Chardo frowned for a moment in thought. "No."

Hvar leaned in on the table and stared at Chardo. "Are you

familiar with the name Ballec?" A small smile crossed Hvar's face.

Jewyl jerked and turned to stare at Hvar. Chardo quietly repeated the name as if it would help him associate it with a face.

"No," Chardo finally said. "Who is he?"

"That is Azre's brother, you dolt," Jewyl spat. "Now think of the ramifications our actions would have on him."

Chardo sat silent then started to smile. "I guess all Hagontha's Chaos would break loose." He leaned back and thumped his index finger on the table. "You can bet Hagontha is going to be smiling about this one for some time."

Jewyl grabbed her tankard and lifted it to throw the contents at Chardo.

"Stay." Hvar held her hand down. "No need to make a scene." He looked about, but none seemed concerned with them.

Jewyl turned to Jopab. "Why? What do you have to gain?"

"I gain nothing," the priest replied. "I have been set free of Hagontha's priesthood."

Jewyl watched Jopab for a few minutes. "For a priest of Hagontha, you certainly know your way around a sword."

Jopab shrugged. "I've not always been a priest." He gazed at the group. "Now, do you want to know why?"

"I, too, would enjoy hearing that answer," Hvar said. "You seem to have many agendas."

Jopab leaned in over the table. "I have only one agenda: Ballec's death."

"The purpose?" Hvar asked.

"I am the son of a field peasant. I had nothing except the promise I would work the fields like my father and, in time, die. In my youth I secretly trained with a friend, both of us pretending to be guards in the Dragon Lord's service. During an incursion by the Wolf Beast, Lord of Abriela, my father was killed, as were many of the people of my village. Lord Azre's men came and killed all of Lord Niaga's men. There were only a few survivors from the village. I was taken to be trained and become a guard at Dianiya. During my training, Ballec learned of my dedication to Hagontha, and I was re-assigned to him. With his guidance, I soon became a priest to our goddess, Hagontha."

"That explains a few things." Chardo lifted his mug and saluted Jopab. "To your honor, sir."

Jopab frowned. "There is more. Ballec is not only the Holy Father of Hagontha..." His voice lowered. "He has instituted the ways of Yendisa."

"He what?" Jewyl took a deep breath. "Who would follow Yendisa? That goddess has been cursed by her siblings. Yendisa is a myth. She is no longer honored."

Jopab shook his head and wrung his hands. "There are those who relish and savor the torments of a live human sacrifice."

Hvar blanched at the words and glanced at Britha, an innocent young girl who could be whisked away to a gruesome death at the hands of Yendisa's followers.

"We must stop him," Hvar said. "What must be done?"

Jewyl tapped absently on table. "I agree, but we must not be rash. There are threads about us which seem to be coming together."

"Threads?" Chardo repeated.

"Yes." Jewyl slowly tapped an index finger to her lips. "Remember the disturbance at Lord Azre's chambers." She paused. "Just before you started that ridiculous dance?"

"Wisdom, indeed," Jopab replied. "You are correct in your guess. I, too, fear the incident was a disturbance by some of Ballec's men."

"But why?" Jewyl asked.

"Ballec wants his brother out of the way," Jopab said. "He wishes to rule and place Yendisa as the number one goddess, replacing all the other gods. Human sacrifices would happen daily throughout the kingdom to appease her anger, and Ballec's need." He slowly looked into each person's eyes at the table. "Ballec wishes to unite Dianiya, Abriela, and Meisa once more under one reign — his."

"Need? You said Ballec has needs." Chardo echoed.

"Yes." Jopab grimaced and lowered his head for a moment. "He delights in the debauchery of the sacrifice. A virgin is brought to the altar and as the host for Yendisa, Ballec takes her."

Hvar turned and hung his head with the images raking his mind.

"Then in the throes of ecstasy, a sacrificial knife is slowly drawn across the victim's neck. It is at that moment when Ballec leans forward to taste her fresh blood from the wound, relishing the act. There is more, but I could no longer watch."

"You saw this?" The three voices blended in a whispered rush.

"I was Ballec's Number Two Apprentice." Jopab swelled with pride then hung his head ashamedly.

"You were Priest Mage Acolyte?" Hvar whispered.

"Yes. As one so close to the Holy Father, I knew of Ballec's presence at all times, or so I thought. One night I needed to discuss a matter with him, and when I entered his chambers, he was gone."

"Let me guess," Chardo said. "A secret passageway?"

"Yes." Jopab smiled. "A secret door I had not been aware of was ajar just enough for me to notice. I doubt it was supposed to be that way, but I entered and proceeded slowly since this tunnel was new to me. I could hear voices chanting, but could not ascertain the words. They were strange. Suddenly I was in an area overlooking a large chamber where Ballec and five other priests performed the ceremony I had described. I was frozen both in terror and awe at what was happening before me. There were others in the shadows, watching, chanting."

"Human sacrifice?" Jewyl murmured. Her eyes widened in realization. "More? You mean Ballec has a following for Yendisa?"

"Yes," Jopab hissed. "Beasts, all of them. Ballec filled a chalice with the victim's blood and... and..."

Chardo stared in disbelief and noticed how pale Jopab's face appeared. "We understand. You needn't continue." He paused. "How long have you known?"

"Months," Jopab replied. "I'm sure Ballec was involved in my being apprehended by Azre's men. I have sat in that cell for too long."

"I was wondering how you came to that end," Jewyl said. "First, how did you face Ballec the next day?" She lifted the tankard and sipped gingerly the ale.

Jopab shook his head and then slugged his ale down.

" A novice barged into my chambers shouting the Holy Father was sick or had injured himself. I awoke with a start, to say the least. He stood there with tears. 'What did you say?' I asked. The young boy was distraught. 'The Holy Father has bled onto his bedding. His face is smeared with dried blood. What shall we do?' 'Nonsense,' I said and pushed him out the door. The novice was appalled at my actions. He went on his way to report me."

"That got you kicked out?" Chardo asked.

"No, my friend." Jopab took a deep breath. "I hurried to Ballec's chamber and found many of my brethren already attending to the Holy Father's needs. I asked if I could assist and was told it appeared Ballec had lost a tooth during the night. All was well. Two of the priests who aided Ballec were ones I recognized from the ceremony. I noticed my friend, Percho, assisted but seemed distant from the activity. I was finally able to get him to join me in a quiet discussion."

"You told your revelations?" Jewyl asked.

Jopab nodded. "Yes, I needed to confide in someone. Percho was one I knew to be a safe person. We hatched a plan requiring more than two and we gained a secret group to put it into action. The lot fell to me to go out and find the assassins. I had to be removed from Hagontha's elite, and that is how I came to be found in the prison. After being dismissed, I headed to Azre's castle since I knew he sought you. It would allow Lord Azre to lead me to you. His men found me, challenged me and I was locked in the prison until Chardo released me. That wasn't my original plan."

"As was Chardo's, I'm sure." Hvar scowled at Chardo.

"Against my better judgment," Jewyl started. "It appears I'd rather have Ballec dead than Azre. Although both deaths aren't totally out of the question."

Chardo clapped his hands together then rubbed the two palms together. "Finally, some action. What do we do next?"

CHAPTER FIVE
The Dancing Dragon

Britha appeared at Hvar's shoulder. "Anyone for more?" She reached into the group and took the empty plates. "I'll bring more drinks. Who is thirsty?"

"Child, never you mind our conversation." Hvar waggled a finger to dismiss her. "Keep the other customers happy. We've enough to drink."

"I'll have another ale, if you please." Jewyl held her tankard for Britha. "Do you have something sweet to eat?"

"I will bring you honeyed bars," Britha replied. "Chardo? Jopab?"

They nodded agreement and Britha hustled away.

"She will leave me, I'm sure," Hvar mumbled and glanced at Jewyl.

"I know not what the paths of destiny have deigned." Jewyl reached out and took Hvar's large hands into hers. "You love your daughter, but cannot make all her life's decisions. If she decides to ride with us, I will not stop her." She gazed into his eyes. "For what is, has already been written, and cannot be undone."

Hvar hung his head and a tear traced a path down his robust cheek.

"Praise be to Hagontha," Jopab chanted. "Chaos reigns."

"Chaos be damned!" Hvar glared at Jopab. "Britha is all I have."

Chardo drained his ale and clanked the empty tankard on the table. "You still have Vico."

"Bah." Hvar scowled at Chardo. "His life is now entwined with The Dancing Dragon."

"We need to plot our plans." Jopab thumped his index finger on the table. "We can't lose our focus."

"Focus," Hvar echoed, and heaved a hallowed laugh.

"Tomorrow is the celebration of the festival will start," Jopab

44

said. "Tomorrow's evening, it is then the Holy Father will be most vulnerable. If we enter by the front gate as entertainers, we can gain access to the temple."

"And then?" Jewyl asked.

"There are many passageways." Jopab smiled. "And hidden chambers. I can gain you access to Ballec's private chambers. I can offer you a clear path to our goal."

"He shall die in his bed." Chardo raised his hand, his thumb stroking his fingers. "The coins are almost ours now, I can feel them." He closed his eyes. "Mm. Just taste that gold."

"We are committed?" Jopab asked.

"Committed," Jewyl confirmed.

Chardo nodded in agreement and turned to Hvar. "But, first thing tomorrow morning, I will go to The Dancing Dragon."

# # #

Chardo awakened early and gazed out the window at the new day. The sun glowed, just peeking above the trees and it promised to be a good one. He looked over at Jopab. Should he? Shouldn't he? Chardo scowled in deep thought. It had been so simple when they'd first met. Chardo was sure he could convince the man to a quick session of non-commitment. That was before he found out Jopab was a priest. It was a common fact priests of Hagontha took an oath of celibacy. Still, Jopab was no longer a priest, but there was just something that bothered him about a tryst with one of the goddess' holies. Somehow it just didn't seem right, especially since Jopab didn't truly seem interested. *Be damned Chaos, Jopab is attractive.*

He stood up and proceeded to the freshening bowl. *The fresh water should snap me out of this reverie*, he thought. He glanced back at Jopab then splashed water onto his face. It just wasn't helping. Jopab was desirable. Chardo stared longingly at the muscular back of the man curled away from him.

The Dancing Dragon, Chardo thought. "At least in that neighborhood I'm sure to find what I'm looking for at one of the establishments." The whispered words came unbidden to his lips. "Especially if Vico is there and ..." He let the thought drift away.

He hastily put on his clothes, avoiding all possible glances at the almost naked Jopab. He silently closed the door behind him as he slipped from the room. Chardo sighed heavily and considered going back.

"You're up early," Hvar said, startling Chardo.

"As are you," Chardo stammered. He gathered his wits about him which had been scattered by the old man's sudden appearance. "I have promises to keep." He smiled at Hvar.

Hvar frowned and stared out the window at the bright sun. "I assure you, Chardo, it is not that early for an innkeeper. Promises?"

"I told you I would visit Vico at The Dancing Dragon." Chardo placed a reassuring arm over the older man's shoulder. "I will see what has happened, and why he has left."

Hvar slapped him on the back and smiled. "Come. Eat. It is a small journey to the other side of town, but still a journey." He grabbed Chardo's chin to look him in the eye. "You truly plan to visit The Dragon?"

"I don't know what has transpired, or why Vico is there, but I will find out." Chardo pulled away and tromped down the stairs before Hvar.

"Marela!" Hvar shouted. "Bring a hearty breakfast for my friend." He pushed Chardo down the last step and across the room to an area by the window. "Here, eat and enjoy the early morning activities." He nodded out the window. "The streets are busy at this time." He smiled. "Always something to amuse one while eating."

Marela sauntered across the room. She carried a streaming tray filled with sausages, potatoes, eggs and fresh breads.

Chardo's eyes raced up and down to take in the sultry beauty of the woman as her hips swayed beneath the thin cotton tunic.

"My cook," Hvar stated. "An excellent cook at that." Hvar's face shone with the boyish charm of puppy-love.

"The foods smell absolutely delicious. Jopab and Jewyl will truly enjoy this feast." Chardo smiled at Marela who feigned innocence. Chardo looked into her cerulean blue eyes. He knew hidden secrets boiled in earnest behind those blue eyes, and all of it could be unleashed in a bout of passion. Suddenly Hvar's toothy smile filled his mind. He calmed himself and let his own passions ease. First Jopab, now Marela, he needed to get to The Dancing Dragon for a quick session of release.

"Thank you," Marela said. She blinked, an eternity passed, then she turned and languidly moved back to the kitchen, allowing

46

her hips to sway even more.

Chardo cocked an eye to Hvar. "Just a cook?" he asked.

"Yes," Hvar sighed with a sideward glance at Marela. A sheepish grin slowly worked its way across his face, curling the heavy mustache that edged his upper lip. "At least, for now. Enjoy your meal and good luck on your endeavors. Tell Vico I still love him as a father always will."

A baker's apprentice strolled the street beyond the window, hawking his wares, barely controlling the stack of goods. Chardo enjoyed his meal, watching the other activities beyond the walls where vendors noisily established their daily markets. He caught glimpses of Marela from time to time, and he was sure she was stealing quick looks at him.

"Hold yourself," Chardo chastised in a mumble. "You've already riled Hvar with Vico, there is no reason to add another notch to Hvar's anger stick with Marela."

Chardo enjoyed the sausages and a couple of hard-boiled eggs in silence, grabbed a small loaf of bread before easing himself out the door when nobody was looking. He smiled at the morning light as it hit has face. He tore the loaf of bread in half to begin eating. Chardo wandered his way toward the other side of town where The Dancing Dragon awaited him. There he would find Vico. Thoughts came unbidden, shoving and crowding Chardo's mind.

Could it be true Vico preferred men to women? I remember he asked me many questions, and... there had been that touch.

Chardo steamed with the memory of Vico touching his leg and the sensations that coursed through his body. He started to get aroused at the thought.

"You are vain to think one so young and appealing would be interested in the likes of you." Chardo looked about, he'd been wandering without really watching. The streets were seedier, there was an air of stealth and shadiness. He was definitely narrowing the distance to The Dancing Dragon.

"Hey, gorgeous!" A voice called from the window above him. "Interested in a bit of fun?" She lifted a hand into the air. "A lovely morning for it."

Chardo looked up at the woman who leaned precariously out the window. She had on too much makeup, her hair was disheveled, yet it attempted a certain semblance of style. The thin wrap of mint-green fabric barely covered her wiles.

"Oh, you are a darling," she cooed. "A pretty one, indeed. A silver deca will get you in the door, love. The name's Barda. Come on up and see me."

"I'm sure your services would be a pleasant start to my day." Chardo smiled at the slightly robust woman. "Unfortunately, I have business I must attend to. Perhaps another day?"

The woman sighed. "That's what all the good ones say. I bet you'd be a great bout in a bed, or even a moment in the hay." She cackled then looked about for another prospect.

Chardo continued on his way. This part of town hadn't changed too much since his last visit. Behind him he could hear Barda shouting to another prospect.

He turned the corner and The Dancing Dragon stood blatantly out in the middle of the row of buildings. Its purple dragon with white wings on a faded black background beckoned to all patrons to enter the establishment. Chardo trudged forward, and ducked quickly through the doorway.

"Good morning." A voice filled with sugar and false vibrato caught Chardo's attention as he headed for the desk. "Can I help you?"

Chardo stopped and nonchalantly glanced at the man standing near the window.

"Lost your tongue, honey?" The man sashayed toward Chardo.

"I'm here to see Vico," Chardo stated.

"Now, just what does Vico have that I don't?" The man slowly traced his finger gently down Chardo's left arm. "My, my, how very nice."

Chardo curtly removed the finger and hand. "If you don't mind." He should have been excited somebody was interested in him, but wasn't.

The man sighed and pushed his lower lip out in a pout. "So you want to see Vico?"

"Yes," Chardo replied and turned to again move toward the desk and what appeared to be a sleeping attendant.

"Chardo?" the man called. "You don't even remember me?"

Chardo stopped and turned to face his admirer. Recognize him? Chardo stared at the man. About the same age, extremely

48

handsome in a rugged way with a hint of femininity, long dark hair, amber eyes. The eyes looked familiar, too familiar. *Amber eyes*? Chardo raced through his memories. *Who was this man before him? Klajany?*

"You really don't remember me, do you?" The man pouted. "After all those fabulous nights together?"

"Klajany?" Chardo offered. "Is that you? You've changed."

The man smiled and his eyes beamed with excitement. He leaped forward and flung his arms around Chardo and nuzzled on his ear.

Startled, Chardo embraced him lightly then gently eased him back. "Good to see you, again."

"Like I said earlier," Klajany cooed. "Exactly what does Vico have to offer that I can't give you. I'm sure you remember my skills." He batted his eyes innocently. "Vico is a mere lad. He's an amateur; clumsy, at best." Once more the man slowly dragged his index finger down Chardo's chest. "You need somebody who knows what they are doing."

Chardo smiled at the memory of his nights with Klajany. "I only need to speak with Vico," Chardo said. "I'm not here for any type of affair with him."

Klajany stepped back, pulling his hand away. "Then you won't be displeased. Vico isn't interested in any liaison with a man." Klajany placed a consoling hand on Chardo's shoulder. "I grant, he's a cute person, turns almost every man's head. He doesn't even try."

"Well then, what does Vico do here?" Chardo asked.

"He's a tease." Klajany rolled his eyes. "He's walks about the building, but with that youthful physique and skimpy apparel ... he excites the customers, but they must find another for their frustrated release."

"He does what?" Chardo asked. He couldn't believe his ears.

"He cleans," Klajany said. "Vico is nothing more than a studly janitor who struts his stuff in front of the clients. He can really excite some of them. Then when they find he is not available ... Well, being frustrated, there are others available to ease the strain."

Chardo glanced about the room. It was clean and although there was nobody other than the two of them, he could see where anywhere up to perhaps twenty patrons could sit and meet the merchandise available. The place was clean. Vico seemed to be doing a superb job.

"Is he here?" Chardo asked.

"I'm sure he is, somewhere." Klajany inhaled deeply. "Would you like to go upstairs for a short length of time?" He brushed his hand across Chardo's chest and let it slide downward. "I remember you." Klajany leered at Chardo with a downward glance to where his hand rested below the waist. He grinned. "Seems you might be remembering me?"

"Chardo!" Vico called. "What brings you here?"

"You!" Chardo stepped back from Klajany's hand. "Good to see you."

"I see my services are no longer needed here," Klajany snipped. He glared at Vico before placing a finger under Vico's chin. "You can be innocent only for so long, child. Enjoy it while you can."

Vico pulled his head back leaving Klajany's finger sticking in the air.

"Chardo, my friend." Vico placed his arm over Chardo's shoulder. "It is so good to see you, again. Come, let us go up to my room."

Chardo followed Vico up the stairs to a small cubicle. There was mixed emotions of concern and excitement stirring within his body. Chardo stared at Vico's muscular body.

"This is your room?" Chardo asked. He glanced about the sparse room. It appeared more like a priest's habitat than that of a young man.

"I like to keep it simple." Vico lounged back onto the bed. Vico wore no tunic, his vest opened to reveal a well-muscled chest with a small amount of hair.

Chardo stared at Vico's chest and arms before his eyes strayed to the way the cloth of his pants clung to the young man's legs. He breathed deeply. Was Vico offering, or teasing?

"Why are you here, Chardo?" Vico reached up and nonchalantly twiddled with a necklace string hanging from the shelf.

"Uh," Chardo stumbled and collected his thoughts. "I came to find out why you left your father's place?"

"My father doesn't understand me," Vico replied. "I have certain needs."

"What doesn't he understand?" Chardo sat down on the chair.

"What needs?"

Vico reached down, scratched his knee then slowly drew his hand up his leg and across his crotch. He hesitated, finally moving it rest on his chest momentarily before touching his chin with his fingers.

Chardo paused. Klajany might have been right. Vico was definitely teasing, or completely naïve of his actions.

Vico sighed, put a finger to his lips then let his hand slide to his chest. "I want to be on my own. I want to be able to say what I do is what I do because I want to do it."

Chardo shook his head and closed his eyes. "You've confused me."

"My father tells me everything to do, Chardo. He tells me when to get up, go to bed, feed the patrons, eat my meals, what I am to eat, if I can get a drink. He dictated my every move."

"Here you do what you want?"

Vico silently stared at Chardo. "No. They tell me what to do, but I do what I want. Let me explain. They tell me to clean the lounge area. I decide if I want to dust or sweep, polish or mop. It is my decision of what I will do to do what they ask."

Chardo quietly nodded his head, understanding. "What would it take to have you come home?"

"I enjoy my life here." Vico smiled and let his hand slide to his waist.

Chardo stood up and moved to the edge of the bed. *Time to call his bluff.* He leaned across Vico. "Is this what you want?"

Vico smiled and placed his hands behind his head. He closed his eyes. "Whatever you want, Chardo. I'm here."

Chardo placed a hand on Vico's chest. "Are you sure?" He pushed Vico's vest to the side and let his hand gently brush the bare skin, moving his hand to the nipple. His hand traced a path to the waist and played with the belt, loosening it. Vico's pants fell open revealing the youth's manhood.

"No!" Vico grabbed the top of his pants. "This isn't the way it should be." He pulled his pants together and hooked his belt.

"Have you ever been with a man?" Chardo asked, standing by the bed.

"Just as Klajany said," Vico whispered. "Innocent. I have had men offer, but have never allowed them to touch me. I was waiting

51

for you. I've always been waiting for you, Chardo."

"I'm honored," Chardo whispered. "But, I could never share a bed with you. I need to honor your father's friendship."

"You want me?" Vico asked and massaged Chardo's thigh.

"That isn't the question." Chardo pulled away. He was being aroused and knew Vico would catch his body betraying his words.

"Then I've been the fool," Vico said. "Perhaps I should have taken Klajany's offer."

"Perhaps you don't really want a man." Chardo stared at the floor between his feet. "Have you slept with a woman?"

Vico shook his head. "No, I'm a virgin. My thoughts have only been of you."

"Come with me." Chardo grabbed Vico's hand. "You need to find your own identity, and I know just the place to go."

Vico stood up, flung his arms around Chardo in a deep embrace and pressed his lips to Chardo's in a passionate kiss. He finally stood back.

Vico stared at Chardo with a questioning expression. "It wasn't what I thought it would be." He touched his lips and slowly drew his fingers across them.

"Only you were involved in the action," Chardo said. "I didn't reciprocate."

Vico frowned. "Why? What is your plan?" Vico asked and tightened the buckle of the belt for his pants.

"Just follow me." Chardo led him out of the room.

"Where are we going?" Vico asked as they raced down the stairs.

Klajany watched the two of them come down the stairs and quickly arose from the divan to cross the room and join them. "The deed is done?"

"No, if you must know. Vico is still a virgin." Chardo pushed Klajany out of their path as he pulled Vico toward the door.

"Where are you taking me?" Vico asked again.

"You'll see." Chardo pushed the young man out the front door of The Dancing Dragon. "Now to your right, then around the corner. I know just the place."

Chardo saw her.

"Ah, darling," she called. "You're back." Then she frowned, recognizing Vico. "You were to The Dancing Dragon? I thought you wanted a little bit of fun with me."

"Fun you shall have." Chardo waved. "Not with me, but with my friend here. His first experience, darling. Treat him good and enjoy his manhood which I can truly say should make you more than happy."

The woman leered at Vico, taking in his muscular chest and arms, narrow waist and filled crotch. She slowly licked her lips. "A virgin? Come into Sleepy Arms and ask to see Barda," she replied. "I'll be waiting."

"Make it last, Barda." Chardo smiled and winked. "Remember, his first time. Be sure he has the time to enjoy…" Chardo shrugged.

Chardo pushed Vico through the door and shoved four decas at the attendant. "This one is to see Barda. I'll take the room next to her."

"You want him to bed with Barda? And you want Honna?"

"Yes," Chardo said. "Let Barda take his innocence." He pushed Vico up the stairs and found Barda's door open and her sitting on the bed.

"Come in darling." Barda beckoned with her index finger. Vico stood at the doorway to her chamber, hesitant.

"Are you sure?" Vico gave a questioning look at Chardo.

"When you are done here, you will be able to better make a decision of what you want," Chardo said and smiled. "I think you will enjoy a woman more than a man. Beyond that, I think when Barda finishes with you, helping your father will no longer be an issue."

"But, I don't want—"

Chardo pushed Vico into the room, the conversation ended, shut the door, and hustled to the next door. "Honna, darling," he said barging into the room, removing his vest and loosening his belt. "Be quick about your duties for my friend next door won't last too long under Barda's expertise tutelage." The belt, pants and sword clanked to the floor.

# # #

"I never realized being with a woman could feel so wonderful," Vico gushed. "There is a strangeness growing within me."

"Today you are a man, Vico." Chardo slapped his companion on the back. "Do you still wish to sleep with me?"

"I'm not sure." Vico looked at Chardo with a sheepish grin. "The feelings are still there. Perhaps, a future day we can have a simple moment together."

"To a future day," Chardo said, smiled and hugged him. "Now, about your father."

"I will talk with him and possibly we can come to some terms about my life at The Red Horse Inn."

Chardo slapped him affectionately on the back. "A good step in the proper direction."

"Life wasn't all that wonderful at The Dancing Dragon," Vico muttered. "I tried to tell myself things were going well, but, it wasn't. Remember Klajany?"

"What of him?" Chardo was suddenly curious and defensive.

"He called me to his room several times when he had a client just to show me what he could. I found it offensive."

"Offensive?" Chardo asked. He stared quizzically at the young man.

"I know that is contradictory, Chardo." Vico waved his hands in frustration. "I know what we would do to be the same, yet it wouldn't be performed as a function, but with love and emotion. There is a difference. It wouldn't be so blatant."

"Yes, there would be a difference," Chardo agreed. "You are right. Now back to your father. I know he loves you dearly and misses you."

They turned the corner and The Red Horse Inn stood before them.

"I have missed him, too." Vico stared at the inn. "He waits for me, I know." Vico moved forward with a determination. "I hope he forgives me."

"Vico!" Britha shouted as he walked through the door. She placed her tray on a table and raced to embrace her brother. She kissed him. "You've changed," she said.

"More than you'd think." Chardo winked.

Hvar came running and then stopped to stare at his two children. A tear welled in one eye.

"Father!" Vico paced across the room to embrace his father.

"I have missed you, and hope you can forgive me "

"There is nothing to forgive," Hvar cried. "You have come home."

"We will need to talk, father," Vico said. "There are things I should make known."

"Father?" Britha's voice was strained as she called to get his attention.

Three guards stood at the doorway, their faces in shadow, but the dark herald very obvious designating Lord Azre.

"We are seeking the one called Jewyl," the head guard said. "She has been reported staying at this inn. She is to make herself known immediately, or action will be taken."

"There are none here by that name." Hvar approached the guard. "This is my inn and who claims the person you seek is here?"

"For twenty pieces of silver," the guard said. "One of your very own has told us the outlaw known as Jewyl is staying here."

CHAPTER SIX
The Chaos of Plans

Hvar turned to face those with him. "Who claims this?" He stared at the confused faces then searched the inn for a traitor. The room was empty.

"I do." Marela sauntered from the kitchen into the room. "She came in here yesterday with two men and joined you last night at the table." She glared at Hvar.

"What are you doing?" Hvar whispered.

She languidly ambled to the door, stepped up to the guard, placed a hand on his chest and slowly turned a gaze to Hvar. "Old man, you have nothing I want. Do you actually think I would want to be a cook? To work in an inn the rest of my life?" She paused. "Or to consider marriage to you?" She turned to the head guard. "The one you seek is here, top of the stairs, second door on the right. One of the men you want is standing there. He's in the red jerkin." She pointed at Chardo. "The priest is probably babbling vows up in his room." She pressed against the guard and, as Chardo remembered, offered a smile full of promises. She slipped out the door.

The guard was momentarily befuddled, but regained his senses quickly. "You have two choices." The guard faced Chardo. "Go peaceably, or go otherwise. Which would you prefer?"

"By the blade." Jewyl leaped the last few steps of the stairs to the floor. "You have two choices, dog guard of Lord Azre. Leave in peace, or leave in pieces." She played her sword in a threatening circle at them.

Chardo joined her and Vico stepped backwards to grab a sword from the wall. He stood clumsily at the ready.

"Guards," Jopab yelled. "You have caught us, but we need our freedom for but a short length of time more. I am a priest of the goddess, Hagontha. Blessed chaos. Leave us until tomorrow, and we shall give ourselves freely."

"Why should I trust you?" the guard asked and pulled his

sword. The sound of two more blades could be heard behind him as his companions pulled their swords.

"Trust me?" Jopab repeated. "I am a priest of Hagontha. Is there not a temple of Hagontha within this city? We are to perform today. Join us and you may take us into custody when we finish."

Jewyl looked at Jopab in total surprise. Chardo frowned in confusion.

The two guards behind the main guard stiffened in shock and their blades fell noisily to the ground. The main guard turned to face their assailant and stepped backward into the inn to avoid the blades' points. Klajany smiled at the group as he stepped through the doorway holding two swords.

"Perhaps I'm not wanted," Klajany said. "Perhaps I have made a mistake, but this was the only way I knew I could see Chardo and Vico."

The guard lifted his sword and Klajany's one blade pushed against the guard's stomach flesh, only to protrude from the guard's back.

Vico stood gawking at Klajany.

"What do you want?" Chardo asked.

"Why did you leave The Dancing Dragon, dear Vico?"

"To lay with a real woman," Vico spat. "I no longer wish to be a servant in The Dancing Dragon. Why are you here?"

"Chardo," Klajany said. "I heard you talking with Barda. I had hoped we could spend a few moments together. It would appear..." He waved his hand to encompass the area and nodded. "Yes. You've been a bit busy." He smiled. "Although I think things have cleared up."

"Klaj, darling." Chardo reached out and pulled him in and placed an arm over his shoulder. "Your timing is impeccable in one regard, and totally wrong in another. It seems my friends and I will be leaving shortly." He winked at Klajany. "I think you understand. Of course, first, we must remove this evidence before we depart. No reason to leave Hvar holding a dragon by the tail."

"Do you have a wagon you are willing to give up?" Klajany asked. "One that doesn't point back to you?"

Hvar nodded.

"Bring it around and we'll put these bodies into it and I'll take them back somewhere near The Dancing Dragon. None would question any of Lord Azre's guards being killed in that neighborhood."

Chardo frowned.

Klajany rolled his eyes. "The royal guard is always looking for quick service and then leave without paying most of the time. Sure, a dead guard or two will raise an eyebrow, but deep down inside, most residents of that particular area will be relieved." He grinned. "Even dear Barda at Sleepy Arms has lost a coin or two with Azre's men."

"Quick," Hvar said. "Vico, bring the wagon around. Britha? Do we have any large flour bags we could place them in?"

"We could just carry them out as if they were drunk." Britha stood with her arms folded in front of her. "They're always doing that over at The Foamy Tankard."

Hvar scowled at Britha.

"Well, they do, father." Britha returned the scowl. "I'm not the little girl you think I am. I do see what goes on around me."

"Please," Klajany said. "Let's just get the bodies out into the cart, cover them up and then we'll get it over to the other side of town and let what happens..." He shrugged. "Just let it happen."

"She's right." Jewyl appraised the situation. "Klajany and Jopab, you carry out one. Chardo and I will carry out one and Vico and Hvar will take the other. Jopab and Klajany will take the cart and Klajany can return to The Dancing Dragon. Jopab will come back here with the horse."

Vico moved forward to speak.

"I believe it to be the best plan for all." Jewyl gazed at Vico. "The less involved you are, Vico, the safer and better for you, your sister, and father." She looked about for agreement.

"Sounds good," Jopab offered. "As soon as the bodies are gone and I return, we must make our plans for the celebration. Thank the goddess for chaos."

Klajany turned over one of the guards he had stabbed. "This one is sort of cute, such a pity I killed him without first seeing his face."

#

"If we plan to attack Ballec in his own house, we must think

58

of something very unique so we may have our swords with us." Jopab turned his ale's container using his palms to move it in a circle.

Jewyl fingered the lip of her tankard. It was still morning, and she wasn't sure an ale would be good, but she needed something. Britha sat beside her, the young girl's excitement barely contained.

"I know my father says I shouldn't bother you." Britha's words were quick and whispered. "But, I am anxious to have an exciting life." She gazed at Jewyl. "Like yours." Britha smiled sheepishly.

"My life is not exciting." Jewyl shook her head. "I live in fear every day Lord Azre or his men will find me, and be killed, or worse, forced to marry the man."

"Why does he search for you?" Britha leaned forward to see her father struggle from the kitchen. She gazed down, knowing her duty should have been to be helping him since Marela had left, but she needed to talk with Jewyl.

"He seeks Jewyl as the princess heir to Shiyula. He wants her to be his wife," Jopab said. "It will give him extreme leverage over the other sovereignties."

Britha inhaled. "A princess?"

"So I am told." Jewyl nonchalantly shrugged. "My grandfather was king of all Shiyula, but was killed. My grandmother became ruling queen, but was in hiding. The kingdom of Shiyula was broken and lost. Queen Vaela was pregnant with my father at that time." Jewyl grabbed Britha's hands and held them in hers. "Our fathers knew each other for years before I was born."

"I wish my father would talk about his life before—"

"Before what?" Hvar stood defiantly behind her, hands on hips and legs spread apart. The apron he wore was already dirty with unknown blood stains. "We must leave these people alone so they can plan their actions." The left eyebrow lifted in a question. "The less we know of their plans, the safer they, and we, shall be."

"I am sorry, father," Britha eased away from the table. "Perhaps I will see you later?"

"It would be nice," Jewyl replied with a smile. "More than likely not. Thank you for all your kindness."

"Why not be a sword fighting group for the celebration?" Britha asked. "Would that not be chaotic enough to honor

Hagontha?"

Jopab stared at Britha. "From the mouths of the innocent. I have been praying for an answer of how we could hide our swords in some costume. Young Britha utters the obvious. Who would look for a hidden sword in such a routine?" He reached out and grabbed her hand and pulled it to his lips for a kiss. "Hide them in plain sight. You, my dear, are the most ingenious person I've ever met."

Britha smiled proudly, yet blushed.

"Come, Britha." Hvar placed his large hands on her delicate shoulders. "We must leave these people to their plans. Someone should stand watch at the door for more guards." He paused. "And, perhaps tonight I will tell you a rousing tale of when I and Jewyl's father spent a night in Eichla's prison."

Britha's eyes widened. "Eichla's prison?"

Hvar smiled while making a circling motion and pointed toward the inn's door indicating she should turn and attend to duties. She sighed and walked to the front door, looked back at the table, then stepped into the sunlight of the street.

"You won't take her, will you?" Hvar spread his fingers apart on the table as he leaned over it. A tear welled in his eye. "She so wants to travel, to have excitement in her life."

Jewyl reached out and patted Hvar's hand. "No, my dear Hvar," she whispered. "You have your family. Vico has returned. I will not allow Britha to join us. Now, go share your tale and enchant her with your dubious youth with my father." She smiled. "Maybe I should listen to learn of my father's past. Eichla's prison?"

"A four person sword fighting group could be interesting." Chardo stood innocently in the middle of the room. "Two men and two women—now that could prove to be very interesting."

Jewyl cocked an eyebrow at Chardo. "I said 'No' and I mean it."

"Very well." Jopab shrugged. "A three person sword fighting routine it shall be. Two men and a woman should be intriguing enough to tempt Hagontha's stewards with chaos."

"One woman and two men," Jewyl repeated. "Don't you think that to be a bit too obvious? Isn't it exactly what Lord Azre is looking for?"

"Fine," Jopab said. "Two women then. I remember that Chardo looked quite attractive when he rescued you at Lord Azre's castle."

Jewyl closed her eyes and shook her head. "Hmm? Let me see – two women and a man. I think Lord Azre would see through that charade as well."

"Fine." Jopab was exasperated. "We are either all three men, or all three women. What are your thoughts?"

Jewyl sipped her ale and glanced back and forth between Jopab and Chardo thinking. Three women. Chardo could do it. Jopab's strong build would definitely draw attention to him not being a woman. Still, a heavy scarf could be draped across his lower face to hide most of his manly facial features. "Three women—"

"Do you think you could pass yourself as a man?" Jopab asked cutting Jewyl's comment. He sat there examining Jewyl. "A more manly gait perhaps? To be honest, there is no way I could possibly be a woman."

Jewyl grabbed the tankard and drained the contents then swiped her wrist and hand across her lips to wipe away the excess. She lowered her voice.

"Perhaps," she said. "Will I need to bed a woman to prove my manhood?"

"What manhood?" Chardo jibbed.

Jopab blushed. "I'm sorry."

"Should we plan our moves?" Jewyl asked. "I would hate to have myself run through during our demonstration."

"Ah, that's the chaotic aspect of this plan." Jopab smiled. "We will never need perform. We will gain access to the courtyard and then—" He spread his fingers in the air before his face. "Poof. Disappear."

"Secret rooms?" Chardo asked.

Jopab smiled a silly grin. "Yes."

"Your plan is?" Jewyl asked.

"Once inside and we are accepted as a sword troupe, we can mix with the others and disappear through a secret chamber. Within the secret tunnel, we can work our way toward Ballec's chamber and prepare for his return. You kill him . We escape through another secret passageway. Deed done. All is well."

"Two hundred pieces of gold, easy." Chardo clapped and rubbed his hands together.

"Nothing is ever as easy as it is planned," Jewyl said. "What if we are discovered?"

"I know the passageways and the other clerics." Jopab grabbed his ale. "If we were to encounter one, they know me, and would never question my presence." He slugged down the drink and then raised it toward Hvar for another.

"Do you still believe your position is safe within the priesthood?" Jewyl asked. "Why? Wouldn't Ballec have notified the others of your treason? Yes, you have friends, but what of those who are loyal to Ballec?" She hesitated. "And those too naïve to know better?" She cocked an eye in Jopab's direction. "You *were* defrocked."

"I still have many friends and allies within the priests of Hagontha — defrocked or otherwise." Jopab's facial features tightened in anger.

"What happens if we meet one of Ballec's men?" Jewyl pushed the thread of questioning.

"You have a sword." Jopab huffed a breath. "Use it."

"I could get you new clothes." Hvar placed new tankards before the group. "Forgive me for listening." He hoped the tension could be broken.

"New clothes," Chardo said. "Something bright and colorful. Flamboyant."

"Yes." Jewyl agreed and smiled profusely. "Make us stand out. Let's make sure Lord Azre can find us." Jewyl scowled and glared at Jopab.

"No," Jopab replied. He was excited and animated. "Would Lord Azre be looking for a group that was so blatantly obvious? No, I don't think so. His eyes will be trained on the group moving among the shadows in stealth. Anyone drawing attention would be noted, but quickly ignored." Jopab nodded. "The more flamboyant, the better."

"There is a streak of truth in your words." Jewyl nodded her head in agreement. "Again, hiding in the open."

"Blessed chaos," Jopab offered while raising his hands. "Within your swirling worlds there is a pattern to the madness."

"I'll have Vico and Britha go get them for you," Hvar said.

"Take these." Jewyl reached into her leather bag and placed two gems in his hand. "This should help defray some of the costs we have caused."

"You need not pay for anything." Hvar began to hand the jewels back. "It is a service I gladly give."

Chardo reached out to retrieve the stones.

"But, I will keep them nonetheless." Hvar pulled his hand back with a glinting smile. "Keep your hands to yourself." He winked at Chardo. "This will help with improvements to my inn."

Chardo pulled back a bit reluctantly and scowled at Jewyl. "Must you give all our money away?" he whispered.

"We share with our friends." Jewyl grinned. "How many times must I tell you that, Chardo? What do we need with wealth?"

"You may give excess to the glory of Hagontha," Jopab added and grinned at Chardo. "A donation of such would cause more chaos than the brotherhood would be able to handle. They would truly be in bliss."

Chardo scowled then slugged down his drink. "Bliss," he thought. "He'd bliss them. Two hundred gold pieces was indeed a tidy sum, but giving away the small handful of gems was plain stupid. If they didn't keep any booty, how would they survive when the sword was no longer their forte?"

"You brood, dear Chardo." Jewyl reached out to pat his hands. "There are still plenty of gems in the bag you have. You remain a rich man."

"There are gems and coins within the compound of Hagontha," Jopab whispered. "If you feel you must collect a few on our retreat, please do so. To be rid of Ballec, any expense is adequate. Take what you feel is right."

Chardo's eyes gleamed at the prospect. *More than the allotted payment*. He rubbed his hands together at the prospect.

"Now you must wait until Vico and Britha return." Hvar nonchalantly nodded toward the stairs. "Perhaps you should return to your rooms and rest?" He glanced at the entry; two guards spoke with possible patrons just beyond the door.

"A wise decision, Hvar," Jewyl said. "Send Britha to me as soon as she returns."

Hvar cast a glance of doubt at Jewyl.

"She will remain, Hvar." Jewyl reached over and patted Hvar's hand. "She won't be happy, but I will not allow her to join us."

Hvar sighed. "She may not join you, but she may leave on

63

her own. I fear I will lose my daughter no matter what."

"I will talk with her," Jewyl confided. "I know I am not her mother, more like a big sister. She may listen to me. I hope she understands."

"Innkeeper," a voice yelled. "Two ales."

Hvar turned to attend to the guards who had come into the inn. Jewyl hastened behind to grab two tankards and hand them to Hvar. He grinned at her. Jopab slipped quietly up the stairs and Chardo remained sipping his ale.

"Innkeeper," the one guard began. "We are looking for our friends, three others who came earlier?"

Hvar placed the tankards in front of the guards. "Enjoy, good sirs. There were other guards earlier, but they left."

"Did they find what they were looking for?"

"No," Hvar replied. "They said they were looking for three people. If I remember correctly a red haired woman and her two companions?"

"Thieves, the lot of them," the guard replied. "They stole from Lord Azre. I hear tell they removed over one hundred gems from the statues of the gods and even took the emerald eyes of the dragon. Each of those emeralds had to be the size of my fist."

Jewyl brought a tray of cheese and a few breads. "Enjoy." She bowed, and then started to leave.

"Ah, a beauty," the other guard grabbed her hand. "Let me see your full beauty. Pleasure me."

"Sir," Jewyl replied. "I am but a lowly cook to wait upon you. My husband and children await my return for their meals"

"Let them wait," the guard said. "What I wish is to only behold you. That will only take a few moments."

Jewyl struggled back in mock innocence. She could feel the clench of the man's hand and knew she could quickly twist and snap free.

"Let her go," his companion ordered. "We are here on official business." The guard turned to Hvar. "Have you seen the ones we seek?" He twisted back to his companion. "I said let her go!"

Jewyl jerked her hand free, pulled it close to her waist and pretended to massage it. The guard had barely held her, yet she needed to appear to be a helpless woman.

"You may go." Hvar nodded to Jewyl.

Jewyl slowly walked to the kitchen area and hesitated at the doorway. She glanced back at the guards and Hvar. Her admirer watched her. She went into the kitchen and closed the door. There were back stairs for her to get to her room. She glanced at the door to the back of the inn. A few quick steps. She opened and slammed the door.

"Let me go and apologize to your cook," the guard said and stood up.

"Please." Hvar boldly placed a hand on the guard's shoulder and pushed him to sit. "You've done more than you need. I just heard the back door. She has probably already left for her home. Fleeing, if you must know." He grinned feebly.

"Fleeing is correct," the guard said and smiled snidely. "Her husband has no idea how lucky he is, especially today."

The other guard slapped him in a friendly manner. "Yes, if only."

"If you need anything else, just call me." Hvar bowed and left.

# # #

Jewyl smoothed the cloth of her jerkin and adjusted the belt of fabric that bound her breasts. Pulling her hair up over her head, she cocked her face one way then another for the sheer joy of admiring her manly appearance. "Would this pass Jopab's inspection?" she whispered. She placed the leather helmet on her head and darkened her lower cheeks and jawbone: a facade of a beard's shadow. She nodded approval. *Jopab will have to agree*, she thought.

A knock at the door broke her reverie. She lowered her voice. "Who's there?"

"Britha. May I come in?"

"Come in," Jewyl replied in her own voice. "I've been waiting for you."

Britha opened the door. "Oh!" She stepped back in surprise. "Jewyl? I hardly recognized you. At first I thought you had another person in your room." Britha entered the room, leaving the door ajar. She gently touched Jewyl's vest. "This is a very good costume."

"Ah, good." Jopab poked his head through the open door.

"You're ready. We must make haste."

Jewyl grabbed Britha's hands. "I will make this very short. Your father loves you dearly and fears you will leave him for a life of adventure with us."

Britha's eyes widened, and she smiled. "I'd love that. May I join you?"

"I can't take you with us," Jewyl said. "We are hunted, and any who travel with me are also hunted. If you traveled with us, your life would be forfeit."

"But, I don't want to spend my life as an innkeeper." Britha pouted. "I'm bored."

"You needn't worry about that." Jewyl smiled. "In another year or two some man will come along and make you his wife. That will be much more exciting than the life I lead. I envy any woman who can stay at home, have children, and a loving husband."

"Do you think so?" Britha gazed hopefully at Jewyl. "Somebody would want to marry me?"

"A lovely lass like you?" Jopab smiled. "I, myself would ask your hand if I weren't a cleric in the service of Hagontha." He paused. "And, I'm too old."

"May your plans go smoothly, and Hagontha be appeased within the chaos," Britha said.

"Come." Jopab grabbed Jewyl's hand. "We'll slip out the back and none will be the wiser of our departure. We should be able to reach the temple in a short time and finish our deed."

Chardo appeared at the door.

Jewyl laughed. "Somebody really should have closed the door."

"I'm sorry," Britha replied. "I guess I should be on my way. May Hagontha smile on your endeavors."

"Aren't we the swordsmen?" Chardo asked as he strode into the room. He dusted off Jewyl's shoulder, lifting the aqua-colored fabric attached there, draping to her leather wristlet. "Our costumes are perfect." He lifted his arm with the yellow-colored fabric. "Do you think we should have a name? I've been thinking about it."

"A name," Jopab echoed. "An excellent idea. Britha?" Jopab swung his arm, the orange-colored fabric rippling in the air.

"I have no idea." Britha lingered by the door, watching. She giggled. "The addition of the fabric to the costumes helps draw the attention from your faces." She leaned in. "Here, let me attach a piece of fabric from the other wristlet to your ankle." She stepped back to admire her work. "Aqua and yellow. Yellow and pink. Pink and aqua." She giggled. "If you were truly a sword-fighting team, it would be quite colorful to watch." She placed a hand to chin in thought. "A name. Hm? I'm not sure."

"Well, I have a name," Chardo said. "I thought perhaps we could name ourselves Hagontha's Blades of Chaos for this situation." He stood and struck a stately pose with his feet a bit apart and the sword pointed directly at the door. The yellow fabric draped dramatically from the lifted arm." He gazed at his opposite leg where the pink fabric draped along the side.

Jopab shrugged. "A good as name as any, I suppose."

"I think it is a delightful name." Britha nodded approvingly at Chardo.

Chardo stuck the tip of the sword into the wooden floor and leaned on it. He placed one hand on his hip. "You agree?" he asked.

Jopab glanced at Chardo's disgusted look and realized he had hurt him. "Please, Chardo," Jopab said. "It is a very good name, although none will ever see the group. Remember, all this is strictly for the purpose of getting into the compound of the temple."

Jewyl stretched to ease the bindings about her chest. "You mean I went to all this trouble, for nothing?"

"An excellent disguise, Jewyl," Jopab said. "Excellent. They are looking for two men and a woman. We will face the world as three men. Shall we go?"

"No." Chardo's chest swelled. "We shall face the world as Hagontha's Blades of Chaos." He pulled the sword from the floor and lifted it in a grand arc to the ceiling.

"You'd best be on your way." Hvar huffed into the room. "Guards are filling the streets even as we speak."

"Ah, Hagontha," Jopab invoked. "We greet your chaos in blessed thanks. Within your swirling skirts we will stride to fulfill our destiny."

"Enough with the chaos," Chardo muttered. "Let's go."

Hvar and Britha ambled down the front stairs to the inn's large room where Vico hurried from table to table in service. Jewyl, Chardo and Jopab quickly and quietly slipped down the back stairs to the kitchen and escaped out the door.

"Should we amble one by one into the street or go as a group?" Jopab asked and nodded toward the lone guard standing at the end of the alley.

CHAPTER SEVEN
Temple of Hagontha

"We have our swords," Jewyl replied. "We might as well approach the guard and prepare for the worst. This will be a test of our costumes."

"Let's go." Chardo started toward the street. "The mobs await us."

Jewyl glanced at the mass of people milling in the street before them.

The guard turned and scrutinized them. "What are you three up to?" He stepped toward them.

Chardo placed a hand on his hip and sashayed three steps in the guard's direction.

"Well, handsome." He batted his eyes and minced even more. "We were looking for a discreet area. Would you like to join us for a little fun?"

The guard stepped back from the encroaching alley into the safety of the open-air street and sunlight.

"None of that here," he barked. "Find another place. The Dancing Dragon is on the other side of town. Be on your way."

He turned and hurriedly stomped away.

Chardo turned to his companions and smiled proudly. "Well, that took care of what could have become a messy situation."

Jewyl laughed. "Perhaps we should do as we were told and be on our way."

She led the group from the alley to the street, turning the opposite direction the guard had taken. They were quickly met with a group of party revelers and a small parade.

"Give way for the followers of Hagontha," a voice bellowed. "Chaos rules."

Gaudy banners flashed in the bright sunlight above the multi-colored dressed revelers.

"Join in the festivities," the voice said. "We go to Hagontha's temple."

"Perfect," Jopab whispered to his companions. "We'll mingle with this group until we get to the temple."

"Then waltz inside, do our job, take our money and leave," Chardo added.

Jopab frowned at Chardo and Jewyl elbowed her companion. He realized he had spoken out of turn.

The three were quickly engulfed in the mire of people and joined in the cheering and songs. The throng wove a chaotic path to the temple of Hagontha, growing in size with each block they passed.

Jewyl stared up at the spires of the temple. The towers careened skyward in a full outward assault of building rules. Jewyl felt dizzy as vertigo wrapped its arms about her. She leaned in toward Jopab. "The temple — I didn't realize Hagontha had such a large following," she whispered. "Are you sure we can accomplish our mission?"

"With chaos there is change." Jopab placed an arm about each of his companions. "Come, Chaos has spoken yet again." Jopab shoved Jewyl and Chardo out of the mainstream and toward a clutter of stones and a wall. "This is easier than I had hoped." He leaned down to the base of the temple wall.

Chardo fumbled with his costume, nervously arranging his sword. Jewyl tried not to show any concern and watched as Jopab re-arranged the stones. She never let her hand stray from the hilt of her sheathed sword. Jopab's movements intrigued her and could see no meaning to the stack of the stones.

"We must move quickly when I say," Jopab said. "This wall only moves the slightest amount. You may need to squeeze in."

"You're going to open it now?" Jewyl asked. "Here? In front of everyone?"

Jopab smiled and silently nodded. "In front of Hagontha herself."

"How?" Jewyl asked.

"I will push this in with my foot," Jopab explained. "When I do, the wall will move approximately an arm's length toward us."

"It will?" Chardo asked.

"We will appear to walk around the corner and disappear," Jopab said. "Only those who are to our left would be able to see what we are doing, and there are none to watch. Hagontha is smiling on our mission."

"If you say so." Chardo skeptically kicked the ground with his sandal.

"Now," Jopab hissed. "Follow me."

The priest scurried around the corner and disappeared into the aperture that opened. Chardo felt the stones crumble beside him.

"Hurry," Jopab said. "The door is going to close."

Jewyl slid into the opening and felt Chardo pushing against her as he came in.

"Not much space here," Jewyl muttered

The wall closed.

"Stuffy. Dark," Jewyl said. "Stuck between solid stone and two men. Every woman's dream."

"Not for long," Jopab whispered and a spark glistened in the darkness. "Here," he added. "A torch." The lone spark burst into flame along the stick Jopab held.

"Chaos seems to be pretty well prepared." Jewyl gazed about the area. "Not as small as I originally thought."

"Come," Jopab ordered.

"So, where are we headed?" Jewyl whispered. "I mean, where inside the temple?"

"Almost seems like a sacrilege with what we are about to do." Chardo gazed back at the closed entrance and saw nothing to indicate it was an opening.

"Think about that, Chardo," Jopab said. "We are not only intruding, but we will be committing a major desecration against the goddess. You should feel awkward. I do. Follow me."

Jopab headed down the tunnel. Jewyl and Chardo stumbled quietly behind in the dimness of the torch Jopab held aloft.

Jewyl glanced up and noticed the intricate carvings on the ceilings. The torchlight played on the glistening multifaceted angles and curves. Muted colors played and moved, shifting in the flickering flames.

"Jopab." Jewyl reached out to touch him on the shoulder. "Exactly what is that on the ceiling?"

Jopab jumped. "It would be best that you avert your eyes from that view. I can say no more at this time."

Chardo looked up.

"By the shadows of Rorc," Chardo exclaimed. "It almost looks like the ceiling is moving."

"Avert your eyes," Jopab commanded. "Keep your focus on the torchlight or on the back of the person before you and stay close to the torch. I've warned you."

"Warned?" Jewyl grabbed Jopab's shoulder to hold him. "You'd best be explaining. Are we safe?"

Jopab glanced upward then quickly averted his eyes. "If we continue to move and move quickly."

"Get going," Jewyl demanded with a glance at the ceiling. "Chardo is right. The shadows move above us, something is alive and I don't think I want to know what it is."

In the small hesitation of Jopab answering Jewyl, she'd heard the sounds from above: a raspy, sliding sound mixed with faint repetitive patting or thumping.

Jopab stopped abruptly and fiddled with the wall. The sound of a few clicks echoed in the long tunnel then the tedious sound of stone grinding against stone. Blinding light assaulted them as the door opened into the chamber. There were other sounds but they came from above.

"Inside," Jopab yelled. "Now." He pushed Jewyl and Chardo into the room.

Jewyl bumped against Chardo, losing her balance to stumble against the wall and unceremoniously plop to the floor. She glimpsed a long item dangling in the passageway beyond the closing door and noticed something that skittered in which Jopab quickly kicked back into the darkness of the tunnel.

"What was that?" Jewyl asked.

"You saw it, too?" Chardo's eyes were wide in surprise. "Whatever it was, it was vile appearing. Jopab?"

"Guardians," Jopab replied, and took a deep breath before leaning against the stone wall. "Mere guardians of the temple."

"You kick your guardians?" Jewyl struggled to stand up. "I find that hard to believe."

Jopab doused the torch. "Any entrance that connects with the outside has guardians. They are unique creatures which only exist within the temples of Hagontha. You saw them slithering on the ceiling and that which I kicked was an offspring."

"An infant?" Chardo asked.

"A female is capable of producing from one hundred to five hundred offspring," Jopab crossed the room. "Those that survive not being consumed, they have the opportunity to breed. They are cannibalistic creatures eating their young — as well as anything else they can find. They have voracious appetites."

"I'm confused," Jewyl said. "They slither and skitter? The little one appeared to be a fur ball and what I saw dangling had to be over twenty feet long. They're related?"

"The pliocas are similar to snakes but have small legs which help them to move about and cling to things and also to keep their skins shiny. When they first hatch, they're covered with silky hair-like appendages."

"Hair-like?" Chardo asked.

"They are actually covered with legs, very soft legs which can barely carry them," Jopab replied. "The legs bend under their weight and hence appear to be skittering when they move. Only as they age and the body elongates do the infants start to resemble the parents." He smiled feebly at the two. "As the body gets longer, the legs are aligned and resemble a centipede."

"We don't have to go back out there?" Chardo pointed at the hidden entrance. "Not that I'm scared, but they appear to be somewhat awkward to kill."

"Consumption is their only means of death," Jopab said. "To slice one would allow it to become two pliocas. If we'd not made it to this point..." Jopab shrugged.

"How many people are able to find, let alone open, these little portals?" Jewyl asked.

"Don't know." Jopab again shrugged. "Don't care. We're safe."

"Well I do care," Jewyl said. "I don't like all these little surprises you seem to have forgotten to detail in our plans. What other snags will be awaiting for us around the corner?"

Jopab reached up and grabbed a jug and tankards from the shelf. "As you can see," he said. "This room is supplied much like the one at Azre's castle." He poured water. "I think we all need a chance to regain composure before we go on."

Jewyl reached to her side and the sword sliced through the air to stop mere inches from Jopab's hands, barely a hair's breadth from the table's top.

"Trust me, my composure is regained," she said. "Now tell me what I want to know. What other secrets are lurking about?"

Jopab slowly raised his eyes to meet Jewyl's gaze. He sat down and motioned for Chardo and Jewyl to join him.

"First." He lifted the tankard. "You need to trust me. Second." Jopab played a finger across his lips. "The worst we will meet from this point on will be another priest." He looked about. "Still, there are the strays."

"Strays?" Jewyl echoed. "What strays?"

"Pliocas that somehow escaped the chamber hallway we were in." Jopab smiled wryly." He lifted his tankard. "Drink. Refresh yourselves."

"You mean we can still run into those things?" Jewyl sat down to face Jopab.

"Usually only one or two will escape," Jopab said, placing the tankard down. "Normally as an infant. If they are able to feed on rats and other creatures of the darkness, they grow. They seldom have the opportunity to breed."

Jewyl shuddered, reached for a tankard and drank deeply. She was amazed at how thirsty she was. Chardo followed suit, finishing his first and slamming the vessel back on the table.

Jopab smiled and his eyes narrowed. "You will sleep now. Just rest and I will be back shortly. Remember, stay here."

"Sleep?" Jewyl asked. "I'm not tired." Her eyes blinked once, twice, and lingered when they closed. She pushed back in her chair and forced her eyes open, staring. "Sleep? You drugged us?"

"You..." Chardo slipped to the floor.

Jopab watched Jewyl's eyes cross just before the lids closed for the last time. She slumped forward and Jopab caught her head and gently laid it to rest on the table..

"No need to hurt yourself," he whispered.

#

"Chardo?" Jewyl called. "Wake up." She slapped her companion's face. "C'mon, friend," she whispered. "You have to wake up."

"What?" Chardo slurred. "Hey, stop hitting me." He waved an arm in Jewyl's direction in an attempt to push her hand away.

"You had me worried there."

"By Rorc's ass." Chardo crawled up onto the chair. "What did he give us? I've never felt like this even on the best celebration night."

"Get your wits about you," Jewyl said. "Jopab seems to be calling all the moves. You're a thief, so get us out of here."

"I'm so thirsty," Chardo said.

"Damn your thirst," the red-head yelled. "We need to get out of here, so do your job. Get us out of here!"

Chardo wiped the drool from the side of his face. "How long have we been out?"

Jewyl scowled at him. "Let me see ... nope, no windows. How would I know? I'm hungry so we've been out for more than a couple of hours. That much I'm sure of."

Chardo ambled to the wall and started fingering the cracks and crevices. "This is where we came in so maybe I can find the mechanism to open the door."

Jewyl shoved the table aside and then pulled up the small rug it had stood on.

"Well the table moved and I don't see anything that appears to open downward," she said.

"There has to be something to trip," Chardo said. The exasperation in his voice blatantly obvious. "Just wait until the Thieves Guild finds out about this." He shook his head.

"You may not want to share this information." Jewyl moved items around on the shelf, checking everything carefully.

Chardo leaned back against the wall and drew his knees up.

"Are you giving up?" Jewyl asked.

"No." Chardo scowled at his companion. "Just reviewing what I can remember." He glanced about the room.

Jewyl cast a curious glance at him then moved to sit beside him.

"Okay, Chardo," Jewyl whispered. "What do you need to remember?"

"Outside." Chardo frowned. "We came into the courtyard. He abruptly pushed us over to the wall. Jopab opened the door and we all slipped in. We walked perhaps twenty... twenty-five paces? Then into this place." He raised his hand and hit the wall above his head with a closed fist. "Of course, those pliocas are on the other side."

"Now I question if we moved with the mob, or if Jopab had planned this all along." Jewyl grimaced in thought. "Things have been just too quaintly perfect."

Chardo sighed and stared at the ceiling where the lantern was connected. He frowned.

"You're unusually quiet," Jewyl whispered after a few minutes of silence.

Chardo pointed at the ceiling. "See that? Help me up there." He stood. "Do you see that small, dark dangling thing just to the left of the chain?"

"Yes," Jewyl replied. "How curious."

Chardo moved and grabbed the table. "You were at the table so he didn't escape by sneaking out below it." He beamed a smile, stepped on the chair and up onto the table. "But there is nothing saying he couldn't have slipped out over our heads."

"His chair was out from the table," Jewyl said. "I remember that. Of course, it wouldn't seem out of place to anyone looking about."

"They are a very tricky lot, these priests of Hagontha," Chardo said. "Their chaos seems pretty much planned."

He pulled on the short nub of cord sticking out between the blocks. There was resistance.

"There has to be some sort of release." He stretched to feel around the edges of the block.

Jewyl stood on her chair, leaned in and grabbed the lantern for balance. It gave.

"I can't believe it," Chardo hissed. "Something that simple. I should have thought of that immediately." He pulled and could feel the cool air from the overhead tunnel when the block was completely turned on its pivot point.

"It's counter-balanced." He pulled the knotted rope down. The knots made it easy to climb. "They think of everything." Chardo started to ascend the rope.

"Very quaint," Jewyl added. "If the cord hadn't been sticking out, I doubt we'd had even thought of looking at the ceiling for an escape route."

Chardo peered from the opening down at Jewyl. "We will make sure the cord is definitely up," he said. "Ready to join me?"

Jewyl placed the two chairs back on the floor, slightly under the table. She looked up at the smiling face in the dark opening.

"That should keep anyone guessing how we got out." She brushed her hands against her thighs to dry them. "This shouldn't be too difficult."

Jewyl grabbed a knot high above her head then wrapped the arches of her feet around a lower knot. She quickly moved into the opening.

"You needn't worry," Chardo offered her a supporting hand to assist. "This passageway is tall enough for us to stand."

"Dark, isn't it?" Jewyl stared down the tunnel.

"I was wondering about that," Chardo said. "There seems to be a glow in the distance. We'll close the stone and let our eyes adapt."

"Oh, my," Jewyl said in mock terror. "In the dark? With you? Alone?"

Chardo cast a weary gaze at Jewyl. "You're worried about your virtue?" He pulled the knotted rope up.

"Not really," Jewyl said. "I was wondering why you didn't use your cat-like thieving skills to negotiate the darkness."

"Even a cat would have problems seeing in the darkness we're going to be in," Chardo said, and gently pushed on the stone to close the opening.

Just as the last of the light disappeared, Jewyl glanced up at the darkness of the ceiling – was there anything up there? She strained to see and listened intently.

There was a glow, very faint but enough to see the passageway itself.

"What is it?" Jewyl touched the wall with her finger. She pulled it back to see the end of her finger glow. "Lichen?"

"It is almost like a dust," Chardo said. "Phosphorous? It might be a type of lichen."

"Never mind." Jewyl leaned over and wiped the small amount from her finger onto Chardo's jerkin. "Which way do you think we should go?"

"Do you feel safe stepping on the stone opening?" He leaned across the stone and rested his hand on the wall. "Plus the passageway ends here so you won't be going too far this way."

"Then I take it we will be going in this direction." Jewyl headed down the tunnel. "Any idea of how we will know when we get to an opening?"

"Anything that seems out of normal should be a pretty good indicator." Chardo smiled in the darkness.

"Do you mean something like a non-glowing hand print?" She pointed in the shadowy darkness of the limited light.

"Interesting," Chardo said. "Could this be where someone stumbled and placed their hand to balance them self?"

"Or left the tunnel?" Jewyl added.

"Obviously pressing on the wall wouldn't move the stone," Chardo said. "There has to be a trigger mechanism."

"Such as?"

Chardo knelt on the floor. "Anything that would indicate usage: lack of lichen light, another hand print or even lichen out of place."

"Chaos rules," Jewyl whispered.

"Right." Chardo shook his head. "Chaos this, chaos that. Here, like this little tidbit right here." He leaned in close into the base of the wall opposite the marking. "See this?" He pulled Jewyl down for a closer examination. "This is probably the trigger." He fingered the area where there was collected lichen on the floor.

Click.

"That's the sound I love to hear," Chardo said. "Now push the other wall."

Jewyl placed both hands on the wall and exerted pressure. Nothing moved.

"You may have to help me," she said. "Nothing is giving."

"Here," Chardo offered. "Let me do this." He placed both hands on the opposite wall then placed a foot on the wall above the trigger. "Push!"

Chardo's foot fell from the wall as it gently gave way.

"Damn them," Chardo hissed. "I should have noticed the missing lichen on this wall. They have to put a foot on this wall and push themselves with their hands against the opposite wall."

"We're in," Jewyl said. "You figured it out. That's what counts."

"But where are we?" Chardo whispered.

"Let me answer that question," Jopab said. "This is my chamber. Welcome."

"You traitor," Chardo said, pulling his sword and charging.

"Hold," Jopab said. "Let me explain."

"Choose your words wisely." Jewyl slowly pulled her sword. "Your actions have spoken louder than your promises. You joined us at Chardo's request. I owe you nothing."

"Perhaps we should all put our blades away," a voice commanded from behind Chardo and Jewyl.

"Klajany?" Chardo asked. "How?"

"Your voices and actions were anything but subtle," Klajany said.

"Let's all sit down and I will explain everything." Jopab tried to placate everyone. "I fear all my plans need to be placed in the open."

"None too soon, it would seem." Jewyl glared at the newcomer. "Why are you here?"

"Sit," Jopab commanded. "Here." He motioned for Jewyl to join him on the bench. "Klajany and Chardo, you both can sit on the bed." He smiled. "No games, please."

"Speaking of games..." Jewyl sat as requested, but glared at Jopab. "Exactly what is yours?"

"I must apologize," Jopab started. "It was when I witnessed the speed and cleanness of Klajany's actions this morning at the inn." He paused and stretched his neck in an arc. "That was when I realized a dual point of attack might be better."

"Chardo and I weren't sufficient?" Jewyl cocked a questioning eye at the priest, leaned over, her hand pressed against her knees and finally glanced at Chardo. "Maybe we should just back out?"

"No," Jopab yelled. "I truly do need the two of you to kill… to eliminate Ballec."

Chardo eased back on the bed, leaning on his elbows, his legs dangling over the edge. "Why?"

"The goddess herself has commanded it," Jopab said.

"I'm not buying that." Jewyl stood and paced a few steps. "You're not telling us the full truth. The proposition was good, but I fear there is more behind the curtain than you have revealed."

Jopab glanced nervously about the room, his eyes darting here and there.

Jewyl drew her sword and dropped into a defense position. Chardo leaped from the bed to join her, his sword slicing the air in an arc.

"If nothing else, priest," Jewyl whispered. "One thing I've learned with you: the walls are suspect at all times."

Klajany dropped from the bed, rolled across the floor to fall behind Jopab. The assassin had the priest's arm locked behind him and a gleaming blade against Jopab's pale neck.

"You've seen my work," Klajany said. "Before you could even open your mouth to shout, I could have your neck sliced and be out of the room. What are they talking about?"

"Please," Jopab begged, his voice cracking. "All is fine. Jewyl is correct. We are not alone."

"Get them out here and in full view," Jewyl commanded. "All of them. I've tired of your priestly tricks."

"Potan. Harkow. Ishnat," Jopab whispered, not moving too much which might cause Klajany's blade to cut. "Come out."

Two stones moved from opposite walls and the three men entered the room.

"I said all of them." Jewyl waved her sword at Jopab.

"Percho, you too," Jopab sighed. "That is all of them, Jewyl."

"How did you know?" Klajany asked. He'd released Jopab and put away his blade.

"He had told us of his friend, Percho," Jewyl said. "When I didn't hear a name I recognized, I figured there still had to be one more hiding."

"She is indeed very talented and worthy of the challenge." Percho entered through the same portal Jewyl and Chardo had used.

"How long have you been out there?" Chardo asked.

"As Klajany said, you're not that quiet." He smiled. "Now, shall we listen to Jopab's plan with no more interruptions?"

"Do we now have all the parties involved present?" Jewyl asked.

CHAPTER EIGHT
Even Good Plans Change

"Yes," Jopab said. "Everyone, please find seats. Jewyl, if you will again join me on this bench?"

Jewyl sheathed her sword and slowly walked back to the place Jopab was graciously pointing to. Her mind scurried with questions, the foremost, why he wanted her beside him?

Percho smiled and shifted from foot to foot nervously. "Jewyl, we need to have Ballec removed. His mind has been poisoned, and it is spreading to others."

"Poisoned?" Klajany repeated.

Percho sighed and stared into the corner. Jewyl followed his gaze. There was nothing.

"Let it be said, Ballec now follows someone other than our mother goddess, Hagontha."

"Chaos be blessed," Jopab muttered which was quickly echoed by the other priests.

"Chaos be damned." Chardo scowled at the mumbling priests. "We had a plan. Why the sudden change?"

Klajany smiled at Chardo. "As you well know, I'm better. It was only natural Jopab would approach me to assist."

Chardo's eyebrows furrowed in a scowl.

"Our plan was indeed well founded," Jopab said. "I only included Klajany, secretly I might add, to assure if something went amiss, there would be another chance."

"Another chance," Jewyl repeated. "How?"

"Klajany is to be included within the priesthood," Percho said. "I was going to attempt to move him into a very high position that would allow him closer access to Ballec."

Klajany smiled broadly.

"Closer access?" Chardo asked. He turned to Klajany. "A wolf living in the hen house, how perfect."

"In addition to the money..." Klajany shrugged. "Enclosed

81

within these walls with this many men, there are certain amenities I'm sure I will enjoy" Klajany flashed a knowing eye to Chardo. "Envious?"

Chardo pointed to the priests sitting on the floor. "And they're worried about Ballec poisoning the priesthood?" Chardo returned a raised an eyebrow at Klajany.

"Gentlemen," Jewyl interrupted. "If you please, we have other issues other than who is going to have more sex."

Percho and Jopab smiled. The other three priests snickered.

"Fine," Jewyl said in exasperation. "Play your silly games. If you wish to have Klajany as another method of attack, so be it."

"We are committed then?" Jopab's head bobbed affirmatively. "Ballec's life must end."

"As you have so aptly discovered, I am also known as The Emerald." Jewyl stood, pulled her sword and lifted it to the ceiling. "I will complete the mission I have been given. My blade will end Ballec's life. I swear this as Jewyl, Princess of Shiyula."

"Percho," Jopab called. "Take Klajany to the garment room and prep him for his new position within the priesthood."

"What do we do?" Jewyl asked.

"You wait," Jopab said.

"Are we safe here?" Jewyl questioned. She looked about the sparse room: a bed, one table, a bench, two chairs, a small library of books and a chest which obviously had to contain clothes.

"Perhaps." Jopab tapped nervously at his lower lip. "Then again, maybe we should move back to the hidden room."

"Fine with me." Chardo stood and walked to the wall.

Jopab crossed the room to join Chardo at the wall. "I do hope you remembered to close the trap ceiling." He cocked a questioning eye. Yes?"

"Better than you," Jewyl snapped. "I even placed the chairs under the table." She glared at the man then had a maddening thought. What if he had deliberately left the cord for them to find? Suddenly her mind raced with obscure scenarios. What other treachery could be at hand?

"You seem distressed, Jewyl," Jopab said. He pushed the wall and it opened to the tunnel they had used to come in. "Not knowing who may come in here, I feel we should move back to the waiting chamber."

"How long will we need to wait?" Chardo asked.

"Until we are needed, obviously." Jewyl took lead and strode into the darkness of the tunnel. "To the left. What? About 20 paces?"

"Very good," Jopab said. "Actually let me step them off, but it should be exactly twenty-two paces from here. Of course, the rope will be there."

The tunnel darkened momentarily, then Jewyl could see the glow from the walls.

"This stuff is very convenient. Was it always here?" Chardo asked. "How does it exist?"

"Notice the breeze?" Jopab responded. "It's very faint but still there. It seems to have enough nutrients in the air for the fungus to live on. It was brought in from the caves near Bilorek. Have you ever been there?"

"No," Jewyl said bluntly. "But, our travels are none of your concern. We are here on official business. We will do what is needed, and collect our payment and be away."

Jopab turned back to her and smiled. "I am sorry you feel that way, Jewyl. I really do enjoy your company."

A shudder coursed down Jewyl's back as she glanced up to see his face in the green light.

"Jopab?" Chardo called. "What would happen if one was to climb up the rope rather than use it to get into the chamber below?"

"A very good question," Jopab replied. "Those who don't know may be inclined to do so. It is not a wise decision. There is only one escape route on the way up to the spikes of death."

"Spikes of death?" Jewyl questioned.

"I am not the traitor you think," Jopab said. "I am on your side, Jewyl. I will share any information you want. The escape is on the south wall when you feel the big knot. The north wall is easy to discern, the fungus grows best and brightest on the north side."

"What are the spikes?" Chardo asked.

"Here is the rope," Jopab said. "The spikes are embedded in the roof. They are thin, sharp, metal points set no more than three fingers width apart. If you remember when you used the rope, you are forced to stretch up, grab a knot then quickly pull yourself up. The spikes are one palm's width above that knot. The sheer energy you use to pull yourself up will impale your head into the spikes."

"A rather gruesome death." Jewyl shuddered.

"I would assume so," Jopab replied. "It is another of our methods to keep the passageways secret."

"Yet, you share this secret freely with us," Jewyl retorted.

"I harbor you no ill will." Jopab stepped on the stone and it opened to the chamber below them. "I want us to be friends."

"Secretly hiring Klajany proves that to me." Jewyl cast a glance at the priest. "That's what a real friend does."

"In my defense," Jopab said. "I did it so if we failed, Ballec would feel secure, and Klajany would be free to assassinate him."

Jewyl sighed. "There is a certain wisdom in your words," Jewyl finally replied.

"I think I'll go up and check out those spikes," Chardo said. "Do you know, is anyone up there?" He paused. "I mean, dangling, right now?"

"I don't know," Jopab replied. "But, I really wouldn't suggest it. Please, join us below in the chamber, Chardo."

Jewyl grabbed the rope and slid down to the table. Chardo followed with Jopab quickly behind.

"We must allow a couple of hours to pass before we begin our path to Ballec's chamber," Jopab said. "There are some food stuffs and refreshments to be had on the shelf."

Jewyl frowned at Jopab.

"Safe food and liquids," he hastily added. "Nothing to make you sleep."

# # #

"So this is to be my new chamber watch?" Ballec scrutinized Klajany. "Why have I not seen him before?"

Percho and Klajany, both already on their knees, bowed deeply before the man who held the highest position in the priesthood of Hagontha.

"He transferred yesterday from Mensyra's temple," Percho said. "My lord, if you have doubts, let me know."

"Mensyra?" Ballec repeated. "I haven't been there in over two years, yet he does strike a familiarity with me. Tell me, how are things there?"

"Very well, Lord Ballec," Klajany said. "Father Asrap sends his blessings and wishes for your Celebration of Chaos."

Percho smiled innocently realizing how easily Klajany had absorbed the information necessary to speak with some authority as a priest from Mensyra.

"He does?" Ballec questioned. "Follow me, please."

Percho and Klajany stood to follow.

"Just him." Ballec pointed to Klajany. "You will wait here while we talk."

Ballec placed his arm about Klajany and guided him to his private bed chamber.

# # #

Percho paced the room, waiting.

The door opened, and Ballec entered the room. Klajany followed.

"I accept this priest as one of my new attendants," Ballec announced. "Thank you, Percho, for locating one with such interesting attributes and talents. He will serve my needs quite well."

Percho smiled, bowed, and backed out of the room. Klajany followed the young priest to the door. Klajany winked and smiled at Percho before closing the door to Ballec's chamber behind Percho.

The plan worked. Percho tried not to frown as he remembered Klajany's face, and the disconcerting smile. *Why the smugness?*

"Ishnat," Percho called the priest forward. "Notify our guests that all is in place."

# # #

The stone entrance from the hallway with the pliocas opened. A priest hurried in then shoved the stone shut, a small, dark ball scurried in. Ishnat quickly stomped on it causing a loud squish followed by an oozing from beneath his foot. He turned and faced Jewyl and Chardo who had drawn their swords.

"All is as desired," Ishnat choked, his eyes wide with fear. "Klajany now guards Ballec."

"Was that a plioca?" Jewyl asked, a shiver tracing a cold finger down her spine as she pointed to the mess on the floor.

"Again, an infant," Jopab replied. "Nothing of concern since it could do little harm to any of us, alone. Now, if there had been a group..." He left the sentence unfinished and turned his attention to Ishnat, rubbing his hands together. "Good, we will now proceed with our plans."

Jopab climbed onto the table. "Ready? Up we go and through the passages to Ballec's chamber."

"Finally!" Jewyl leaped onto the table beside Jopab. She glanced at the mire of green and black on the floor then smiled at Jopab. "Today, Chardo and I will prove our skills." She grabbed the rope and scaled into the darkness above.

"Please." Chardo motioned to Jopab. "You next, I'll follow. Ishnat? Will you be coming?"

The priest shook his head. "I will attend to things here." He glanced at the dead plioca. "I will join you later."

Chardo glanced up to see Jopab disappear into the opening. He scaled the rope quickly and Jopab pulled the rope up and pushed the stone to close it.

"This way," Jopab said. "We only need to move approximately fifty paces, a tunnel will lead to the left, another thirty paces and we will be at Ballec's chambers."

"Lead on." Jewyl stepped back and leaned against the wall to let Jopab take point.

"Remember." Jopab placed an index finger to his lips. "We must remain quiet as we approach Ballec's chambers. Klajany and I heard you both out here when you came to my chambers. These may be stone walls but even the slightest of sounds is magnified."

"So that is how Klajany was able to hide," Jewyl said.

"My dear," Jopab replied. "We could hear the two of you stumbling, even before you attempted to find and open the gateway."

"Then be silent," Jewyl hissed. She was sure Jopab could see her disdain in the low lighting from the walls.

A few minutes later Jopab held up his hand as he slowly crept forward. He spread his fingers out and pressed them against the wall, turned his head and listened. He frowned.

Jewyl eased close. "Is there a problem?" she whispered.

Jopab raised his hand and shook his head negatively. He stood and raised his index finger then leaned down and there was a click. The wall opened.

Jewyl blinked in the bright light that glared from the room

and raised one hand to shade her eyes.

"Who dares to enter my chamber?" Ballec demanded.

"Pardon," Jopab said and stepped into the bright light.

Jewyl drew her sword and could hear Chardo doing the same. They entered the chamber behind Jopab.

Ballec stood on a raised platform beside his bed. Curtains hung down from the ceiling at the corners of the bed. Ballec had his hand on a silk drape beside him. A sneer of a smile crossed his face. There was an air of confidence.

"Enter, traitorous Jopab!" Ballec stood tall and didn't cower. "Guards!"

Chardo leaped forward and charged at the smiling man. Ballec laughed aloud and stepped aside. Jewyl moved to the side to stop Ballec. Klajany pushed back the curtain hiding him and stood beside Ballec, his sword pulled in defense of the Holy Father.

"You?" Jewyl yelled. "Klajany, what have you done?"

"Just assuring myself a place." Klajany raised his sword toward Jewyl.

"This is your doing, Jopab," Chardo yelled and charged Klajany.

The blades rang loudly in the first strike between Chardo and Klajany.

The room became a flurry of chaos. Priests, some with swords, some with make-shift clubs charged into the chamber to attack. Jewyl parried and thrust, trying only to maim the guards and make her way to Ballec. The deal had been to kill Ballec. Nothing had been said about the possibility of killing innocent priests. She looked for Chardo, he was still locked in battle with Klajany. She questioned the amount of time Chardo spent trying to subdue Klajany. She remembered his charge which was definitely not one to echo memories of some tryst or romantic ties between them. Suddenly, a burst of pain on her left wrist shocked her as a staff clipped it. She dropped her dagger. Jewyl raised her right arm to strike with the sword, and felt the staff hit her right rib. She yelled in pain. This attacker was from behind, while another kept her occupied from the front. The odds were against them. Her sword dropped and she felt the assailant's arm go around her neck while his other hand grabbed her right wrist to constrain her. She glanced again at Chardo. Her yell had caught his attention and in that split second,

Klajany had disarmed him. Chardo, too was being held captive.

"Fine," Ballec yelled. "Pull the traitors to the center. I wish to see who my adversaries are. I know of Jopab, Percho and I'm very sure there are other priests involved." The man paced nervously on the raised bed platform. "Klajany, my newest," he called. "Come here and tell me who I can trust and who I can't of those you see before us."

Klajany strutted silently to the platform and looked out over the four prisoners and the gathered priests who held them. He studied the group.

"Two who hold Percho are not to be trusted. There is one each with Jewyl and Chardo. I don't recognize any who hold Jopab. Along that wall," Klajany pointed. "There are two more and the one on the end over there. The others, I'm not sure." Klajany turned to Ballec and bowed. "As you wished, my lord."

"Thank you," Ballec said and motioned for guards from the back to move forward. Klajany turned to smile at the prisoners.

"All the traitors are to be killed," Ballec ordered. "Starting with the worst." He lunged forward and shoved the small dagger into Klajany's back between the shoulder blades, directly into his heart. Klajany's eyes widened before he crumbed to the floor.

"No," Chardo yelled, and pulled away from those that held him. He moved to Klajany and grabbed the dying man's sword.

Jewyl broke away from the grip the one guard on her left hand. She recognized the one on her right. He let go immediately. Her sword was only a couple of steps away.

"We come to arrest Ballec," a voice commanded at the door's entrance. Four of Azre's soldiers entered the room. "What foolery goes on here?"

Jewyl stabbed the priest closest to her. Azre's henchmen drew their swords and joined in the fray. Soldiers. Priests. Assassins. Again, mayhem befuddled the priests, and suddenly Jopab was beside her.

"Quick! Follow me," he hissed. He moved toward Chardo who had retrieved his sword. Percho was behind them.

Jewyl followed, her sword slicing through the air at the priests, any who ventured near. She glanced at Klajany, he lay in a heap on the platform. He was dead, she knew that.

Suddenly they were in the darkened chamber and Jopab was

closing the stone door.

"Follow me," he said and raced down the tunnel.

Jewyl, Chardo and Percho followed.

She couldn't see the priest, but could hear him as his sandals slapped against the stone floor of the tunnel. The small amount of light from the fungus was barely enough to see in.

We must be running north or south, Jewyl thought. *It has to be since the light is so dim.*

"Here," Jopab shouted. "Quick, inside."

A room opened and Jewyl led the group in.

"We will only have a small moment of reprieve before somebody discovers us," Percho said. "I have cast my lot with you, if you will have me."

"Well, I'm not exactly sure where we will be going next," Jewyl said. "But offhand, I'd say all the plans we made, together and separately, have gone astray. There was enough chaos in that room to keep Mother Hagontha happy for the next few days."

"Taunt not the goddess," Jopab whispered. "In her wisdom, she has allowed us to escape."

"I know my talents offer you nothing," Percho continued. "Although, I do have some knowledge of the other temples." He looked at Jopab. "Of course, so does Jopab."

Jewyl straightened her hair, pulling it back and wrapping a small piece of cord to hold it. She leaned back on the table. "If you wish to toss your lot with us..." Jewyl shrugged her shoulders. "I have no problem with that."

"Are you aware Ballec will be headed to Zornal?" Percho asked. "I do have some knowledge which I can share. With Azre wanting to arrest him, I am sure he will flee in that direction since he has already made plans to go there tomorrow."

"What would one day's difference be?" Jewyl questioned. "Besides, why does the mighty Lord Azre want to arrest his brother, Ballec? What am I missing?"

CHAPTER NINE
To Zornal, Maybe

"Perhaps the dragon has awakened and finally figured out the chaos of his court is being caused by Ballec," Jopab said.

A door opened and a priest peeked in, hugging tightly to the door.

"What goes on?" he demanded. "Are you the ones who Ballec seeks?"

"You have two choices, Rane." Percho grabbed the young priest and pulled him into the chamber. "Join us, or become our prisoner."

"Father Ballec demands if anyone knows of your whereabouts—"

"Bind and gag him," Jopab said, cutting off the young man's words. "We've no time for this."

Rane moved to leave, but Chardo was behind him. The priest fell to his knees. Disabled, Rane sat quietly gagged in the corner. His eyes were wide with fear, but he listened to all that was spoken.

"We will leave here and head for Lord Azre's castle," Jewyl said.

Chardo frowned then caught Jewyl's quick eye movement at Rane.

"When we get there we will sneak in via the method we got out, using the tunnels and secret passageways," she continued. "Ballec seems to be having his own problems and I am sure he will not be headed in that direction. We'll let Azre deal with his brother."

Jopab, Percho and Chardo nodded in agreement.

"Since we all agree," Jewyl said. "Let's get a move on. This priest has found us, it won't take long for another to follow. Which way out of here?"

"Down," Jopab said. "The table. We'll take the supplies here." Percho and Chardo reached up and grabbed the bags of foodstuffs and jugs of wine. Jopab turned to Rane. "You will be sure to notify the priests when you are released to replace all of this?" He hesitated. "Need I mention you shouldn't repeat what you've heard?"

Rane vigorously nodded his head.

Jopab opened the trap and looked into the darkness. "Follow me to our freedom." He jumped into the opening and disappeared.

Jewyl, Chardo and Percho followed.

# # #

Jewyl followed Jopab through the catacombs. She could hear Chardo and Percho following behind her. They weren't too far, yet they seemed to be lingering, and she could hear whisperings.

"How many are aware of these tunnels?" Jewyl asked Jopab.

"Most of the senior priests know all the different tunnels so that would be… perhaps maybe seven or eight," Jopab replied. "Of course, Ballec knows all of them, and obviously more than the senior priests." He paused. "The initiates only know of the major ones for escape, perhaps another twenty-five."

"So, about thirty-five, total," Jewyl stated.

"The novices are unaware of any secret passages," Jopab added.

The group walked in silence for a few minutes when Jopab stopped. He held up his hand in the low light, barely visible. "Listen," he whispered. "We are not alone."

"So," Jewyl said. "Our chances are extremely slim of meeting another within these tunnels and now we get lucky to encounter somebody?"

Jopab waved his hand and then pushed Jewyl against the wall.

In the distance Jewyl saw the flickering light on the distant wall, revealing an opening of this passage to another. A torch came into view and the sound of marching sandals preceded the five soldiers.

"Stop the grumbling. Lord Azre says we are not to return until we have found evidence of Ballec's escape, or we have captured him. The same holds true for the elusive red-head, Jewyl. He wants her alive. Ballec, he doesn't care whether he lives or dies."

"There is a tunnel to your right, sir."

The group stopped and the lead guard ambled closer to the

tunnel where they hid.

"Small opening, obviously a tributary to this main tunnel. We'll search it on our return." He motioned the other four to continue on in their search. The torch light faded in the distance.

"All is as chaos designs," Jopab said with reverence. "We now may move forward safely, I think."

"Blessed chaos," Percho murmured.

Jewyl sighed, and continued to follow Jopab in silence. Suddenly, she butted him when he stopped abruptly.

"We are near the exit," he hissed. "We could be ambushed when we leave the tunnel."

"We what?" Jewyl asked. "How many exits are there? Why would they be guarding this one?"

"There are only two escape routes from that particular room," Percho said moving in closer to the three.

Jewyl noticed the smirk on Chardo's face. It bothered her, but she didn't know if it was why he smirked, or the fact she could see it so bluntly in the hideous green light.

"Percho, do you really think Rane has kept silent?" Jopab shrugged, and smiled at the group.

"He is one who was of my equal. Since we've not been followed, it appears he hasn't revealed our secret. Still..."

"Fine," Jewyl huffed. "My sword is ready to see more action." She lifted it before her.

"Careful," Jopab said. "I only said there could be an ambush, not that there was an ambush planned."

Jewyl glared at the priest. *Why phrase it that way?* she thought.

"You said there was another exit?" Chardo asked. "Why didn't we take that one?"

"Two reasons," Jopab replied. "One. The other route escapes into town. Two. This route is away from our misguided and highly anticipated direction."

"There was a way to get into the temple from town?" Jewyl dropped the guard on her sword. "Why didn't we use it?"

"It is an escape out." Jopab lifted one hand in an attempt to appease her. "There is no latch to open it from outside."

"A wise decision," Chardo said. "Otherwise every thief in town would be using it to access the gold of the temple."

"Tell them the truth," Percho said. "The full truth."

Jopab leaned against the wall of the tunnel and sighed loudly. "The other way would lead to what appears to be a dead end. If one knows the correct latch sequence, which I do know, then a secret passageway is available."

"So what is the secret?" Jewyl said.

"Pliocas," Jopab said. "It is a long walk through hundreds, perhaps thousands of pliocas."

Jewyl shivered at the thought of walking a long, dark tunnel of moving, shifting creatures. She remembered when one of the infants ambled across her right foot and she almost screamed.

"We've dealt with them before." Chardo swelled with authority.

"As I said, the distance is great," Jopab said. "The pliocas can be confused with one, maybe two bodies running the tunnel. A group of this size stumbling their way to freedom is but a meal to them."

"I've been in the tunnel," Percho said. "Jopab speaks the truth. The floor is riddled with the bones of their victims."

"Do you think Ballec used it?" A wicked smile crossed Jewyl's lips. "Maybe the pliocas have done for us where we failed."

Percho snickered. Jopab sighed.

"I know I mentioned the pliocas were specifically brought to the temple," Jopab said. "In doing so, they were ingrained with a fear of the head priest."

"They what?" Chardo exclaimed.

"Whoever is a head priest," Jopab said. "All our blessed fathers of Hagontha's can walk safely among the pliocas. The creatures are the pets of the father priest."

"So we were forced to this exit." Jewyl sighed. "Nothing like playing into their hand. Let us be ready for the ambush since there is obviously no hope, otherwise."

"There is always hope," Jopab said. "Chaos gives us that. Follow me into the light and freedom."

"Light?" Chardo asked.

"Within our very grasp," Jopab said. "Do you not see the difference in the distance before us? We will turn this corner and you will see the opening."

"Be ready," Jewyl whispered. *Be ready for the worst*, she thought

She lifted her sword and the group gingerly approached the opening.

"We'll not come out without a fight," Jopab yelled.

Jewyl jumped, startled at his words.

"Why let them know we are here?" she yelled.

"Why not?" Jopab said. "These corridors echo even the slightest of sound."

"For the glory of chaos," Jopab said and stepped into the light. He raised his hand to ward off the bright sunlight.

Jewyl leaped out from the tunnel. She swung her sword in a full arc, all the while taking in the surrounding area.

Chardo followed suit and Percho ambled out.

"There's nobody here," Jewyl said. There was surprise in her voice. She again glanced about her noting to conceal an assailant. There were none.

"We seem to be quite safe." Percho casually leaned against a tree.

Chardo frowned. "Yes, it appears that way." He sheathed his sword.

"I suggest we be on our way," Jewyl said. "But, not before we cover our tracks here." Jewyl sheathed her sword and looked to Jopab. "What happened? Why aren't they here?" She grabbed a small clump of weeds and swept casually at the footprints in the dust.

"Percho," Jopab said. "Get away from that tree and the grasses. We don't want to leave any tracks."

"For a simple priest, you seem to know a lot about skulking about places," Jewyl said. A frown knitted between her eyebrows. "In fact, you don't seem at all surprised nobody is here."

"Oh, trust me," Jopab said. "They will be here — in time. They first must find Rane, gather their wits, learn the truth, and finally, tromp out here to capture us."

Jewyl looked about.

"Yes," Jopab said. "They could show at any minute."

"Percho, straighten the grasses," Jewyl demanded. "Chardo, could you cover our tracks back into the tunnel a short distance?" Jewyl pointed at a cluster of large stones. "Jopab, stand on those stones. Percho, you join him."

"Because I'm a priest, I can't help with this?" Jopab asked. The sarcasm not lost on Jewyl.

"No," Jewyl said. "I want you to carefully move on the stones beyond us so you may scout the area. Leave as few traces of being here, and let us know if they come. I'm entrusting our lives to you. You recognize the whistle of a blue chipper?"

Jopab nodded.

"Fine," she said. "When you hear the whistle, we're ready to depart. If you see something to warrant an earlier departure, I'm sure you will let us know."

Jopab glared at Jewyl for a full minute before stomping off, leaving deep footprints, seething she had spoken to him in that tone.

He watched the nearby road, listening for Jewyl to whistle. Behind him he could see Percho standing on the rocks while Jewyl and Chardo cleaned all traces of their mere existence. A movement. He caught it at the edge of his vision and jerked to see what it was. A sound carried on the wind. He frowned and scrutinized everything — only thing moving was Jewyl and Chardo. Suddenly, a fawn stumbled from the brush, and froze, staring at the road to the west. The deer's ears twitched, trying to locate the sound.

Jopab immediately glanced down the road. There was nothing. At least, nothing he could see. Yet, there was a sound on the wind blowing from that direction. Both the deer and Jopab heard it. *Is that muffled voices?* he thought.

The sound of a blue chipper whistle cut through the air. Jopab silently eased back to the group.

"We'd best be on our way," Jopab said. "I didn't see anyone, but there was a sound, like the mumblings of people talking. A startled fawn heard it and we both watched the road."

"Fine." Jewyl pointed toward the woods. "Move out that way. Follow Chardo. I will cover our final footprints."

"We're not using the road?" Percho asked.

"The woods, shrubs and brush will be our friends," Jewyl said. "They will keep us hidden, and if we don't break too many branches, not reveal our escape route." Jewyl nodded in the direction to go.

Chardo motioned for the two priests to follow him. "The road is for guards and others, not for us."

"East? I thought we're going to Zornal," Jopab asked.

"In due time," Jewyl said. "We could walk the distance, but if we take a round-about journey, going first to Lisbeth Harbor, our group can enjoy some leisure while aboard a ship bound for Zornal."

"A ship?" Chardo yelped. "Out on the open waters?"

Jewyl smiled. "Yes, out on the ocean. Is there a problem?" She smiled, enjoying Chardo's fear of water and his uncontrolled nausea.

"I've never been to sea," Jopab offered sheepishly. "How many days?"

"If the wind is with us, I would chance two days at best," Jewyl said. "Of course, if the wind is against us, perhaps another day longer. Still, it is better than walking, and it will give us some leisure time."

"Leisure," Percho echoed. "To sit and enjoy doing nothing. How marvelous, me sitting with my head over the side the whole trip. It will take Ballec at least three days to get to Zornal." Percho carefully pushed a branch aside. "We could even beat him if we hastened our steps."

"We will proceed with caution to protect ourselves," Jewyl said. "We're not safe, yet. We could encounter priests or guards at any moment."

Chardo snickered and Jopab shook his head.

"We'd best be making plans for this evening," Jewyl said. "The woods will end shortly and then it will be open fields — not the easiest place to hide."

"Could we skirt them?" Percho asked.

"Add more walking?" Jopab questioned. "You of all people, you want to take a longer route?"

"I prefer to keep my life," Percho said. "The inconvenience of walking for the convenience of breathing is welcomed by me."

Chardo held up his hand and everyone froze. He placed a finger to his lips then whispered. "Who would like fresh meat for our evening meal?"

Jewyl looked beyond Jopab. A stunning stag with an enormous rack stood motionless, watching them.

"So much meat to waste," Jewyl hissed.

"Not the stag." Chardo slowly motioned to the right. "There, near the clearing. Do you see that good sized hen? It would feed us well."

Jewyl followed Chardo's pointing hand as he dropped to a knee, bow in hand, arrow ready.

The bird squawked and the stag dropped. The stag lay dead on the ground, an arrow piercing its body.

"Nice aim, but I thought you were going for the hen." Jewyl gazed down at Chardo. She stared at the arrow still in the bow. "Nice shot, but exactly how did you do that? I thought you aiming for the hen, not the stag."

"There's plenty for all," a voice cried out from near them.

Jewyl spun to face the body of the voice, her sword held at the ready. Chardo stood, following suit.

"Please, Jewyl," the voice continued. "You'd dare to lock swords with the love of your life?"

"Bezner?" Jewyl asked. "Is it truly you?"

The tall stranger stepped into view.

"Bezner!" Chardo shouted. "You dirty flea bitten scoundrel of Winmore. How did you get here?"

"Yes," Jewyl's voice matched her icy glare. "Exactly how did you get here? Is there a beauty hidden among the bushes waiting for you?"

Bezner moved to Jewyl and wrapped his arm about her waist, pulling her close. Tipping her head up, he gently kissed her.

Jewyl pulled away from him. "So, after three years, you believe you can walk into my life, and everything is forgiven?" She wiped the back of her hand slowly across her lips, all the while watching him. She only hoped her body wouldn't give away her true feelings. Already she could feel her heart starting to beat faster.

Chardo came up and slapped Bezner on the back. "So what have you been up to?"

"News travels fast," Bezner replied. "I've heard about your incident with Lord Azre, and today's little fiasco at the temple has everyone's lips flapping in the breeze."

"How did you happen upon us?" Jopab moved forward. "I am Jopab, a priest of the temple." He offered out his hand as a gesture of friendship.

Bezner shook it. "You walked directly under me. I had my eye on that stag for a few minutes and ready to shoot when you appeared. I couldn't believe my eyes. It took me a few seconds to recognize Jewyl…" He reached out and stroked her hair. "Now, Chardo? Who can forget Chardo?"

"Why are you out here?" Jewyl asked.

"To be honest?" Bezner stroked his chin and grinned slyly.

"That would be refreshing, and definitely a good start." Jewyl walked away from Bezner.

"There is a farmer a short distance from here," he said. "He has a daughter who I have had my eye on for some time."

"Oh?" Jewyl said, her voice cold.

"Ah, you're jealous, my love." Bezner smiled and winked at Jewyl. "Hiurla is not one who I will tarry a bit of time and then run. We are to wed after the harvest."

Jewyl frowned, and turned away from the group. A tear welled in one eye.

"Uh-oh," Chardo whispered and nodded at Jewyl.

"How was I to know you still existed?" Bezner moved closer and placed his arms about her. "We crossed swords and when the guards finally entered the tavern, you escaped. I haven't seen or heard about you until the last few days." He paused. "It has been three years."

"I had no ties on you," Jewyl said, and turned to face the group. "I hope you and this farmer's daughter have a full life together."

"Hiurla," Bezner said.

"Fine," Jewyl said. "There could never be an 'us' until I settled accounts and reign on the throne of Shiyula. I don't have time to involve myself with any man."

Percho had retrieved the stag and quickly cleaned the carcass.

"Then let us enjoy this meal." Bezner nodded at Percho. "I thought of letting you shoot the hen, but that would have meant I would need to follow the stag later and get it for Sanat and his family." He gazed at the sun. "This late in the day? I would have to give it up." He scrutinized the four. "You may stay there tonight, if you so wish."

"Your offer is very kind," Jopab said. "If Sanat has no problems then we will stay there."

"No!" Jewyl announced. "We need not put anyone in harm's way." She stood firm in her words. "We should continue on and stay elsewhere, even out in the open, if need be."

"Whatever you wish, Jewyl," Bezner said. "I'm not all that hungry, so I'll take the remainder of the stag with me, if you don't mind. Good fortune in your endeavor, whatever it may be."

"May Mother Hagontha smile upon you," Jopab said.

"Chaos is at every turn," Percho piped. "Blessed chaos."

"You're going to let him go?" Chardo whispered to Jewyl.

"Yes," she replied. "He loves another, and I'm not free to love him. It is best."

Bezner stopped and stared at Jewyl.

"Good fortune, my love," Jewyl said, hearing her voice tremble the words. "Hiurla is very lucky."

Bezner nodded, turned, and disappeared into the brush.

"You let him go?" Jopab asked.

"I don't want to talk about it." Jewyl wiped the tear from the corner of her eye. "Percho, hurry with that hen. I'm famished."

"Somebody start a fire," Percho asked. "By the time it has glowing embers, this slab of venison will be ready to cook. A feast, indeed."

Chardo and Jopab quickly built a fire. Jewyl kept a watch for anything out of the ordinary.

"Maybe we could rest here a while," Jewyl said, turned and looked to the edge of the woods. "Then just as the sun sets, continue our journey out of the woods and across the open fields. Traveling under the shroud of darkness will be to our advantage." Jewyl turned back to the group of men. "That smells good," she said turning her attentions to Percho and the roasting hen. The scent of crackling juices over the open fire gripped her stomach. "I don't know if I can wait until it is done."

"It will be ready shortly," Percho said. He opened a pouch he pulled from inside his garments. He pinched his fingers into the leather sack and gently sifted the retrieved, minute contents over the meat. "That will add a nice flavor," he added. "Just two more minutes." He smiled.

Jewyl feasted on the venison, slathering the juicy meats into her mouth. She watched the others enjoying their meal. She suddenly wondered if Bezner had gotten the stag back to the farm and into Huiurla's arms. It really didn't matter. Bezner would be back at the farm, and with his bride-to-be. Jewyl winced at the thought of him holding another. She dropped her eyes to cover a tear. How could she expect any man to wait for her to finish her self-assigned task of claiming her kingdom?

"How soon before we go?" Jopab asked while gazing at the

setting sun.

"We can depart soon." Jewyl threw dirt onto the fire in an attempt to hide any signs of their having been present.

"Your friend said there was a farm nearby." Jopab gazed at Jewyl with hope. "Perhaps we could stay there?"

"I would rather move on and not involve them," Jewyl replied.

"I agree," Chardo said.

The group moved about the small area, removing as many traces of their presence as possible. The fire was covered, it disappeared, leaves and debris were strewn casually about to hide any tale-tell signs of their presence.

"This time of the evening is perfect, just as the shadows play about," Jewyl started. "That will be to our advantage and we can move, just like a shadow between the trees."

"Until we get to the fields." Chardo grinned evilly. "Exactly how do you plan to hide us in the fields? Have you not noticed the moon in the sky? Full. It will shine brightly tonight."

Percho glanced nervously at Jewyl. "You have a plan?"

"Perhaps we should take the time to discuss—"

"I have a plan!" Jewyl stood with hands on hips, glaring at the three men. "Yes, I am a woman, but I have survived by my wits, perhaps better than some men."

CHAPTER TEN
Longrel

Jopab sputtered. "I beg forgiveness, Jewyl. If you have a plan, please share."

Jewyl strutted close to the edge of the woods, near where the field began. "See the cattle just a ways into the field?"

The three men gazed out into the open area. Not far away, cattle grazed in a cluster.

"I hadn't noticed them,"

"We should be able to gain them," Jewyl said. "Once we are within the herd, we can urge them to the other side. Who would question grazing cattle, moving in the darkness."

"A wise idea," Jopab said.

"We could milk them," Chardo said. "A bit of nourishment for us."

Jewyl shook her head. "You really have never learned, have you? If these beasts needed milking, the farmer would have taken them in before dark. These are probably being raised for butcher." She grinned. "They might all be young bulls."

"Could we take one?" Percho asked.

"Again, too much waste," Jewyl said. "Plus, I would prefer not to rile Bezner, nor his future father-in-law. We can move these cattle quickly across the fields and be back into the cover of the trees."

"Then we will sleep?" Percho asked. "Yes?"

"Yes. A short walk into the forest on the other side...to hide us," Jewyl said.

Chardo nodded agreement.

Jewyl glanced up at the sky. "The moon is about to hide behind some clouds. There will be some momentary darkness. Now is our chance." She stepped out into the open field. The four moved silently into the cluster of cattle.

"Just keep down," Jewyl whispered as she gently stroked her

hand across the cow's shoulders. "The silhouette of a man will stand out easily in the moonlight.

She watched the moon break away from the clouds and shed a bluish light on the scene. The cattle were a bit nervous, but failed to stampede which Jewyl was thankful for. She had noticed them as they approached the clearing, and the plan solidified in her mind. Her only fear was of spooking the beasts. Once more she felt the flames of anger build as she remembered Jopab's attempts to continue to control the group. It was quickly replaced with remorse at the thought of Bezner and Hiurla being wed. Jewyl felt the tear trace a path from the eye and felt her nose start. She sniffed and wiped the tear away.

In the distance, she could see flickering lights of what she was sure to be the farmer's home. Bezner would be there. She urged the cow beside her to plod along a little faster and wiped one last tear from her eye.

"What is your hurry?" Percho lagged behind with his cow.

"The quicker we are across this opening, the sooner we are safe." Jewyl glanced back the young priest. "Now, hustle these cattle."

"You've pushed them far enough," Jopab said. "We are but a few strides from the other side. Let our disguises rest and feed here."

Percho shoved the shrubs apart and leaned against a small tree. "How far before we rest?" He slid down the tree allowing the bark to rake up his spine. "A fire will be nice."

"No fire," Jopab said. "Jewyl wanted to get a bit further into the woods before we rested."

"On second thought, I say we rest here." Jewyl contradicted Jopab. "I see now the fields can be our friend. While we rest here, we can see if anyone draws near."

"Then we should set a guard," Jopab countered.

"No," Jewyl retorted quickly, and glared at Jopab. "We all rest. We need our strength. A weak link could be our downfall."

Jopab fumed and stomped about in a fit of anger.

"Doing that, my dear priest," Jewyl said. "Leaves a difficult track to hide."

Jopab froze and stared at the severe damage done. "Hagontha's bane," he whispered. "The goddess has caused this chaos."

"Enough of Hagontha," Chardo said with a yawn and a stretch. "Let's sleep."

He lay down and quickly curled into a fetal position. Percho smiled and moved near Chardo. Jewyl scanned the shadowy area and started to move toward an area a few feet away.

"I think we should all sleep very close," Jopab said. "If you don't mind, you can sleep by Chardo and I will take up a position on the outside."

"I need no protection," Jewyl said, and glared at Jopab while placing a hand on the hilt of her sword.

"Nonetheless, you will sleep as I have said, or we assign a watch."

Jewyl sighed loudly and slumped into a sitting position, folding her arms in front of her defiantly.

"I'm not sleepy so I will sit here until my eyes feel ready to close," she said.

"Fine. I will sit with you." Jopab grinned at her, yet even in the darkness he knew she was frowning at him. "When you decide to sleep, so will I."

Her eyes flashed in the moonlight. "As you wish," she said. "I'll lay down and go to sleep." She flopped down on the ground, her back to Jopab.

In the distance, Chardo grinned at her. She rolled her eyes in exasperation.

Jopab lay down.

Jewyl lay there, seething at Jopab's demands. *Who does he think he is?*

Ever since Bezner had showed up and left, Jopab had become impossible. *Bezner*, she thought and the memory of his strong arms and flashing smile filled her mind, and time passed.

A gentle touch caressed her back as a finger traced a pattern on her shoulder. It felt good. Bezner had done that, but this time there was a strangeness, this wasn't Bezner. She froze. Her eyes wide, she noticed Chardo and Percho were not to be seen.

"Relax," Jopab whispered. "You are much too tense. Your muscles are taunt." His fingers traveled her spine. "Our friends have moved to a more discreet area, and away from our prying eyes." Suddenly there were two hands on her back, massaging, thumbs working the knots of tension. A warm breath heated the nape of her neck as Jopab gently exhaled before kissing her.

"You really shouldn't," she murmured, then turned to face him.

His arms embraced her, pulling her close. Their lips met in a kiss and a passion Jewyl had not felt in a long time surfaced to be released. She moaned as Jopab's left hand caressed her breast. His right arm again pulled her closer to him before inching to the base of her back. Their bodies meshed. She could feel his arousal.

A third hand stroked her back. The ecstasy of the moment caught her unaware. Suddenly it hit her. *A third hand? Whose was it? Chardo? Percho?*

"No, Chardo," she heard Percho rasp in the distance. "This way."

She felt Chardo's hand leave. In the distance behind her she could hear the two men whispering.

"Your attention should be here," Jopab whispered and nibbled on her ear.

Jewyl pulled his head back, looked at the rugged features in the moonlight, then giggled.

"Are you sure you want my full attention, Jopab?" she asked in a sigh. "It has been a long time."

"The night is short, Jewyl," Jopab replied. "Let us not waste it in questions." He placed his lips over hers and kissed her deeply.

# # #

Jewyl twisted in the morning light, turning to shade her eyes. She'd slept well and a small smile curled her lips at the memory of the intense love making. Suddenly she was awake, realizing her current location. She cursed quietly at herself for allowing Jopab to seduce her. How could she lower her defenses? Scents assaulted her nose.

"Good morning." Jopab stirred the fire and smiled cheerily. "Are you hungry?" He stood.

Jewyl glanced about. Chardo and Percho were in the distance, locked in a naked embrace, barely hidden by the nearby shrubs. She frowned. She had never considered Percho could be the type to catch Chardo's eye, he always seemed more interested in men with a physique like Jopab's.

104

"Jewyl, dear," Jopab whispered. "Breakfast?" He knelt and offered a woven grass platter to her. "Enjoy."

Jewyl eyes flared at the spoken intimacy then quickly scanned the contents of the platter with its fried vegetable patty and roasted chicken. She moved one arm to cover her bare breasts and grabbed her blouse. "I'm not hungry," she murmured and slid her blouse over her head. She stood, pulling her breeches up in a swift movement. She glared down at Jopab who stared at her, and then she again surveyed her surroundings. She wanted to erase the memory of the shenanigans she had allowed to happen. She glanced again at Jopab and knelt beside him.

"Last night was a mistake." She placed a hand on his shoulder and gave him a comforting squeeze. "It should never have happened, Jopab."

"Unfortunately, Jewyl, it did happen," Jopab replied. "I've adored you since the first time I set eyes on you. Remember? You were a fury in Azre's court, blades moving everywhere. Do you remember the first time I touched you? I know you felt it. I'm sure you know my feelings. What we shared last night was not an accident."

"You're a priest—"

"I'm a man first," Jopab cut off her words.

Jewyl adjusted the blouse about her waist. She tried not to remember when he had helped her down and into the boat; his hands had slid along her legs. Yes, it had felt good.

"Still, last night should not have happened." Jewyl inhaled deeply. "If I have led you on, I am sorry."

Jopab slid the grass mat toward her. "Here, eat," he said and looked away toward the small fire and noticed the smoke curling upwards into the sky.

"Are we having a lover's quarrel?" Chardo asked, ambling toward them. He wore only a smile. "That food smells great. Is there more?"

Jopab nodded toward the fire. "Be quick. I need to put it out since it is giving off a dark smoke which, if anyone is watching, could see."

"And this?" Chardo asked, pointing at what lay before Jewyl.

"Eat it," Jewyl said. "Or give it to Percho." She shrugged. "I don't want any, but first, at least put some clothes on." Jewyl pulled her knees up and rested her chin on them.

"Percho prefers I don't," Chardo said, grinning like a love-struck teenage lad. "Since when has modesty been an issue with you? We've seen each other naked many times over."

"Get dressed." Jewyl ordered and caste a glance at the distant bushes. "We'd best be on our way. We have a mission."

Jopab strode over to the fire and kicked dirt onto it. "Percho! If you plan on eating, you'd best be getting a move on."

Chardo bent down and leaned into Jewyl. "Personally, darling, I'd give anything to have a bout with Jopab. Why are you tossing him aside? Was he that bad in bed?"

Jewyl slapped Chardo's face. He grabbed her hand and held it firmly.

"So," he whispered. His eyes searched hers. "You do care. Why are you being so cold?"

Jewyl's eyes flared as she stared at Chardo. "You don't understand," she said. A tear welled in her eye. "I'm but a trophy, nothing more. He will leave me just like the others."

Chardo pulled Jewyl closer. "They don't leave. Jewyl. You send them away." He glared at her. "I've been around long enough to know you. Last night was no fling. You don't just give yourself to anyone. You weren't drunk. You wanted it... probably more than he did." Chardo flung her hand away as he released it and threw his hands into the air with exasperation. "Why?" he shouted. "Why?"

Jopab and Percho both glanced at Chardo's outburst.

Jewyl leaped back away from the sudden stranger before her. Was Chardo jealous?

"I give," Chardo grunted, shook his head, grabbed the mat of food and stormed toward Percho with the plate of food in hand.

"Looks like we have company," Jopab yelled. "Appears to be Bezner."

Jewyl looked up and could see her lost love nearing. She quickly finger combed her short tresses and attempted to pull them back in a knot. She gave up. Straightening her clothes once more, she stood to greet Bezner.

"I can only stay a moment," Bezner said as he slid off his steed and faced Jewyl. "Last night we were visited twice — once by guards of Lord Azre, and later by priests of Hagontha."

"It was expected," Jopab said.

Bezner glanced at the priest before turning a questioning gaze to Jewyl. He pushed a stray hair behind her ear. "What mess have you gotten yourself into?" he asked. Bezner grabbed her hands and searched her eyes. "Must I continue to shadow you for protection's sake?"

Jewyl pushed Bezner's hands away and stepped back. "You infuriate me," she spat. "I am not a waif to be watched over and cared for. I am quite capable of taking care of myself."

"I only meant..." Bezner fell silent.

"If you need to care for someone, go back to your new love, take care of her." Jewyl reached down, grabbed, and strapped her sword belt about her waist. "As you can see, I don't need you to protect me."

Bezner nodded. "As you wish," he whispered.

"Which way did the guards go?" Jopab asked.

"You will probably meet them in Lisbeth Harbor," Bezner said. "As well as the priests."

"We can handle them," Jewyl said and scoured the camp area. "Remove all signs we were here." She looked at Bezner. "We won't be needing your assistance, if that is what you were thinking." Jewyl forced a smile. "We wouldn't want to detain you from your wedding."

"You should make the port city by mid-afternoon," Bezner said and bowed. "I wish you good travel." He leapt onto the horse's back. "Safe journey." He pulled the reins taunt. The horse turned its head back toward the farm.

Bezner glanced down at Jewyl. She stood there defiant, waiting for him to leave. "Rather harsh," Chardo whispered to Jewyl. "Like I said, you always push them away."

Jewyl turned away, there was no reason for Chardo to see the tears. "He has a new love." She made sure her voice didn't tremble or crack. She inhaled deeply before slowly letting it escape.

"We'd best be on our way," Jopab said. "Hagontha hasn't given us an easy path. Percho, get things moving."

The group moved quietly through the woods, watching and listening.

#

Jewyl gazed down the hillside toward the massive city and the ocean which disappeared in the horizon to match the sky.

"Our journey is near its end." Jewyl nodded toward the city. "We will find our ship, rest, and not worry about Azre's guards or Ballec's priests while at sea."

"Mother Hagontha will confuse them," Jopab added. "Chaos be blessed."

Jewyl stepped from the woods onto the road leading to Lisbeth Harbor. "We will find an inn, enjoy a meal, and make our final plans."

# # #

Lisbeth Harbor
The World's Largest
Harbor of Ocean Trade

Percho read the large sign aloud to them as they prepared to enter the gate into the city.

"Welcome, kind travelers," the rag-tag man said as he hobbled beside them in an attempt to keep pace. "Welcome to Lisbeth Harbor. Share a coin with one of Hagontha's lost souls?"

"Hagontha has no lost souls," Jopab spat. "If you work, you will earn the money you need. Why bother complete strangers?"

"My story is long," the man replied. "Let me share—"

"We really don't have time." Jewyl cast a casual glance at him then wrinkled her nose at the man's odors.

"I was a seafarer," the man began, ignoring Jewyl's comment. "A good one, at that until Hagontha..." His voice trailed. "I lost my leg at sea, and my wife left me upon my return. My son was killed by bandits, my home burned, and the captain set sail without me."

"Truly a sad tale," Percho said. "But, why do you blame Hagontha for your misfortune?"

"Is she not the goddess of chaos?" the man asked. "Is not my life's story one filled with chaos?"

"Hagontha is the goddess of chaos, indeed," Percho replied. "She reigns over chaos and will lead you through the paths of chaos, but you have forgotten — our lovely goddess doesn't cause chaos. She controls it.",

"Still, if you would be so kind to share a coin?" The man held out his scrawny hand, his fingers wiggling in anticipation.

"Find another to bother," Chardo said. "We've no time for your sad story. Now be away."

"And you say I'm harsh," Jewyl whispered to Chardo. She quickly turned her attentions to the city as they approached the wharf.

"We need a home base." She pointed at the inn just a few doors away. "The Crooked Skull might suffice. Let us get an ale and plan."

Chardo licked his lips. "An ale."

A woman with a cowl to cover her hair and face neared them. The woman tapped Jewyl's shoulder, whispered '*Join me at The Crooked Skull, Vaela,*' and continued on her way toward the inn.

Vaela? Who would call me that here? Jewyl watched the woman disappear into the inn. "Follow her," Jewyl said and hastened to the door of the inn.

Jewyl stood momentarily at the doorway to let her eyes grow accustomed to the darker room. She noted where the woman sat in a corner, alone. Jewyl strode quickly to the table.

"Who are you?" Jewyl demanded.

The woman pulled the cowl from her head to reveal her face.

"Britha? What are you doing here?" Jewyl quickly sat and motioned to the others to join her.

"Britha?" Chardo and Jopab said in unison.

Percho motioned for ales to be brought.

"There is much to tell you," Britha said. "A priest came to my father. He claimed to be a friend of Jopab and Percho. He said Ballec has fled to Zornal and Lord Azre's men are in pursuit of him and you. It was assumed you would go to Zornal, but there was also an assumption you might come to Lisbeth Harbor. Vico went to Zornal. I came here."

"But why?" Jewyl asked. "Why did you seek us out?"

"The Holy Father intends to deify Lord Azre." Britha shrugged. "The priest, Nethan, said you'd understand."

Jopab nodded. "It is a ceremony, but I truly don't believe Lord Azre understands the full consequences of the action."

"Plus, now I can join your group," Britha said, her eyes bright with anticipation and excitement.

Jewyl shook her head. "I promised your father I would not take you. Therefore, you must return home to him."

Britha stood and stamped her foot. "I am of the age to make my own decisions. I have stood watch, waiting for your arrival. None have bothered me. You and my father have no say."

Chardo quickly surveyed the area to see who had seen Britha's defiant act. He swung his drink drunkenly in the air. "And, so it should be," he said loudly.

Jewyl stood and placed a comforting arm around Britha. "I told you, a young man will come to save you from the dull life at the inn. What he brings — that I can't promise, but trust me, he will love you, and you will love him."

Britha began to whimper and tears flowed. "I want something exciting to happen now."

"Go back to your father, and the inn. Tell him we have received the warning, and understand the message." Jewyl hugged Britha. "You don't see it now, but someday you will thank me."

A young man approached and bowed. "My name is Longrel, most people call me Lon. Tell me, young maiden. These men are not of the age to be your father. Where is he, for I wish to know you better."

"Bashiwa. My father owns The Red Horse Inn."

"I will take you there and then bask in your beauty."

Britha blushed.

Chardo stood protectively to Britha's side. "Just who are you, Longrel, that we should trust you?"

"I have sailed for three long years on The Albatross Wing, and now weary of the sea life. I seek a permanent existence away from Lisbeth Harbor, and its shady inhabitants. This one," Lon nodded to Britha. "She has a fire about her to add to her beauty. She has been in my dreams these last months, and now, to see her, my dreams were but hazy visions."

"I will return to my father as you wish, Jew— Vaela." Britha curtsied to Longrel. "This gentleman may escort me." She drew back her cape. "I have protection, and know how to use it." The sword's handle glinted in the low light before she allowed the cape to cover it once more.

Longrel smiled. "A fire, indeed."

Chardo leaned in to whisper in Longrel's ear while placing a strong hand on the lad's shoulder. "If you are less than honorable, I will seek you out, and I will remove those which you want and cherish." Chardo raised an eyebrow. "Your days of having offspring will be no more." He squeezed Longrel's shoulder to drive home the point. "Britha is like a sister to me, and her brother, Vico, will more likely rip out your heart. Tread carefully."

Longrel nodded acknowledgment of Chardo's threat.

Jopab raised a hand to detain Longrel. "Tell me, Lon, which ship do you suggest we hire for a journey to Zornal?"

"Steer away from The Black Fury as well as Sea Ghost. I've heard tell they take on strangers who are never seen again. I know I've seen Full Sail Racer and The Sea Dragon at both harbors." He gazed at the group. "Then again, you might wish to stay clear of The Sea Dragon if you have issues with Lord Azre." Longrel shrugged and gave a knowing smile.

Jewyl leaped to her feet, a dagger discretely pressing at Longrel's waist. "A loose tongue dies quickly. Explain your words"

Frightened, he glanced at Britha. "Less than an hour before Britha entered, Lord Azre's guards stormed in looking for a woman and three men. The descriptions almost matched except for the darker red of your hair, Vaela."

"Is the Albatross Wing a fit ship to sail to our destination?" Jopab continued his questioning of Longrel. "You said you've seen other ships at Zornal. I assume The Albatross Wing sails there also?"

Longrel slowly nodded his head and whispered, "Yes."

Jewyl released the young man and put her dagger in its sheath. "Perhaps now is the best time for you to depart with Britha on a trip to Bashiwa." She turned to Britha. "I know you won't betray me." She glanced at Longrel. "If he tries, I'm sure you know what to do." The obvious was left unstated.

"I will return Britha safely to her father in Bashiwa. There, I will enjoy her beauty and bide my time until I decide that which I will do as my lifelong ambition." He grabbed Jewyl's hand which took her by surprise. "Your secret is safe with me." He turned to Britha. "Shall we depart?" He took her hand and led her to the exit and they disappeared.

"So, Chardo, do you have enough the gems to get us passage on a ship." Jewyl turned to look at Jopab. "Do you want to help make the arrangements? You can join Chardo." Jewyl nodded at the inn doors.

A lone guard stood in the entrance.

Chardo lifted a filled pouch to the table. "I have plenty of gems; more than enough. I was able to acquire more."

Jewyl frowned. "We don't need you pick-pocketing to have us arrested."

Chardo pulled back the pouch, a look of hurt on his face. "I didn't thieve these from the people of this fine city. Nobody should sound an alarm."

CHAPTER ELEVEN
Escape In A Storm

A guard stepped into the shadowed room. He was not one of Azre's men. Jewyl sighed relief as he slumped into a chair in a distant corner and growled for ale.

"Perhaps a quick split of our group would be beneficial to our efforts." She nodded toward the guard. "Percho and I will remain here at the Crooked Skull Inn. The two of you find us a way out of Lisbeth Harbor."

"Fine," Jopab said, shrugged, and stood. "As you wish, *Vaela*. You ready, Chardo?" He put his arm about Chardo's shoulder conspiratorially, and led him toward the door. "Once outside, do we continue down the cobbled street or take ourselves up the stairs to the docks? I say stairs. We should find us a nice galley quickly. I've heard the merchant owners are always willing to take on paying passengers."

Chardo smiled at Jopab's touch. "I should be able to get us all passage without any difficulty." Chardo narrowed his eyes slyly. "I gleaned a couple of extra pearls from the tunnels during our escape."

The bright sunlight made them squint momentarily. A group of guards slowly made their way toward the inn. Thirty paces in the opposite direction Jopab saw the stairs leading up to the docks.

He stopped abruptly. "Pearls? Tunnels?" Jopab repeated and stared at Chardo. "May I see them?"

Chardo looked about before pulling a cluster of small pearls from his belt and let them roll about in his palm. The iridescent globes glistening in the sunlight.

Jopab smiled and poked at a couple of the pearls in Chardo's hand. "Collected from the walls?"

"No," Chardo replied. "I picked these up from the floor. Is there a problem?"

"Not really," Jopab said. "Now, if you plan to use these pretty ones I suggest you make sure you won't be staying around too long."

"Oh?" Chardo asked. "Why is that?"

"I would say these are still quite young." Jopab held one of the pearls between his index finger and thumb, rolling it gently. "Perhaps another eight to ten days, at best." He giggled. "No more than twelve."

"Ten days to what?" Chardo asked retrieving the pearl. "Twelve?"

"Depending on conditions," Jopab replied with a sly smile. "Hatching is the term I'd use. What you have grabbed are plioca eggs."

"You'd say anything." Chardo frowned. "These are pearls." He put them back in the belt's pouch.

"Suit yourself," Jopab said. "Just remember, I warned you. If you continue to keep them in the dark, the eggs will grow, until suddenly one day you have a belt full of young pliocas. Do you remember those spidery things?"

A shudder coursed through Chardo. "A plioca?"

"How many pearls do you have?" Jopab asked.

"I probably have near fifty or so." Chardo held the ball up close and scrutinized it carefully. "You're sure these are plioca eggs?"

"I'd rather not be near you when they hatch," Jopab said. "In fact, I don't think any of our group should be anywhere near you when they hatch." Jopab winked at his companion. "Just remember one fact, young pliocas are voraciously hungry."

They hustled up the stairs and Chardo froze at the sight of the open bay and collection of ships.

"Must we travel by water?" Chardo grabbed his stomach with one hand and covered his mouth with the other.

"Good sirs," a voice called to them. "Are you in search of passage? I have an excellent fleet of fast ships porting all the known coast." He bowed. "Merchant Auro at your service."

"It would appear our luck has changed." Jopab smiled at the stranger. "We need passage to Zornal."

The thin man stood silently appraising them, stroking his beard with one hand while the other nervously fumbled in the pocket of his long, red coat. "Zornal?" he finally asked. "Just you two, young, strapping men?"

"There will be four," Jopab said. "How much?"

"Payment in pearls," Chardo added.

"If you were to pay me pearls..." The man once more stroked his beard while he thought. "I would need five pearls per head." He grinned at Chardo. "Oh, there is also the harbor tax." He cocked an eye at them.

"Harbor tax?" Chardo exclaimed. "Harbor thievery is more like it."

"You seem to be in a hurry," the man said. "Also, I feel you wish to avoid too many questions being asked." He cocked an eye and gave a small shrug. "That, too, my good sirs, will cost extra."

"How much?" Jopab sighed. "What will it cost us for passage of four to Zornal?"

The man leered and his lip curled at the edge of his mouth. "Fifty pearls," he said.

"Fifty!" Chardo yelled.

"Hush," Jopab said. "Pay the man. When will the ship be ready?"

Chardo slowly counted out fifty pearls from his belt. He had seven remaining.

"Perhaps I should have charged more." the man stated and smiled at the bulge of Chardo's leather bag.

"I asked when the ship would be ready," Jopab repeated.

"An hour before the sun sets," the merchant said dropping the pearls into a leather pouch attached to his belt. "The Albatross Wing will be ready to depart for Zornal as the tide goes out, whether you be aboard or not."

"We'll be here," Chardo sneered.

"I'll inform the captain of four passengers to arrive before departure."

Jopab nodded. "Just be sure to inform him we've paid our passage."

"I am not a thief," the merchant said. "I run a profitable and proper business." He placed his hands to his forehead then swung his arms down in graceful arcs. "Safe journey." The thin man turned quickly, his red coat flaring out as he headed for the ship.

Chardo looked up at the ship's bow — The Albatross Wing. His stomach turned and he felt clamminess coating his skin. He took a deep breath, inhaling the scents of the dock.

"We'd best be getting ourselves back to Jewyl and Percho,"

Chardo said. "Are you positive these are plioca eggs?"

Jopab smiled before slapping Chardo on the back. "Ask Percho when we get back. Show him one and ask him what it is."

Chardo cocked an eye to Jopab.

"I'll remain silent," Jopab said.

# # #

Jewyl stood on the gangplank, glaring at the man obstructing her way.

"I'll not have a woman aboard this ship." The man stood his ground.

Chardo moved forward. "We've paid passage for four, and she is one of the four."

"If payment is the problem," the scruffy man said. "Then I'll personally return from my pockets her portion of fare."

"I'll slice you from stem to stern," Jewyl said, and patted the hilt of her sword.

"What is the ruckus?" The captain strode toward the gangplank, his blouse fluttering in the light ocean breeze.

"We have paid passage for four. Your lackey won't allow one of them aboard," Chardo replied.

The captain motioned the sailor aside with a wave of his hand. He cast a casual glance at Jewyl. "Captain Murdo at your service." He nodded his head. "So, you're the one causing all the commotion." He fiddled with one side of his mustache, twirling the end with his fingers.

"Amazing," Jewyl said. "Me. A ruckus?"

"It's bad luck to have a woman as part of the crew," Murdo replied. "I have a very superstitious lot aboard the Albatross Wing."

"Part of the crew?" Chardo sputtered. "We happen to be paying passengers."

Captain Murdo raised an eyebrow. "Everyone works aboard my ship, even paying passengers."

"I can carry my weight," Jewyl said. "I really don't see my being aboard as a problem, and I certainly don't see how I could bring you bad luck."

"All I ask is that you not dispatch any of my crew." Murdo pointed at Jewyl's sword. "If you can agree to that, then please, come aboard, Jewyl."

Jewyl jerked back and examined the captain. "You know me?"

"Let me say I know of you," Murdo replied. "There were guards at The Bawdy Maiden and they were quite boisterous in their comments of what they were looking for." He watched the four passengers. "Let me see... three men and a woman." Murdo tapped his lower lip with his index finger. "Oh, yes and the woman has red hair." He reached out and Jewyl pulled back, but not before he touched her hair and brown dust fell away to reveal more red. "Even at The Crooked Skull I could tell your hair was red, but you were with one man. I saw no need to speak." He paused. "But now..." He smiled, his eyelids narrowing.

"Perhaps we should get on board," Jewyl said. "Perhaps even below deck until we sail?"

"That would work just fine," Murdo replied with a flourished bow. "At least, keep out of view until we are out of visual range," he whispered as Jewyl sauntered across the gangplank onto the ship.

"What a gorgeous golden sunset," Percho said.

Murdo raised an eyebrow and turned to view what Percho had noted. Immediately he heard the words scream within his head:

When the sun flickers on a coin
A day's future can be told
But beware the open seas
If the evening sky turns gold

"Already two bad omens," Murdo mumbled. "We haven't even cast off, yet." He turned to the crew. "Prepare to set sail."

The crew cast off and The Albatross Wing drifted into the harbor under the guidance of a light breeze.

"A wind to save your sorry souls," Captain Murdo yelled. "Store the oars and scurry above to drop the sails."

He watched the sails unfurl in the golden sunlight and smiled at the commotion on the wharf they'd left. He knew the incident would catch somebody's attention, and it had. Guards, the ones he was sure he'd seen at the tavern now hurried forward to the wharf, causing even more commotion and chaos.

He leaned against a banister. *Who are these four?* he thought.

117

What have they done to rouse the anger of Lord Azre? Why do they need to get to Zornal? He paused in thought, a curl showing at the edges of his lips. *A better question — how much money do they carry?*

The Albatross Wing heaved, catching Murdo's attention. The wind picked up as the ship rounded the safety of the harbor. Waves crashed against the ship.

"*At least no ship has raised a sail to pursue*," he thought.

"Do we need to take the sails down, captain?" the helmsman asked with a wary eye to the sky.

"Let us get a bit more distance," Murdo replied. "If the wind picks up stronger, call me. I'm going below to get answers from our guests."

Murdo could feel the eyes of his crew watch his every step. He grabbed the doors' wooden handles and yanked them open.

"If there be a question or problem, I'll be in my room," he shouted, ducked his head, and started below. He turned quickly about and scanned the deck, scowling. "If it be about our guests, keep your tongue, or I'll have it for a meal." He pulled the doors shut.

"Captain?" The voice called from the darkness below.

Murdo stepped back and smiled as his eyes acclimated to the stairway's murkiness.

"Jewyl," he replied.

"You made comment to us having duties aboard your ship, that none traveled for free." Jewyl cautiously stepped back toward the door she'd come through. "We paid for our passage to Zornal."

"Aye, that you did, my beauty." Murdo leaned toward Jewyl. "You paid for your passage. Yet, something tells me you'll pay even more for your safety."

"Safety?" Jopab repeated, opening the door to the room.

Murdo pushed forward, shoving Jewyl and Jopab back into the room.

"Aye," the captain said. "Safety, indeed. A sweet, young thing like Jewyl would need some protection from the likes of those above deck. In fact," he cast a casual glance and nod at Jopab, Chardo and Percho, "they might need a bit more protection. My men are very ambivalent in how their needs are taken care of — as long as they are taken care of."

Chardo pulled his sword out in a smooth movement which was countered loudly by Murdo's sword. Murdo felt a point's pressure on his back.

"If you plan to protect me..." Jewyl held her dagger against Murdo. "Perhaps you should not waste your time on those who will defend me. Drop it."

Murdo held the sword. "You would cheat me of a few coins?"

The ship lurched, Chardo fell forward toward Murdo who turned quickly to avoid both the blade from Chardo and Jewyl as she lost balance and sword.

"It would appear I am more familiar with the surf of the sea than you," Murdo said. "I have my sea-legs. You landers don't."

He stood gloating over Chardo. Murdo held his sword near Chardo's neck, teasing with a slight movement back and forth. Jewyl still held onto the table she'd grabbed to stop her fall. She eyed her dagger.

"I don't think you should," Murdo said with a quick glance at her and the dagger just out of her reach.

"If money is the issue," Jopab said. "Please, we have more than enough. Chardo, give this man the remainder of your pearls."

"Ah, yes, Chardo," Murdo sneered. "Jewyl's companion. So he holds the coin purse. I've often wondered what he did."

Chardo frowned then cast a glare at Jopab.

"I have some pearls," Chardo said. "I gave fifty of them for passage."

"Fifty!" Murdo shouted. "That cheating merchant. He told me he only was able to get twenty."

"Fifty per person," Jopab said and winked at Chardo. "I would say he more than cheated you."

Chardo quietly and quickly removed his bag and handed it to Murdo. "Here."

Murdo grabbed the bag then hefted it for weight. "Not many left," he said.

"I wouldn't believe so after paying for our passage," Jopab said.

"Captain Murdo," a voice from above yelled. "We have two problems."

Murdo tucked the bag under his belt. "Be there," he yelled

back. "Now about your passage. You are duly paid to me and can wander the ship as you please. Just remember, your safety is in my hands, and my hands alone. If any of the crew..." his voice faded off as he put his sword away and walked out the door.

"Well, that went well," Jopab said. "Still haven't lost my ability to arbitrate things without a fight." He rubbed his hands together. "Now, I just hope we're off this vessel before anything happens."

Jewyl frowned at Jopab's statement. "Happens?"

"Uh, Percho," Jopab started. "Chardo was able to retrieve all his pearls from the floor of the tunnels."

Percho's face washed white. "He what? Not them?"

"I told you," Jopab said. He smiled at Chardo. "Now let us see what is going on above since there were two problems for the captain to look after."

The group quietly eased their way onto the staircase and listened.

"Get all the sails but the main one down, now," Murdo yelled.

"Captain, the storm will destroy us," one of the crew yelled.

"That is The Sea Dragon," Murdo said. "It is the fastest ship in the harbor. If you wish to take your chances with Lord Azre's guards, then take down all the sails."

The vessel again lurched in the waves and sea water rushed across the deck and into the stairwell.

"We're wet," Jewyl said. "Guess we might as well help. I don't think the Azre's guards are after anyone else except us."

"What can we do to assist?" Jewyl asked as the doors to below battered open and she was facing Murdo.

"You," he said pointing to Jewyl. "Go back and give assistance to the helmsman. Get us away from the shore's view. Only then will The Sea Dragon dare not follow us. It will head back to shore."

"You three, go help with the sails."

Jewyl stumbled to the aft part of the ship and could see the young man straining at the helm. She smiled at him. "Two can make the job easier," she yelled over the increasing winds.

The helmsman smiled weakly and stood up to allow Jewyl to join him on the large wooden wheel. "She wants to pull starboard," he said and wiped the dripping water from his face.

"You ever been out beyond the sight of land?" Jewyl asked.

"No," the helmsman replied, his voice quivering.

Jewyl smiled, brushed her wet hair back with her hand then grabbed hold of the wheel. "Let's take her out to sea," Jewyl yelled. "What do we have to lose, but the ship that follows?"

"Our lives," the helmsman said. "I know not how far to the edge and the storm has confused our directions."

Lightening blazed through the clouds. The winds whipped the sail.

"See how our adversary falls behind," Jewyl said.

"As does the land!" The helmsman pointed. "There is nothing to see. Even The Sea Dragon has turned around."

"Bring down that sail," Murdo yelled. "Now!"

The ship lurched and waves rolled over the bow. The sound of creaking wood snapped and Murdo stepped back. The sail whipped in the wind.

"Chardo!" Jopab yelled above the howling winds. "Watch out!"

A lanyard cracked through the air catching another sailor as Chardo dropped to the deck. The man snapped out of existence as the rope and sail fluttered into the darkness.

"Grab that corner," a voice yelled.

Jewyl held a death grip on the wheel and looked desperately about the deck before her, trying to locate the men of her group. She could see Chardo clinging to the boom, his arms wrapped around the sail to keep it from billowing. Jopab held a segment of the sail from the wind's grasp, holding it wrapped about the main boom. Percho? Where was Percho?

The rain stung and Jewyl squinted to find the young priest in the boiling darkness of the storm.

"Have you seen Percho?" Jopab yelled to Chardo.

Chardo shook his head and quickly scanned the area around him.

"Here," Percho said. "Above you."

"What in the name of all that is holy to Hagontha are you doing up there?" Jopab yelled.

Percho jumped down from the main mast then slipped as the ship tilted, followed by a quick dip into the trough. He slid across the wet deck, grabbing and scratching to grab hold of anything to stop his current path to the edge of the ship.

Jewyl watched in horror as the young man approached the edge.

"The rope," Jopab shouted. "Grab the rope and hold on."

Percho grabbed the rope and swung like pendulum across the deck.

Murdo moved forward, reached down and hoisted Percho upright.

"I may lose a sailor now and then, but I'll not have my name bandied about as one who loses paying customers." Murdo pushed the straggly priest back toward the mast.

"Helmsman!" Murdo shouted. "Make way to land."

"Land?" the young helmsman yelled with one hand up to his mouth to amplify his words. "Which way is land?"

"That is your job," Murdo yelled back. "Be quick about it."

"He has no idea where land is," Jewyl said. "Pick a direction and we'll hold course until the storm clears. You can then get your bearings."

"What if the storm doesn't end?"

"We'll stay on your course until sunrise," Jewyl said and smiled at the young man. "If the sun comes up in the wrong direction, we'll simply turn the ship around."

"What if the sun is at the edge of the world?"

CHAPTER TWELVE
Island Of The Lost Souls

"Does not the sun always rise to the east?" Jewyl asked. "You worry too much. My arms are aching."

Rain, driven by the wind, pelted against Jewyl. It stung.

"The storm grows stronger," she said.

The helmsman nodded and shrugged. He lashed the hand grips of the wheel with rope tied to the ship's side rail.

"This will help hold the course," he said. "After some time necessary for you to give your arms a much needed break, we'll straighten The Albatross Wing out. Now, you, let go of the helm and relax your arms."

Jewyl eased off her hold on the helm and watched the young man's arm muscles tighten and his face strain as he picked up the tension. "You are much stronger than you appear," he said.

"A compliment, I'm sure," Jewyl said.

The helmsman scanned the skies above, Jewyl followed suit. The clouds rolled and churned as the storm progressed.

"Help me," the helmsman hollered.

Jewyl jumped up and grabbed the helm with him and attempted to move it back to its original position. She watched the rope they'd tied to the wheel whip in the winds. It'd snapped.

"This is not good," the helmsman said. "A very bad omen."

"What do you mean?" Jewyl asked.

"The ship is possessed," he replied and let go of the helm. "See? It does not move."

"Of course not," Jewyl said. "I'm still holding the helm."

She felt the helm move under her hands, not away but in the same direction she had been holding. She let go.

"Possessed?" the helmsman queried and wiped the rain from his face.

"It would appear that way," Jewyl replied and kept an eye on the helm. It held true, not moving. "I wonder where we are going."

"Going?" the helmsman echoed.

Jewyl nodded and kept watching the helm. There, in the collective rain she could faintly see the wet outline of huge, rugged hands, sometimes skeletal, holding the helm. Jewyl stepped back and stared into the space above the helm. The rain channeled and flowed around the large specter, making him both visible and invisible in the wetness.

The specter leaned his head back, lightening shot through the air, and Jewyl could see the face of the skull, the jaw moving to talk. A shriek pierced the air.

All the deck hands turned aft to watch the ghostly character take shape at the helm.

Again, the jaw moved. "Welcome," the specter said and let loose a terrifying laugh to match the howling wind.

Jopab leaped forward and protectively wrapped his arms about Jewyl. "What do we have here?"

She pulled away and gouged an elbow into his chest.

"What in the name of Hagontha is that?" Percho asked.

"Chaos," Chardo said. "This ship is doomed."

"Helmsman!" Murdo yelled. "Take your position. That helm is unmanned."

"It's haunted," the helmsman replied. "Look closely, do you see our speed?"

Everyone quickly glanced over the edge of the ship to see the surging ocean. Then, in unison, the group looked to the bow and watched it slice through the very top of the waves.

"The ship is possessed," Murdo whispered, his eyes wide in terror. "Even now, see how it is being lifted?"

Jewyl grabbed a handrail on the port side of the ship, leaned over and scrutinized the situation — one that, indeed, did have the ship out of the water.

"It is caused by the woman," a voice yelled above the wailing winds. "It is because of her we have endured all this misfortune."

"A woman should never be aboard a ship," another voice yelled.

"Get her," yelled one of the nearby crew. "Throw her overboard."

"Stand back," Murdo yelled. "She is under my protection, and she brought no evil aboard this ship."

A haunting, laughing shriek cut through the air from the phantom helmsman. He turned the helm to a hard starboard even though the ship wasn't in water. The ship responded with a lurch. The wet deck was slippery. Jewyl slipped, fell, and floundered on the wet deck. She tried to watch the barely visible helmsman while grabbing for something to hold onto. The phantom raised his hands into the air, stood there momentarily, and then completely disappeared.

"There are rocks ahead," the young helmsman yelled. "Look out!"

The ship dropped through the air, crashing upon the rough waves, only to be dashed and splintered upon the rocks.

Jewyl felt the deck cracking and breaking beneath her. She grabbed a rope and hung on. The cold sea water engulfed her. There was chaos, splintering wood, and sputtered screaming. She could feel the rope pulling her down. It twisted about her arm, locking her in a death grip. She fought for release, and kicked her feet to keep from being dragged any deeper. Finally, she was loose and quickly bobbed to the surface.

A group of large boulders loomed in the darkness and foaming waters. Wave after wave of water crashed against the stones. Jewyl moved toward them.

If I can make it to the rocks and not be killed in the surf striking them, she thought, and swam furiously with the flowing tides as they lunged toward the stones before being violently pulled away.

"Jewyl?" Chardo's voice called out. "Anyone?"

"I'm here," Jewyl replied. "I'm swimming toward the boulders."

"Already on some," Chardo replied. "Percho? Jopab? Captain Murdo? Anyone?"

The winds howled, but there were no crying voices in it. The rain had stopped.

Jewyl clambered onto the stones and saw Chardo a mere ten feet away on another outcropping.

"Anyone else alive?" Jewyl yelled into the wind.

Silence.

"What happened to all of the ship?" Jewyl asked. "There is only a small amount of wood floating about." She pulled at her clothes twisting them together into knots to remove as much water as possible.

"Are you okay?" Chardo asked. "You were under the water for so long."

"My wrist and arm got tangled in a rope," she replied. "Where is everyone?"

"One of the men said he could hear the surf so there has to be land," Chardo replied. "I know some of the men went that way." He pointed.

"What of our group?" Jewyl asked. There was silence. "Jopab?" More silence. "Percho!"

"Nothing," he replied. "I've heard nothing of them."

"Maybe they went toward land?" Jewyl offered.

"Possibly, but I doubt it," he replied. "I've been yelling their names, including yours, for quite some time. I was about to give up when you replied."

"There is hope," Jewyl said. "Jopab? Percho?" She listened, but was only greeted by the sound of waves crashing near her.

"Per-cho... Jo-pab," Chardo yelled into the darkness.

"I hear something," Jewyl yelled. "It's coming from this side." She pointed toward the land. "I can hear voices."

"Perhaps they are the sounds of the men as they fall off the edge of the world," Chardo said.

"You wouldn't hear surf if it truly was a drop off," Jewyl said. "Jopab! Percho!" she yelled toward the sounds. She listened.

"I'll swear someone is calling to us," Jewyl said. "Listen."

"Race you there," Chardo said and dived into the swirling waters.

"Chardo! You idiot," she screamed and carefully eased into the waters.

"Hurry," Jopab said as he bobbed into view. "Swim fast. There is more in these waters than us. Nasty things we really don't want to meet."

"Where have you been?" Jewyl asked. She started to swim toward the shore.

"I was pushed around the rocks when we crashed," he said. "I was about to try to swim back to the rocks when I heard somebody yell there was land. I've been swimming for land."

"What of Percho and Captain Murdo?" Jewyl asked.

"Murdo is on the beach," Jopab said. "Percho? I haven't seen him, yet. He may have been lost in the crash."

"If you want to beat me," Chardo said, swimming up next to Jewyl. "You're going to have to stop talking to Jopab so much."

"Good to see you, too," Jopab said.

"I can hear the surf now, we're close," Jewyl said. "What just brushed my leg?"

"Stand up," Jopab said. "It is a long walk to shore since the sands come out so very far."

Chardo stood and began to run toward the beach, sloughing through the surf.

"Something has my leg," Jewyl shrieked. "Get it off."

"Stand up," Jopab demanded and looked at the thing attached to Jewyl's leg. "It is a sucker fish, I think."

He took a knife and scraped it down Jewyl's right leg. "This will hurt a little," he whispered.

Jewyl felt the knife brushing along her leg; then she felt it grind against the teeth of the sucker fish. She could almost hear the popping sound each tooth made as it broke contact with Jewyl's leg. The fish dropped off and Jopab stabbed it. He brought it to eye level to view.

"What's happening?" Chardo asked splashing back into the surf from shore.

"Nasty little thing," he said. "Want to look at it?" he offered it to Chardo.

"I've had enough of this water," Jewyl said and proceeded toward the shoreline.

"Aiee!" came the yell. "You do not belong here."

Everyone turned toward the area where the voice had come from.

"Turn back," the voice yelled. "You are in danger."

A short man in tattered clothes ran from the trees. "Go away," he demanded. His hands flailed above him to chase the survivors away. "Go back, now! Your lives are in danger."

Jewyl watched a scraggly bearded man with the disheveled hair charge toward her.

"A woman?" The man stopped abruptly.

Jewyl brought up her sword as did others of the group.

The man stared at the group while tugging on his beard,

twiddling his fingers through the unruly hairs.

"This is not right," he said. He bobbed his head a couple of times, before bringing one hand up to his temple and tapping his fingers on his forehead, as if it helped him to think.

His eyes glazed and lips moved. Jewyl listened to the broken words.

"Not living... Woman... Not lost soul... No men... Ships..."

The man's eyes cleared and focused.

"Yes! Ships," he yelled. "Where are your ships? To rescue me? Yes?"

Murdo stepped forward. "I've no intention of saving you," he said. "If you wish, I can quickly run this blade through you and end your miserable life. Who are you?"

The man's eyes flared wide. "Me? Who am I? I am..." The man bent his head and searched the ground before him. "My name. My name?" He dropped to his knees in the sand, his hands scribbling in the sand. "My name is..." He looked up at Jewyl. "Please, you must save me."

Murdo lifted his sword. "What is your name?"

"Please," the man said then started crying. "My name is-- I don't remember my name," he said between the sobs. He stopped crying and wildly looked in both directions. "We are not alone. It is not safe here."

"You've said that before," Jewyl said, and walked up to the man. She knelt down in front of him and grabbed his hands. "Yes, I am a woman. Who are you? Take your time. Think."

The man quivered and shrunk back from Jewyl, all the while searching her face with maniacal eyes.

"My name is... my name is Hars... my name is Harsbor." He pulled himself up proudly. "No! My name is Harsborz."

Jewyl searched his eyes which once more had changed from the look of a wild man to that of a sane person.

"My name is Harsborz," he said. "I have been on this island over..." He hesitated. "I've been here a long time. We are all in danger. This is the Island of Lost Souls."

"That is a legend," Murdo said. "I've sailed the seas for many years and never once come upon it."

"You're here, now," Harsborz said, and glared at Murdo. "Beware, my good man, for it will steal your soul."

"Are you the only one here?" Murdo asked.

"I am," Harsborz said with a curious smile. "And I am not. There are the undead, and the non-living also exist here." His lips curled in a grin. "Both of them can cause you harm."

"Undead? Non-living?" Jewyl repeated, questioning his words.

"There are those who come and pretend to be the dead," Harsborz said. "I call them the undead. Plus, there are also the non-living. Those I call the true lost souls."

"You try to trick us," Jopab said. "Living. Dead. Not. In Hagontha's name, what is your ploy?"

"Hagontha?" Harsborz frowned and scowled at Jopab. "She is but a newborn goddess, a baby. Beware of her and the Lost Souls." Harsborz's voice deepened and the words flowed in a chant. "For in the true path, the queen of all that is, was, and not to be, will rule the living and not living. Only when the Lost Souls have been put to rest will the true nature of her be known. All hail and may chaos rule."

"I've not heard that one before," Jopab said. "At least, not those exact words."

"What do you mean?" Chardo asked.

"Do you remember me talking about Yendisa?" Jopab whispered.

"Aiee!" Harsborz yelled. "You say the unspeakable name. It is she who the undead come to worship."

"Who are these undead?" Chardo asked. "You keep mentioning them."

The man cowered momentarily then sheepishly looked around. His eyes squinted as he stared down the beach, into the darkness.

"No," Harsborz shouted, and scrambled away a few feet away on all fours. "She comes! Beware the lost souls," he yelled and pointed a gnarled index finger toward them. "You've been warned," he said, leapt up, and quickly disappeared into the shrubs.

"Okay," Jewyl said. "Anyone familiar with these lost souls he's babbling about? Either one of them?" She looked at the men's' blank faces. "No? Fine," she said. "Let's call it a night, start a fire and get settled in."

"You don't give orders to my men," Murdo said. He raised an

eyebrow and glared at Jewyl. "They will do as I tell them."

"We're not your men," Chardo said. "I agree with Jewyl. We should settle in for the night since we don't know where we are. Any rest is better than no rest when fighting an unknown."

Jewyl surveyed the dark shadows beyond the sands of the beach. In the clearing night sky she could tell this island was bigger than she expected. She cast a glance down the beach in each direction.

"Who's that?" Murdo asked and pointed.

Percho? Jewyl thought. She glanced in the direction Murdo was pointing to see a slim shadowy figure strolling toward them. "A woman?" Jewyl softly asked.

"Why a woman?" Murdo asked. "On this forsaken island?"

"It could be a woman," Jopab replied. "By the size of this island I would expect some natives to inhabit it." There was silence. "Of course, Harsborz doesn't really instill the confidence of more inhabitants."

"There is something wrong," Jewyl said. "Watch her. Do you see how the shadows play on her body?"

Before Murdo could say anything, three of his crew rushed forward, stumbling in the sand, to meet the strange woman. She stretched out her arms to greet them as they floundered closer. Suddenly there was a melee of activity — large, muscular sailors tossed about as if they were nothing more than paper dolls. The sand settled and the woman continued toward them.

"I may be stating the obvious here," Jewyl said. "But, don't you think we should consider some course of action?"

The figure moved toward Murdo. His men cautiously gave way as she approached him.

Jewyl had been correct. The lights did play games on this strange woman, and at times she appeared almost invisible.

"A ghost," one of the crew finally yelled. "How can that be?"

"Stand behind me," Jewyl said, and pushed Murdo aside to step in front of him and face the stranger. "What is your business here?"

The shadowy figure halted and tried to see beyond Jewyl to find Murdo.

"You are not in charge," the woman said and floated back, hovering three feet away from Jewyl. "I must talk with the person in

130

command."

"You will talk with me, or you'll talk with no one," Jewyl said and lifted her sword to a ready position of attack.

"Very well, Jewyl," the woman said and lifted her sword in preparation to parry Jewyl's attack. "I tried to warn you." The ghost disappeared in an explosion of showering sparks and smoke.

Jewyl staggered backward from the fireworks, but quickly regained her stance and composure. She brushed sand off her arms and legs, and shook her hair to remove any from it.

"Impressive exit," Jewyl muttered.

"How did she know your name?" Chardo asked.

"You caught that, did you?" Jewyl replied and smiled at him. "When she got closer, she appeared more familiar, yet I couldn't recognize her.

"An adversary from your past?" Murdo asked, all the while listening to the mutterings of his crew.

Jewyl shrugged. "Perhaps." She took three strides toward the crew men then slashed the sword into the sand, dragging a piercing line as she walked toward the trees. "This is my border. Tread across the line and be prepared to battle a fighting demon." Jewyl pointed at herself. "Stay on this side with me and I will attempt to protect you. As our guest so aptly stated, 'You have been warned.' I know how to use this and I am a very light sleeper." She sheathed her sword, turned and walked toward Chardo. "There may be sleep yet tonight," she whispered as she passed him.

"You heard her," Murdo said stepping over the line to join his crew. "My sword will aid my crew with any problems on this side of that line." He turned to face Jewyl and glared at her and her companions. "Cross over your line into my territory, and this sword will be your enemy." He lifted his sword into the air, bowed then turned to his crew. "Now, get about to take some sleep. Who will handle first watch?"

Chardo gathered some driftwood and soon had a rewarding fire. Jopab grabbed a branch with flames and carried it toward the ship's crew as an offering of good faith. Soon, two fires blazed on the beach. Percho and Jopab joined forces to gather food, and the sound of cracking shells could be heard.

Jewyl nibbled the sweet meat from the half-shell and stared into the darkness where Harsborz obviously hid...

What else lurked beyond? Jewyl wondered.

CHAPTER THIRTEEN
Kiss Of The Lost Souls

Jewyl laid on the sands of the beach, her eyelids closing slowly, only to pop back open at the faint sounds of the roaring fire or crashing surf. She couldn't believe it was only last night she had made love with Jopab. Right now it seemed so long ago. The fire crackled softly, and in the distance she could see Chardo squatting, his body tense to take action at a moment's notice. He was keeping watch over her and Jopab. She smiled at the memory of last night, before scowling and scolding herself for the frivolity. Something light touched her cheek. She awoke and tensed, but only in the manner not to give her away. Her first reaction was to jump up, but she held back. She kept her eyes closed. Again, she felt something touch her head, then her arm, and finally her leg. Again. Again. Again. Jewyl opened one eye and slowly scanned the area. Jopab had relieved Chardo of the watch. The fire was low, but still strong enough to ward off any stray animals. All seemed normal.

She touched her cheek. Her finger was wet. The light rain turned into drizzle then into a heavy downfall very quickly. Jewyl could feel the wind picking up speed. She stood and saw the ship's crew was now fully awake and jumping about in the rain.

"Simple rain. Interesting, isn't it?" Jopab nodded toward the men in the distance. "Chardo, I thought you said you were going to sleep over there with the sailors."

Chardo stretched his arms above him, then yawned. "Decided better of it," he said, an smiled.

"I hope they enjoy their second bath in a day." Jewyl picked up Jopab's first line of conversation. "Any ideas on how to get out of all this?"

Jopab shook his head. "Percho had all the equipment," he said. "The fool probably drowned trying to save it."

"He wasn't a fool." Chardo trudged toward the tree line. "We've made due without the comfort of a tavern before."

Jewyl looked at the fire, it was almost dead from the rain.

It's going to be a long, cold night, she thought.

Drums.

"Somebody is happy about the rain?" Chardo asked dragging a few leaves behind him. "Who plays a drum in the rain? Jopab, do you want to help me get these palm branches together?"

"The purpose?" Jopab asked, all the while gathering the fronds like Jewyl and Chardo were doing. He glanced over at the ship's crew. They were looking inland.

"The branches may be wet," Jewyl said. "But they will help keep us dry when we thatch them."

Chardo quickly pulled a thin leaf from a frond and whipped it around a cluster of other fronds. "Find some long sticks, poles, whatever," he said. "We'll use them to make a frame."

Jopab brought some of the longer wood from the stockpile they had for the fire. "This should work," he said and laid it at Chardo's feet. "What do you think of the drums?"

"I don't," Chardo said. "I think it could be just the wind banging a branch against a hollow log."

Chardo moved in a fury lashing the sticks together, adding the fronds, and repeating. A strange structure of precarious stability came into existence.

"There." Chardo stood back to admire his handiwork in the stinging rain. "That should keep us pretty dry as long as the wind doesn't blow any stronger."

"Three of us?" Jopab pointed at the strange tee-pee lean-to shelter. "In that?"

Chardo smiled. "We'll be in out of the weather. Oh, we may be a bit cramped, but we all know one another pretty well by now." He slapped Jopab on the shoulder and smiled. "In."

Jewyl crawled inside first, Jopab followed and Chardo pulled another group of fronds behind him as he clambered in.

"Cozy," Jopab murmured. "Shall I continue my sentry?"

"If you're tired," Jewyl said. "I can stay awake."

"Nobody needs to stay awake." Chardo snuggled into a corner. "We're inside. There isn't any fire. All the wood is wet. What else is there?"

"The drums," Jewyl said. "I'm not swallowing your story about a branch beating itself on any log, Chardo. That is a consistent beat, not the random banging you claim."

"Whatever it is," Jopab said, while pulling his knees up closer to him. "We're sitting out here as obvious as can be. If we'd only built the shelter back into the tree line a little further."

"Would that make you feel safer?" Chardo stood. "All we need do is stand and carry this to the edge of the tree line."

Jopab smiled, but in the darkness, it was missed. "That easy?" Jopab finally asked. "Then let's move this thing and leave the sailors to the outcome of the drums."

"Those are strange words uttered for a priest," Jewyl said. "What are you thinking?" She stood with the two men and carried the structure to the tree line and nestled it among some overgrowth.

Jewyl re-adjusted her position then peeped outside to see if anyone was near. "The rain has lessened," she said. "The drums are still beating. I don't think Harsborz could accomplish all that by himself. When Harsborz said, 'we are not alone,' I don't know exactly what he meant, but I don't think we want to be here... or anywhere on this island, for a fact."

"Aiee!" came the cry.

Jewyl, Chardo and Percho each pulled back a frond to see what was happening. Harsborz stood where they had originally built their hut. He carried a staff.

"Behold the sins of Yendisa," he yelled at the crew. "Behold the power of the Lost Souls." The old man started to dance maniacally about the few struggling embers of the fire Jopab and Chardo had built earlier.

The embers glowed, pulsing in strength and light. Soon a blaze flashed and streaked its way upward into the sky. The rain stopped, the wind held its breath. There was an uncanny silence on the beach.

"Look," Chardo whispered. "See the waters? They don't move. There's no surf."

Jewyl strained to peer out of her little nook she'd created in the fronds. Chardo was correct, the ocean was still, but he also was wrong.

"There is no water," Jewyl said quietly. "That is a wet ocean floor. See the rocks I had landed on? They are now part of the beach. What does it all mean?"

"Yendisa controls the waters," Jopab whispered. "Yendisa

was before there was anything." He pulled back into the hut, crouching. "Yendisa," he whispered, and buried his head between his knees.

"Get control of yourself," Jewyl said. "You've seen worse."

"Behold!" Harsborz yelled while holding both hands in the air. He slowly brought them down to point at the sailors. Before anyone could react, he dashed into the vegetation to disappear.

Jewyl looked out and could see the ship's crew. There was mayhem, yelling, hollering, when suddenly Murdo and his men were completely encompassed by a group of bodies. These things, people, whatever, glowed a sickly green and where their eyes should have been were nothing but dark patches. The beings appeared skeletal yet something bothered Jewyl. She stared at them. They were indeed skeletal, the white bones standing out from the green glow, yet they were not complete. One looked in her direction, she could feel the eyes burning into her soul, searching. Jewyl held her ground. The creature turned and she realized the craziness of the situation. When it had stared at her, she could see the rib cage, the front of the skull and the legs, but when it turned away, all she could see was the back of the creature, blackness.

"Does it make sense to you?" Chardo asked in a low whisper. "Why haven't the crew given up our location?"

"Yendisa," Jopab whispered.

Jewyl could see him wringing his hands together in the darkness. *What has happened to this man?* she wondered.

"They are not creatures of the night," Murdo yelled. "They are flesh and blood. Fight them."

Jewyl turned back to the scene in time to see Murdo's sword slice through the air at one of the creatures.

"Hurry," a voice whispered in the darkness. "Come with me if you wish to live."

"Harsborz?" Chardo asked.

"Come. Come," Harsborz called urgently. "Be very quiet. The waters are going to come back."

Jewyl crawled out of the makeshift hut and could see Harsborz. His wild maniacal look gone, he now appeared quite tame and docile.

"What about the waters?" she asked.

"It will come back, taller, taller than three of me," Harsborz said. "We must make it to the cave in time or all will be lost."

"Who are those men out there?" Chardo asked.

"They are followers of Yendisa," Harsborz whispered. "They are the not dead. We must avoid them." The small man peered back at his followers. "They seek sacrifices." He smiled. "I don't need sacrifice. I have plenty food."

Jewyl frowned. She could hear the change in Harsborz voice.

There was a roar, a loud rumbling and the sound of water.

"Hurry!" Harsborz yelled. "It comes! It comes! We must hurry." He dashed through the overgrowth and undergrowth, the vines and branches whipping at his frail body.

"What about Captain Murdo and the crew?" Jopab asked.

"They live, they die," Harsborz replied. "I can't save all. Pretty woman. Yes, I save her." He smiled a lecherous grin. "Yes, woman for Harsborz."

"Hold it," Jewyl said and grabbed the old man by the arm to turn him toward her. "I'm not your woman." She let go when he jerked his arm free.

Harsborz frowned, mumbled something before once more motioning the group to follow him.

Chardo leaned closer to Jewyl. "I don't think you made a friend."

"If you think I treated other men cold, watch me with Harsborz," Jewyl replied. She pushed a swaying frond from her face and out of the way. "Wait a minute," she said. "Where'd he go?"

"I'm here," Harsborz said and grabbed her hand to yank her down beside him in the shrubbery. "Down. Get down." He put a finger to his lips.

Jewyl motioned to the others to get down and be quiet.

"We are not alone," Harsborz whispered to Jewyl. "I protect you. Shhh."

Jewyl listened, but couldn't hear anything. Finally, she saw the shadowy figures moving in the overgrowth. There was a glow about them, but totally unlike those on the beach. One passed close to them and Jewyl watched in amazement. The figure moved silently through the growth without disturbing it. The frond Jewyl had moved sliced through the figure. A coldness embraced her.

Jewyl looked to Harsborz, but she could tell he'd again went over the edge. His eyes were wild, and he was starting to titter. He started to get up, and she quickly covered his mouth and rolled over his body to hold him down. She wasn't about to let him give away their hiding place.

Harsborz pulled Jewyl's hand away. "Come, we go."

"Who were they?" Jopab asked.

"Those were Yendisa's true undead," Harsborz said, panting under Jewyl's weight.

"Get off him," Chardo said. "Unless you'd like us to leave you two alone?"

Jewyl rolled away and quickly stood. "He almost gave our hiding place away." She dusted herself off.

"Come," Harsborz said, and once more motioned with his hand.

Jewyl shook her head at this quick change of Harsborz's demeanor. A mere few seconds ago he was on the edge, and now he seemed normal. Once again, his eyes were clear. Jewyl grimaced at the thought of how fast he could change his demeanor.

"How many undead do you have here?" Jewyl asked.

"Two," Harsborz said. "The living undead — those on the beach with your friends, and probably now their captives. Plus, the true undead who passed us and go to meet them."

"True undead?" Jewyl echoed.

"Your friends on the beach," Harsborz said and pushed a branch carefully back so as not break it. "They will be sacrificed to Yendisa. If they believe in her, they will attain undead status. If not, they will become food for the undead." He paused and shook his head. "Both of the undead shall feast. Come, here is my hiding place."

They stood at the base of a large grouping of boulders. Harsborz gently pushed a bush aside to reveal an opening and pathway within them.

"Who comes here?" a voice called from within.

"Aieee," Harsborz screamed. "We have been discovered." He fell to the ground, groveling in supplication. "Forgiveness, great goddess," he murmured over and over.

"We are followers of Hagontha," Jopab said. "In chaos she rules."

"Jopab?" came the reply. "You're alive?"

"Percho?" Chardo asked. "Is that you?"

The young man stepped from the shadows into the clearing night.

"Percho!" Jewyl exclaimed. "You're alive! Blessed be the goddess. How did you get here?"

Harsborz stood up and frowned at the sudden excitement by the group for the intruder.

Jewyl saw his consternation. "This is our lost friend," she said. "We thought he had drowned when the ship was destroyed."

"We had best hurry," Harsborz said. "They will be returning soon, and we must be hidden when they approach."

"He's right," Percho said. "I believe they can hear a person breathing. I had to hold my breath when they passed me. Three of them stepped on my hand and I thought my hand was going to freeze to the ground. They are cold to the touch."

"You have touched an undead?" Harsborz asked, and grabbed Percho's hand.

"Not by choice," Percho shot back and pulled his hand away from Harsborz's inquisitive search.

"Let's not talk here," Jewyl said. "We'd best get on inside. Harsborz? Lead the way." She leaned against the boulder and let the small man pass.

"We should be safe," Harsborz said. "Who would stop to think there may be a place within the boulders?"

Jewyl eyed the area and the distant hills. *Could not somebody see this from up there?* she thought, and made a note to check it out in the future, if necessary.

"They're here," said a strange voice. "Captain Murdo? I've found them."

We only needed another second or two, Jewyl thought.

"Surrender to them," Captain Murdo said while striding to her. He stopped and stood, keeping an eye on her. They were quickly joined by a living undead.

"When my sword is taken." Jewyl raised the weapon in preparation to attack while looking at the man hidden under the guise of paints. Where she had seen black sockets before, now blue eyes looked out at her from within the dark paint.

A green mist swirled in and Jewyl felt its coldness as the true undead passed through her body. Like an unwanted kiss, she was repulsed by the feeling. She slumped to the ground. As she fell, she saw the others, her companions, falling to the ground and the swirling mists forming into men. A paralyzing coldness embraced her. She closed her eyes.

CHAPTER FOURTEEN
The Lost Souls

Jewyl awoke, groggy, and her body ached everywhere. She discovered her hands tied and her feet bound. She lay sprawled on her side. A furtive search of the area revealed Chardo, Jopab, Percho and Harsborz in similar situations. They were all prisoners. This she didn't doubt.

Distant arguing caught her attention. It was behind her, and although she was tempted to turn over to see who and what it was all about, she didn't. She noticed Harsborz open one eye to look at her and he barely shook his head. She remained still.

"I don't care if you were offered a thousand gold coins," the voice said. "You won't be able to get a copper coin if you damage the goods."

"I didn't plan to damage her, as you call it," Captain Murdo replied. "You'd deny me a small taste of the tribute?"

"If the Holy Father even suspected she was here." The fear in the other's voice lifted in a crescendo before lowering to a whisper. "Have you any idea of the consequences?"

"Ballec?" Murdo questioned. "Bah! Listen to me, Auro. We need to appease the undead right now."

"Feed me into the burning mouth of Yendisa, if you wish," Harsborz said. "I remain true to Hagontha."

"Blessed chaos," Jopab murmured. "May Hagontha continue to move in mysterious ways."

Jewyl watched Jopab. He lay quietly, not moving. She frowned. *Maybe not*, she thought. There was a small jerk of an arm and little movement behind his back. *He is working the ropes*. Every so often he would nod, and his eyes would move to the left. She followed where he was looking and saw the pile of swords — their swords.

Murdo strode over to Harsborz. "Be still," he said. "If I set you free, it will be to put your puny body on the altar." He guffawed and kicked at Harsborz. "A snack for her. Yet, maybe you are truly worthy of Yendisa." He kicked Harsborz again. "You're a befouled embodiment of Hagontha."

Harsborz glared at the man then spat on his boot. "You're not worthy to even say her name. May Hagontha serve me and give you a foul ending."

Jopab glanced at Harsborz. "Rather harsh," he said.

"This is not Murdo's first time here," Harsborz said. "Am I correct?"

Murdo kicked Harsborz in the stomach. "Mind your manners, wizard," he said.

"Wizard?" Jopab questioned.

Murdo stepped over to Jopab. "Yes," he replied. "You didn't know that, did you?" He smirked beneath the beard. "You should choose your allies more wisely," he added. "Isn't that correct, Jewyl?" Murdo swung around to face her with a smug smile.

Jewyl moved quickly, swinging her legs against Murdo, knocking him to the ground.

"Yes," she said. "All choices must be weighed, and then acted upon."

Murdo scrambled to his feet and glared down at Jewyl; his right foot inched backwards slowly in preparation to kick Jewyl.

"Murdo!" Auro yelled. "Touching her in any way will be your last act before meeting Yendisa in her eternal flames, face-to-face."

Color drained out of the captain's face, emphasized even more by the dark beard and scraggly hair framing it. "You wouldn't," he said.

"Ballec will be here before sundown," Auro said. "He assured me not less than five days ago when we last spoke. In the meantime, I need nourishment, and my assistants need taken care of." He paused. "Of your new scalawags last taken on, which do you feel will be the tastiest, and the best offering to our most holy goddess, Yendisa?"

Captain Murdo slowly let his gaze drop to Percho.

"Of *your* men, Murdo! Not these — they are for Ballec." Auro turned and started to walk away. "Never mind, I'll make my choice."

"Obviously you don't know about what's happened in

142

Bashiwa?" Jewyl called to the distancing man.

"Hush," Jopab hissed.

"I wouldn't bet all my assets," Jewyl taunted. "Things have changed, and last I heard, Ballec was headed for Zornal."

"Zornal?" Auro turned. "For what purpose would he go there?"

"He was going there…" Percho hesitated as he did some mental calculations. "I guess it would have been today."

"Must we give all our secrets away?" Jopab shouted. "This is the same man we paid at Lizbeth Harbor for passage to Zornal on the Albatross Wing." Jopab scowled at his comrades. "Fine. Lord Azre's men came to arrest him the day before yesterday."

"None of this makes any sense," Auro replied. "Why do you tell us this?"

Jewyl scrambled to sit up. "Perhaps we have a bargaining chip." She smiled as innocently as she could at Auro and Murdo.

"There was rumor at the inn yesterday," Murdo whispered. "I, too, heard about Lord Azre attacking Ballec at the temple. Still, it was only a rumor."

"Fine," Auro said. "Taking this rumor as a truth, why would you tell me Ballec won't be coming. I'm protecting you from Murdo who feels he is due some taste of the spoils."

Jewyl squirmed trying not to show her captors how close she was to being free of the ropes holding her hands together.

"Perhaps it was all just rumor," she said, and gazed into the distance beyond Auro.

"I waste my time," Auro said, slightly annoyed.

Murdo pushed Jewyl once more prone onto the ground then raised a hand in a threat to strike her.

"Touch her and your life is forfeit." Auro cocked a warning eye in Murdo's direction, turned, and plodded off into the brush.

Murdo scowled at Auro as he retreated into the shrubs then quietly dusted himself off, glanced at the five prisoners and smiled.

"I may not get my full reward," he said, leering at Jewyl, "but I have this which will keep me quite happy." He patted his leather bag before opening it and removing one the of pearls. "I thank you, Chardo, for this great booty." Murdo held the item between his index and thumb, letting it roll, allowing it to shimmer in the flickering fire light. He leaned back and laughed into the sky above as he slipped it back into the bag with the others. "Why waste my time on one Jewyl when I can buy a bounty of women when I return to the shores of true land." He raised his hand as if to slap Jewyl. "Bah. No need to waste my energy." He followed Auro into the shrubs.

Jewyl watched him leave and scrambled to sit up once more. She surveyed the area. "We are totally alone," she said. "Is it not strange they would leave us?"

"We are on an island," Harsborz replied. "Where would we go? They have Yendisa to guard us."

"They may have Yendisa," Jopab said, "but they also have pliocas — or will soon."

"They have what?" Harsborz asked. His eyes moved quickly as if searching the space in front of him while he remembered. "Did you say pliocas?"

Chardo and Percho nodded their heads vigorously.

"How?" Harsborz asked.

"Chardo guaranteed our place on board the ship with plioca eggs," Percho said. "He picked them up not knowing their true identity, but thinking them to be pearls."

"How many?" Harsborz hastily asked. "How long do we have?"

"I'm uncertain to the actual count," Jopab said. "We paid fifty to Auro, plus Murdo took the remainder. Now, as to when they will hatch? By the look of the one Murdo held, I would say within the next sunset or sooner. We need to escape."

"Voracious pliocas," Harsborz whispered. "Hagontha is truly a goddess of chaos."

"Or the stupidity of my friend," Jewyl said. "Are you through your knots yet, Jopab?" she asked. She was now sitting up, but had bent over and was squeezing her body through the small loop her tied arms created. "I'll have these in front soon," she grunted. "Then I can use my teeth to untie these lame excuses for knots."

"You're not the only one who can do that," Chardo said and was quickly hunched over to pull his arms forward. "Now move over here and I'll untie you."

Jopab, Percho and Harsborz stared at Chardo.

"Being limber is a necessity in this line of business," he quipped and untied the knots binding his feet. "We'd best be moving quickly, and as quietly possible, away from here."

"Auro didn't get blown onto this island," Harsborz said. "Nor was he shipwrecked. He should have a ship, probably a very small one, moored someplace."

The four looked at him for more information.

"I would guess his ship to be in the lagoon," he said with a quirky smile, and raised his hands into the air.

"Are you truly a wizard?" Chardo asked.

"Did you not see the waters recede? Do I not appear and disappear with ease? Are we not at the lagoon?"

Jewyl glanced around and realized that they were no longer at the opening where they had been held captive, but instead on the beach, listening to the waves quietly lap the sands.

"You are truly a wizard," Jewyl said.

"I thought him to be a crazy, old hermit," Chardo said. "A wise wizard, indeed."

"I am more than what I appear." He pointed at the boat. "There is your escape from this island," Harsborz said. "Move quickly for I fear the pliocas are hatching as we speak. Listen."

In the distance they heard the screams; painful screams of victims as small pliocas dined on living flesh.

"They said Ballec will come here," Jewyl said and strained against the old man's pull.

Harsborz's eyes glazed and he let loose the hold he had on Jewyl.

"Ballec moves toward Zornal at this very moment," Harsborz said, his voice very distant. "You must not tarry, but hasten to meet him. He awaits you."

"Well," Jopab said. "At least we know where he is, and it isn't going to be here."

Again, distant screams of pain and agony carried on the winds of the island jungle.

Harsborz's eyes cleared and he moved with the group to the water.

"Go," Harsborz said. "On the ship you will find a small bowl of water with a stick floating on it. Keep the stick aimed at the right side of the ship until you see shore. You have a very long row. Now, go!"

"You must come with us," Jewyl said, pulling Harsborz into the waves.

"No," he said. "I must stay here, it is my destiny. I serve Hagontha here."

Jopab grabbed Harsborz other arm and helped to pull him toward the ship. "You can serve Hagontha at the temple," Jopab said.

Harsborz snapped his arms free from Jewyl and Jopab.

"I must remain here," he said and lifted from the waters to float above the waves. "It is my duty and punishment."

"Punishment?" Chardo echoed.

"Who was Holy Father before Ballec?" Harsborz asked. "Think, Jopab. Do you remember his name?"

Jopab stood quietly in the waters, letting the waves massage him with each surge.

"Percho?" Harsborz called. "Did you learn the Recitation of Holy Fathers?"

"Yes," Percho replied.

"Borhars," Jopab blurted. "The Holy Father before Ballec was Borhars. He dishonored himself and Ballec replaced him. Why do you ask?"

"Do you know the story of Borhars and why he was so-called dishonored?"

Jopab and Percho shook their heads negatively.

"Borhars discovered through the mysticism of magic, the Holy Father had even more power to confound and control chaos," Harsborz said. "Many considered Borhars on the verge of heresy. Lord Azre cared little one way or another if Borhars was being sacrilegious, but Ballec saw this as a chance to gain some power as the younger brother. He convinced his father, Lord Renyon, to place him in the position of Holy Father, and ban Borhars from Shiyula."

"Shiyula?" Jewyl repeated. "You know of Shiyula?"

"Child," Harsborz said, smiling at her. "Shiyula is all. Dianiya has always been only a small portion of the great land your grandfather ruled."

Jewyl pulled back, surprised at his statements.

"Yes," Harsborz said. "I knew your grandfather. As Holy Father I served your grandfather faithfully."

"Served?" Jopab asked.

"Yes, Jopab," Harsborz said. "I served Jewyl's grandfather. I was the youngest Holy Father ever to be seated on the throne of Hagontha.

"You are Borhars?" Chardo asked.

"I am," the wizard said. "But, I no longer answer to that name. Today I am known as Harsborz, and will remain such until my time is committed."

"Come with us," Jewyl pleaded.

"No, my daughter," Harsborz said. "You must go forward and find your destiny. I will remain here to fulfill mine. Pliocas." He smiled, and an evil glint of happiness sparkled for a mere second in his eyes. "They won't bother me," he said. "I am a Holy Father and am protected." He raised his hands again to the sky. "Mother Hagontha, only your chaos can comfort me. Into your arms I offer my services."

Jewyl watched Harsborz walk back to the shore, his feet barely touching the surging waves of the ocean.

"Jewyl," Chardo yelled. "Give me your hand."

She reached up and Chardo pulled her aboard the small ship.

"Plenty of room for the four of us," Percho said. "Of course, I do wish we had our supplies along."

"Those?" Chardo asked and pointed to the bundle behind Percho.

"Thank you, Father Borhars," Percho yelled to the small figure standing on the beach.

Jewyl watched, and waved one last time.

The beach was empty.

She turned back to the matter at hand, grabbed an oar to assist, and wondered at their escape.

Everyone kept an eye on the needle floating in the bowl so it would never waiver from pointing to the right of the ship.

CHAPTER FIFTEEN
Mersayn

Jewyl stretched her arms hoping the pain would go away.

"Any idea of where we are?" she asked, and once more scanned the surrounding area trying to locate something familiar. The shore extended in each direction.

"Hmm?" Chardo said. He stood there, hand covering the lower part of his face with one finger thumping on his lips. He continued to search the horizon. "Uh-huh. Yes. Yes." He sighed loudly. "As usual, we're lost," Chardo said, with a boyish grin.

"Well, there's a fire over there," Percho said and pointed toward the pale gray tendrils of smoke to the north.

"Well, we may be lost, but that fire indicates whoever is there must know where they are." Chardo said. "Sounds like as good of direction as any to me." He slapped Percho on the back. "Great eyesight, Perc, old boy."

"Perc? My name is Percho." The soft gentleness was missing from his voice. "Also, I am neither old, nor a boy." He gathered the bag of belongings and headed in the general direction of the smoke.

"Is there something wrong?" Chardo asked, his eyes wide in disbelief. "Did I do something?"

"Percho isn't lost," Jopab replied. "He came from a coastal village located north of Lisbeth Harbor. I feel he knows exactly where we are."

"Your mouth has gotten us into more trouble," Jewyl muttered and shook her head.

Chardo shrugged. "I'll go talk to him. Give me a little space, okay?" He hustled to fall into a matched stride with Percho.

Jewyl figured it would take only a few seconds before Percho fell under Chardo's charms and was once again himself. She watched Percho push Chardo's arm away. She frowned. *Perhaps this time it will take longer,* she thought. Chardo stepped behind Percho and Jewyl could see her friend's hands come up around the neck and

148

slowly massage the shoulder blades before his hands disappeared from view. She didn't even want to think of what could be happening.

"You're quiet," Jopab said. "You've been watching Chardo so intently. Is there more between you two than just long term friends?"

Jewyl clenched fist struck out at Jopab, lobbing gently against his upper arm. "Trust me, he and I are only friends. Nothing more."

"Hey, you two," Chardo yelled. "Take a break, collect flowers, look at the sky, whatever. Percho and I are going ahead to scout the area."

Jewyl rolled her eyes, let her head drop forward, and slowly shook it.

"His timing is always less than perfect," she murmured.

"I think they want some time alone," Jopab said. He smiled at Jewyl. His lips parted and the smile quickly turned into a silly grin. A grin like that of a little boy.

Jewyl tried to ignore him, but knew that Percho and Chardo would be missing for at least another hour, possibly longer.

"I know we spent a lot of time on the water, but would you be interested in swimming?" Jopab asked and removed his tunic.

His muscles moved with a hypnotic rhythm to keep Jewyl's eyes watching him. He kicked off his sandals.

"Are you going to stare, or join me?" he asked. "You've seen all of this before." He waved a hand at his naked body. "Remember?"

Jewyl turned away. She could feel the heat of embarrassment flush her cheeks. "I don't know," she replied.

"Skinny dipping can be fun," Jopab said, and dashed by her on his way to the lapping waves.

She watched his feet kick up the sand and his leg muscles flex with each grand leap of his jog to the water, before splashing into the water. Jewyl shaded her eyes and scrutinized the sky. She turned to watch Jopab, seeing only his legs dive from sight.

It was too idyllic, too suddenly easy. What had happened?

Jewyl watched Jopab surface and splash in the water. It looked inviting. She removed her garments and slowly walked to the shoreline. Her hesitancy was not if she wanted to swim or not, but if she should be more modest; as Jopab had commented, he knew her body, too.

"The water is very refreshing," Jopab yelled. "I feel my very soul being cleansed right now."

She sauntered into the waters, feeling the coolness surge up and down her legs with each wave as she continued. Finally, she dove under. She surfaced and found Jopab.

"I don't do this too often," Jewyl said, swimming over to Jopab.

"Nor I," he replied. "Since the day I was initiated into the priesthood of Hagontha, I can't remember ever going swimming." He moved closer.

"It has been a long time for me, too," Jewyl said. A movement on shore caught her attention, yet she saw nothing.

Jopab reached out with a hand.

"I don't think we should," Jewyl said and tried to appear nonchalant as she watched the shore.

"Are you afraid Chardo and Percho would return and catch us?" He smiled with a devilish glint in his eye.

"Hey!" Chardo yelled, running over a dune toward the beach. "What you doing out there? Can I join you?"

"That was quick," Jopab said softly. "I figured they would be gone at least an hour." He nodded to Jewyl and they started to swim toward shore.

"As did I," Jewyl said. "Did you happen to see anything moving on the beach just a few minutes ago?"

Jopab shook his head negatively and continued to swim.

Jewyl stopped, treaded the waters and scanned the sandy beach. She knew she had seen something. It had to still be there, but all she could see was Chardo.

"Where's Percho?" Jewyl hollered.

"He's gone ahead to let them know we're coming," Chardo yelled back.

Jewyl trudged from the water, all the while keeping an eye on the location where she'd seen movement.

Chardo glanced in the direction of her gaze. "What's going on?"

"Nothing," Jewyl replied, shaking her head. "Where did you say Percho went?"

"The least you could do..." Chardo smiled while motioning

toward her. "At least show some token of modesty." He placed a hand over his eyes in mock shock. "At least Jopab was prudish enough to cover himself as he dashed for his clothes."

"Behave. You have Percho," Jopab said and slapped Chardo on the shoulder. "And, to answer your question, Jewyl, my guess would be to see his parents."

"Parents?" Jewyl asked, and looked about for her clothes. "Where are my clothes?"

"Probably where you dropped them in your rush," Chardo quipped.

"Actually, I left them right about here," Jewyl said then glanced over at the rock where she'd seen the activity. "Excuse me." She tromped toward the stone.

Jopab and Chardo quietly followed.

"What do we have here?" Jewyl said, grabbing her clothes from the clutches of the small creature.

"Please," a high pitched voice squealed. "Please, don't hurt me."

"What is it?" Chardo asked.

"A small child," Jopab said, and grabbed an arm. "A very dirty little child."

"Please, no hurt," the child cried while trying to pull away from Jopab. "No hurt me."

"We won't hurt you," Jewyl said as she slid the tunic over her head. "Why would we want to hurt you?"

"Clothes," the child said, and cowered closer to the large stone.

Jewyl kneeled down to the child. "Come here," she said. "You're safe with us. We won't hurt you." Jewyl leaned forward and pushed a scraggly mat of hair behind the waif's ear. "What's your name?"

"Her name is Mersayn," Percho said. "She is the child of the hermit, Atchel, who lives near here."

"What a lovely name," Jewyl said. "Are you hungry?"

The little girl nodded her head and reached out to Jewyl. "Food? Please?"

"Where is Atchel?" Percho asked. "Is he well?"

"He sleeping," Mersayn replied, and grabbed the crust of bread from Percho's hand. "He sleep long time."

151

Percho frowned. "Long time?"

"Atchel?" Jewyl murmured. "That name is familiar."

"If you are indeed the person you claim," Percho said. "Atchel is your mother's cousin." He reached down and picked up Mersayn. "This child would be a cousin, somewhat removed."

Jewyl smiled at Mersayn and reached out to hold her. The waif curled into the protective arms of Percho.

Chardo frowned. "Such a young child. How?"

"Atchel's father, Lysirth, came to the aide of your grandfather and was also killed in the siege of Shiyula. Lysirth's wife was with child, a son, who was born six months after Lysirth's death. The son, Atchel, much like you, fought a tedious vendetta against Renyon, then Azre, in an attempt to regain the proper ruling for your mother, Vaela. When Atchel's son, Resnold, was born — Atchel stopped fighting. Resnold took up the fight when he was only sixteen."

"I remember that," Jewyl said. "Strange. I never knew Atchel or Resnold were related."

Percho nodded. "I believe that was the plan," he said. "To protect you, and when you became another pest bothering Azre, the self-proclaimed monarch declared Resnold a traitor to the reign and placed a bounty on his head. Resnold was betrayed by one of his own. He and his wife were killed five years ago. Mersayn was hidden from Azre's men."

"Atchel sleep," Mersayn said. "Come. You see." She jumped from Percho's arms and scurried a few feet. "Hurry. See."

"We'd best follow," Chardo said. "She'll get away."

"I know where Atchel sleeps," Percho murmured. "I fear this slumber is his long sleep. If you would, please take Mersayn to my parent's home and I will take care of Atchel." He stooped down to the waif. "Go with these people to see my parents. You are safe with them." He took Mersayn's hand and curled Jewyl's fingers softly around them. "Okay?"

"She pretty," Mersayn said, and smiled at Jewyl.

"Would you like me to help?" Jopab asked.

"Let me," Chardo said. "You know Percho's parents. Yes? It would be better to have somebody they know approach them."

Jopab nodded and silently headed toward the lone curling smoke in the distance.

"If Atchel is indeed my relative," Jewyl said. "I feel I should

152

be there to see the rites."

"You're right," Percho said. He sighed heavily, grimaced, and turned to Chardo. "Please, Chardo, my friend, take Mersayn and Jopab to my parent's home and await us there."

Chardo frowned at the formality of the request. "Sure," he replied and then looked at Mersayn. "Is that okay?"

"Chardo funny," Mersayn said. "Go."

Jewyl watched the three of them saunter toward the distant smoke. Mersayn skipped between the two men. She finally turned to Percho.

"What haven't you told me," she said and glared at the man before her.

"First," Percho said, "let us attend to Atchel. If rites need to be performed I would prefer to be in the correct frame of mind." He headed off toward the woods which lay to the east of his parent's home.

"I see a hill," Jewyl said, having followed quietly behind the priest. "What do you hide?"

"Here," Percho said, and pointed at a faint trace of a path. "We must maintain silence until we arrive there. Keep your full attention to any possible intruders."

"Intruders?"

"Shh," Percho hissed and placed a finger to his lips. "Silence," he whispered.

He stepped gingerly and quietly through the woods, following the almost invisible path. The tree branches gathered closer above them and Jewyl could swear they were reaching out to snag her. It darkened with each small step.

"Here," Percho said and stepped into a shadowed opening within the trunk of a large tree.

Jewyl jerked back as Percho disappeared into the tree. "Percho?" she whispered.

"Hush," he replied. A hand reached out of the darkness, snagged her tunic, and tugged her into the shadows. "We wait here to be sure none have followed," Percho whispered into her ear. "Say nothing."

Jewyl's eyes slowly acclimated to the shadows and she could see Percho beside her as he watched for anything beyond the tree's trunk. She wondered how large the tree could be to harbor two people inside its trunk.

A twig snap caught her attention and she stiffened every muscle, holding her breath, waiting, and watching.

Percho leaned forward over Jewyl's shoulder. A sword sliced the air before him outside the tree's trunk.

"They were here, captain," a voice boomed. "I saw them."

"Where is the girl?" a distant voice replied. "Have you found her?"

"There was two people," the closer voice said. "The little girl disappeared over an hour ago."

The large man searched the shadows of the trunk before lunging his sword into the darkness. Jewyl and Percho moved, avoiding the blade.

"Bah," the man said then swatted an insect on his neck. He waved his sword before him. "Damned infestations," he murmured.

"I want that child," the distant voice yelled. "Azre wants her alive. Now find her."

Suddenly the woods burst with thrashing sounds as men searched the brush and tall grasses. Yelling and screaming among themselves, they chased small animals of the woods into the open to be slaughtered.

"We're safe here," Percho whispered. "Just remain on your guard."

Jewyl huddled in the darkness of the tree's trunk and watched Azre's men blunder about beyond her. She secretly smiled when she realized Azre also wanted her, and his men didn't even realize she was so close at hand.

She leaned back when one of the guards stomped by the opening.

She was alone. Percho was gone.

CHAPTER SIXTEEN
Atchel

Jewyl gingerly reached beyond into the darkness of the trunk. Somewhere in the darkness there had to be a way to escape. She touched wood.

"I'm down here," Percho whispered. "Slowly and very quietly stoop down."

Jewyl did as requested, all the while keeping a watch on the activity beyond their hiding place.

"Now stretch out your left arm and you will notice an opening," Percho whispered.

Jewyl moved her arm as requested and felt Percho grasp her hand. It startled her, but she held her control.

"There are steps here," he said and placed her hands down on them. "Follow me, and be very careful. These are extremely narrow steps."

The darkness engulfed her and Jewyl followed Percho, sometimes a shadowy figure before her, at other times nothing but utter pitch black. She could feel the steps curling to the right. There was a coolness from the spiraling tunnel, yet there was no light. She suddenly saw a glimmer, or glow, before Percho.

"We're almost there," Percho whispered. "These mosses are similar to those found in the tunnels of our temple."

Jewyl remembered the glow and instantly froze. Pliocas! She held her breath and listened and watched the shadows to see if they moved of their own.

"There is nothing to fear," Percho said guessing her worry. "There are no pliocas here, if that is what you fear. Come."

Jewyl relaxed, breathed, and continued to walk down the steps. Percho appeared as a strange apparition before her.

"Mersayn lives here?" Jewyl asked.

"As does Atchel," Percho added. "This has been their safe haven since the betrayal."

155

"How well did you know Resnold?" Jewyl asked.

"Very well," Percho replied. "I was... I was his best friend." Percho choked.

"Then you know who betrayed him?" Jewyl watched the man before her.

"Yes," Percho said flatly. There was a silence that hung in the air. "Yes, I know well who betrayed him."

Jewyl waited.

"Why?" Jewyl broke the silence. "Why did you do it?"

"It was necessary," Percho said. "My parents were poor. The sea was their only source of income, and my father's boat had been ruined in a storm."

"Sounds more like it was a convenience for you," Jewyl said.

"No, not really," Percho said. "Resnold fought with a veracity I envied. He fought for a return to a time I didn't know, but only had heard in tales. It was a dream."

"You had no faith?"

"I had a faith," Percho continued. "I believed he would overcome Azre, and return the kingdoms to their original glory. I thought he meant to sit on the throne of Shiyula. It was then I realized perhaps we were wrong."

"So you betrayed him?"

"Yes," Percho said. "I gave Resnold the information that would put him in a definite location and position so Azre's men could take him. It was while he was being flogged in public I learned his true path. He fought to regain the throne for the princess of Shiyula." Percho's voice choked. "Yes, Jewyl, he was giving his life so you could rule."

"You didn't take up the cause?" Jewyl asked.

"As part of the deal, for my life, I had vowed allegiance to Azre," Percho said. "I became a priest for Hagontha and was to reveal information about the priesthood's activity back to Lord Azre, especially anything his brother Ballec was involved with."

"You expect my trust now?" Jewyl asked sarcastically.

"Nothing has changed," Percho said. "I am the same today as I was yesterday. My betrayal was years ago. In the priesthood I learned the trueness of chaos, and what Hagontha really means. I realized the errors I made, but learned quickly what I could and couldn't do to correct the wrongs." Percho turned and faced Jewyl. A tear traced a path down his cheek. "I have wronged your family, and in this small gesture, I hoped to atone my wrongs."

"Small gesture?" Jewyl asked.

"When I learned of Resnold's father, Atchel, I secured him to a safe area where he could live out his life. He took with him Aryna, Resnold's wife. She bore a daughter, then departed this haven of safety because she couldn't live in these conditions." He waved his hands to encompass the dank room. "She was discovered, and executed. I learned Azre's men tortured Aryna in an attempt to learn the whereabouts of her offspring. The fact Mersayn exists proves the secret died with Aryna."

"What are you trying to tell me?" Jewyl asked, watching the man before her shutter as he shed tear after tear.

"Mersayn has started to search areas beyond this safety," Percho said. "The fact Mersayn has wandered to the sea amazes me, but it also tells me that perhaps Atchel has died."

"Died?" Jewyl replied.

"Long sleep?" Percho asked. "Did you not hear her say Atchel has been sleeping a long time? I fear Mersayn may be in danger, and there is nothing I can do to protect her if there is none to watch over her."

"You expect me to care for her?" Jewyl asked. She stepped back at the thought of any planned motherhood.

"If not you, then someone who you trust very strongly," Percho said. "We must move on."

"I can't take a young girl like Mersayn with me," Jewyl said. "It just wouldn't be safe. To ask Chardo to watch her wouldn't be the best, either."

"No, Chardo, although a very dear person, wouldn't be the proper tutor for her," Percho agreed, a slight smile crossing his lips.

"I have the person," Jewyl said. "A perfect match and I don't think anyone would question Mersayn's sudden appearance."

Percho turned to face Jewyl, his face alight with a possible answer.

"Who?" he asked.

"It would be– " She looked at Percho, and held back. Could she trust him? He was right, nothing had really changed over the last few days; it was only her new knowledge of an old mistake. "I will take her to my friends when the current job is finished. Can she stay with your parents?"

Percho frowned at Jewyl's sudden shortness and hesitation. "I see no reason why she couldn't stay with them until this is all resolved," he said. "It may make my parents feel young again."

Jewyl wrinkled her nose at the odor.

"It would appear Atchel has been sleeping too many days," Percho said. "If you wish, I can attend to his remains, and you go back up. I'm sure Azre's men have given up their search by now."

"No," Jewyl said. "This is family, so I will assist in any way I can. Lead on."

The stench was stronger with each step, but Jewyl kept up with Percho.

"Here," Percho said and offered a ragged piece of cloth to her.

She grabbed it and quickly tied it about her head to cover her nose. It helped somewhat, and she was now acclimating to the scents.

"Mersayn has lived down here all her life?" Jewyl asked as they entered the small chamber.

Moss covered the walls, ceiling, and most of the furnishings. She looked at the small chair and could see where Mersayn had sat and kept the moss at bay. Atchel lay on a small bed which glowed eerily.

"It almost appears the moss has covered his face," Jewyl said looking at the old man. "How old was he?"

"I have no idea," Percho said. "This is Mersayn's grandfather so he has seen many winters."

Jewyl scrutinized the face trying to see any family resemblance. *Could this truly be a relative?* she thought.

"Your grandmother's brother's son," Percho said. "Do you see any family resemblance?"

"Strangely," Jewyl said, "his ears are similar to my mother's, and perhaps somewhat like mind." She pushed back her hair to let Percho see the resemblance.

"Yes," Percho said. "I see the similarities." Percho smiled. "Also his eyes were a deep green, like yours."

Percho moved about the crowded room, placing items from one location to another.

"I can perform the rites of passage here," he said. "If you

would like."

"This was his home," Jewyl said. "It would only be proper." She looked about then noticed what appeared to be a chest lid. "Perhaps we can let him rest in there?" She pointed at the chest.

"I thought perhaps we could leave him on the bed," Percho said. "I fear moving his body might be too much for us." He covered his mouth and nose with his hand.

Jewyl glanced at Atchel and agreed he should continue to rest on the bed.

"Really won't be using this for quite some time," Percho said. "I stumbled upon this safe haven by accident when I was still a young boy. I was hiding from some guards when I ducked into the trunk of this tree and my foot slipped down into the tunnel. Other than me, only Mersayn and Atchel know of it. Even my parents don't know of this place. Atchel should have a very quiet rest here."

"Who do you think made it?" Jewyl asked, seating herself on the chest.

"No idea," Percho replied. "It had a lot of dust so it hadn't been used in a very long time. Even the tree hasn't rotted over the years. It probably belonged to some wizard and has a lot of magic. Atchel will be safe. Shall I begin?"

Jewyl nodded and Percho began the rites of passage.

"Spearmint to greet the goddess," Percho said and placed a sprig of greens between Atchel's lips. "Silk to shield your eyes of her beauty," he said and placed a cloth over Atchel's eyes.

"Silk?" Jewyl asked in a hushed voice and nodded at the heavy cloth.

"We use what is available," he replied. "A rinse to hide your footsteps." He removed Atchel's sandals and poured a small amount of water on the bare feet. "Now, none may see your path as you walk with Hagontha."

Percho kneeled beside the bed and fumbled with his fingers. "A ring," he whispered in a choked voice. "A ring of friendship from me to you." He placed the ring on Atchel's finger. "If you can find it in your spirit to forgive me, return it upon our next meeting." He stood up.

"Go with the goddess," Percho said and stood there quietly for a few moments. "Enjoy the rewards of chaos," he whispered. He wiped the welled up tears from his eyes.

"Go with the goddess," Jewyl echoed. She didn't normally follow any particular belief of one god or goddess over another, but she felt a comfort in the small ceremony Percho had performed. There seemed a hint of closure. She had never met Atchel, yet she felt a bond existed between them. He would lay here until the green mold engulfed him; eternal peace.

"I feel a... a... There is something." Jewyl stood and gazed about the room. "It is all so strange, and yet, I feel a pull – a tugging. I know not what it is." She shrugged. "Strange."

"Shall we go?" Percho asked and headed for the steps that led up and out.

Jewyl nodded and followed him to the stairs with only a small glimpse back before beginning the climb. She was amazed how quickly they came to the open space within the trunk. It had taken so long to go down the winding steps, and now, the exit seemed no more than twenty steps.

Percho placed a cautionary finger to his lips and stretched toward the opening trying to hear. He was greeted by the sounds of birds and woodland insects. A soft wind rustled the leaves and grasses.

"It's safe," he hissed and stepped into the light.

Jewyl followed and inhaled deeply the fresh air. The woods which had seemed so ominous coming in, was now light and airy.

"First we'll need to meet up with Chardo, Jopab and Mersayn," Jewyl said. She stepped out and around the trunk and started down the path.

"A pleasant day for a walk," Percho said and followed.

"What magic is this?" a voice bellowed. "Halt in the name of Lord Azre."

Jewyl turned and faced the owner of the voice.

"How could you appear in the middle of the woods," the guard asked, his sword at the ready. "What wizardry is this?"

"No wizardry at all," Jewyl replied. She pulled her sword and let it arc in front of her as she swung it toward the guard.

Metal clanged loudly in the hushed silence of the woods. Jewyl raised her sword above her head then danced quickly to the left to avoid the attacking rush of the guard. She twisted and brought the sword down to connect with the guard's unprotected back. The sound of blade hitting spine and rib bones echoed loudly. The guard fell, his sword dropping away from him.

"Now I see why Jopab has such a high opinion of your swordsmanship," Percho said. "You are a dangerous opponent and one who knows how to use it to her own advantage."

The guard groaned and moved in a feeble attempt to grasp his dropped sword.

Jewyl kicked him with her foot and rolled him so she could face him.

"Know your adversary," she said. "I am Jewyl, Princess of Shiyula."

The guard's eyes widened in recognition of the name, and then his whole body winced when her sword plunged through his body.

"Was that totally necessary?" Percho asked with a sneer of disdain.

"Ah, so you *are* a priest of chaos, after all," Jewyl replied. She wiped the blood from the sword on the body. "You attend to death, but avoid death otherwise."

"We could have tied him up," Percho said. "He was innocent."

"Innocent?" Jewyl asked. "He was a guard of Lord Azre. Tie him up? To allow him freedom when discovered so he could reveal our plans? What of Mersayn? We've too much to lose if he were to waggle his tongue."

Percho hung his head and slowly nodded agreement. "Perhaps you've done the right thing. Our whereabouts must be kept secret."

"I'm sure he's not the only guard left here," Jewyl said. "We'd best keep a low profile on our way to your parents."

"Follow me," Percho said, swelling with renewed vigor. "There is the secret path I had when a child. It may be overgrown somewhat, but I'm sure we can use it. It is well away from the eyes that would watch the path."

"You continue to confuse me," Jewyl said.

"That is the way of Hagontha," the priest said with a smile. "Come."

CHAPTER SEVENTEEN
Plots

"Jewyl! Percho!" Chardo exclaimed. "Glad to see you." Chardo stood and waved.

"Lower your voice, you idiot," Jewyl yelled. "Do you want all of Azre's guards on us?" She pulled her sword, turned to keep a watchful eye on the woods and stepped carefully toward Chardo and the small house.

"Don't worry," Chardo replied. "They left earlier — about thirty of them. We're all alone."

"Where's Mersayn?" Percho asked.

"Fishing with your parents," Chardo said.

"They asked us along," Jopab added, coming from inside the hut. "I just couldn't see myself out on the waters so soon." He dried his hands on a towel. "The boar has been gutted and cleaned. Who wants the honors of roasting him?"

"I'll do it," Percho said. "I know where the pit is. Chardo, bring me some green palms, please."

Percho ambled off to the pit and moved things around. Chardo rushed about the area gathering palm branches.

"This should be enough," Chardo said between deep breaths. "He didn't say whether he wanted long ones, short ones, young or old; so I got a mixture." He smiled at the group then hustled over to Percho and deposited the collection near the pit.

Chardo stood there a few moments then placed his arm over Percho's shoulder. Percho brushed it aside. Jewyl and Jopab watched the two men. Some words were spoken. Finally, in exasperation, Chardo threw his hands into the air and stomped back to the hut.

"Problems in paradise?" Jewyl asked.

Chardo glared at his friend, shook his head, and entered the hut. He shut the door behind him.

"Okay," Jewyl said. "Not sure where this is going. I guess we'll wait it out."

"What's the story on Atchel," Jopab asked. "Long sleep?"

"I performed the rites," Percho said.

He surprised them since they hadn't heard him approach. His voice was dull and listless.

"He sleeps peacefully," Percho added.

"What is it?" Jopab asked.

Percho turned and looked at the distant sea. He rested an arm against the hut.

"Do you see the ocean?" Percho asked. "The waves crest, then wash upon the beach, rushing in and flooding here and there. Each wave is different, yet the same. There is water, a crest, spreading out to flood and deposit whatever it had upon the beach. Our days are like that, the same, yet different. Each morning we awake, it is the same, yet always different. We're waves rushing toward the land."

"What are you babbling about?" Chardo asked. He stood just inside the door of the hut. "What did you do to him, Jewyl?"

Percho shot Chardo a piercing glance. "She's done nothing," he spat and returned his gaze to the ocean. His voice became distant. "Every day. Nothing. The same. Different." He turned his attention to Jopab. "When will it all end?"

"What end?" Jopab asked. He walked up to Percho and placed a hand on his shoulder.

Percho shrugged it off and pulled his shoulder away. He narrowed his eyes and searched the beach. "They're returning," he said. "The same, but different."

"What do you want to end?" Jewyl asked with a quizzical look on her face.

"The killing," Percho whispered. "The killing."

"Oh," Jewyl said. "We're back to the guard, again."

"No," Percho retorted. He hesitated. "Perhaps." He shook his head. "No, it has nothing to do with the guard you killed. It has to do with my treachery, and the innocent people who were killed. It is about Klajany, Father Ballec, Vico, Mersayn, Atchel, Resnold, Father Borhars, and even Lord Azre. All of them." He hesitated. "Even my parents."

"Your parents are alive," Jopab said. "Like most of those you named. Why do you bring them into this conversation?"

"Because of me," Percho said. "Because of me, they'll die. It won't be old age, but some treachery curling up in some wave to crash down on them — drowning their very existence."

"We can leave," Jewyl said. "Now, or at least very soon. We'll not stay the night." She glanced at the two older figures tromping from the ocean. She could see a third person, Mersayn, bouncing about. "We'll take Mersayn and leave immediately."

"It's too late," Percho said. "We've already tainted them. No, I tainted it. Years ago." He hung his head, and his body moved slightly as he sobbed.

"Let me help you," Chardo said, and moved closer to the man. "Why do you insist on pushing me away."

"All you want is sex," Percho said. "Everything can't be fixed with a romp in the bed, or wherever."

"I'm not looking for sex!" Chardo exclaimed. "Did I say I wanted sex?" Chardo stomped out of the hut and toward the trio coming from the ocean.

"Please, Chardo," Percho called. "You'll only make it worse."

Chardo waved at the trio. He grabbed the stringer of fish from Percho's mother. He would have taken the larger stringer of fish from Percho's father, but didn't want to shame him in doing so. Having the lighter stringer Chardo asked the old man if he would like to trade. In this manner, no shame would be made. The old man shook his head negatively, and continued to huff under the stringer's weight.

"We'll have to add these to the boar," Chardo yelled. "Mmm. Fresh smoked fish."

"Give me," Percho said and reached out for the two stringers. "I'll add them."

Percho's father silently offered his string of fish and Percho accepted it. He flung it over his shoulder and looked at Chardo.

"I'll help," Chardo said. "There is more to me than what you say." His eyes flared at Percho.

"I'm sorry," Percho mumbled, and headed for the pit.

"That's more like it," Chardo said. He slapped Percho on the back and the two headed for the pit. One could hear Chardo laughing from time to time.

"Did I hear your friend say there was a boar?" Percho's father asked.

"That's right," Jewyl replied. "Jopab cleaned it and Percho

has it in the pit."

"There will be plenty to eat," Percho's mother said. "The fish will be done shortly. I'll go to the garden and collect a few vegetables for us."

"May I help?" Jewyl asked, and received a warm smile in response.

"Me help?" Mersayn scampered around the old woman. "Me help?"

"Of course you can," the older woman replied. "Call me Tenja, please. Anything you want to do to help an old woman is appreciated." She reached out and cupped the small girl's chin. "You are more questions than answers, child." Tenja smiled and watched as Mersayn danced about them. She cocked her head and cast an eye at Jewyl. "Now what is your name?" She looked directly at Jewyl, dark eyes piercing into Jewyl.

"My friends call me Jewyl."

The old woman frowned, the shadow of question lingering just a moment. She let it go and was once again smiling. "Jewyl," she repeated. "My, what a lovely name. I knew somebody with that name, but that was a long time ago. I'm sure before you were ever born."

"Red balls, good," Mersayn yelled and grabbed at the globes of tomatoes. "Me like red balls." She paused and gazed at Jewyl. "Did you get the shiny?"

"Those are tomatoes, dear," Tenja said. "Oh, my, we'll need lettuce, some carrots, small onions and I think we can swipe a few new potatoes, too. Mmm, I can already taste the onions and new potatoes in the sauce." She smacked her lips. Mersayn giggled.

"The shiny?" Jewyl glanced at Mersayn with concern but quickly eased the frown to a smile at the waif.

"Atchel's shiny. He show me. Long. Shiny. Pretty." Mersayn smiled at Jewyl. "Oh, sharp, too."

Jewyl frowned, trying to figure out what she meant.

"We left it with Atchel," Jewyl said. "Is that okay?"

Mersayn nodded.

"Somebody's coming," Jopab yelled. "It looks like guards. Probably from Lord Azre himself."

"Quick," the old woman said. "Lay down and I'll cover you."

"Me hide, too?" Mersayn asked.

"Yes, yes," Tenja said and pushed the waif in with Jewyl. "Keep quiet."

Jewyl raised her head to see what was going on and where Chardo and Percho might be.

"Get down," the old woman hissed. "They'll see you."

Jewyl frowned. What gave this old woman the idea she needed protection from a few guards?

"We hide, yes?" Mersayn asked. "Now we run away?"

Jewyl could feel her companions body start to tense in preparation of leaping up to run away.

"No!" Jewyl yelled and grabbed Mersayn. "We stay hidden. Let them find us, if they can. That's more fun. Now, be very still and quiet so we can hear them."

Jewyl strained to hear, but felt the horse's hooves first. They were very close.

"Old lady," the guard's voice boomed. "We seek strangers. Have you seen any?"

"My wife's eyes fail her," Percho's father said. "Can I assist you?"

The guard's horse strutted to meet the old man part way.

"One of our companions was slain not too long ago," the guard bellowed. "We seek any knowledge of this deed and offer a reward for the proper information of the culprit."

"We are but humble peasants," Percho's father said. "We get a little food from the garden and a few fish from the sea. We are old." He raised his hands. "We don't travel far from our hut."

"I care little about that," the guard replied. "Who is that stranger?"

The old man carefully turned around to see Jopab still standing there.

"That is but a cleric of Hagontha," he said. "He has been with us four days now, and will soon return to the temple."

"Why is here?"

"I'm here to serve my penance," Jopab said. "I am Holy Priest Second Hand to Lord Ballec and have committed an improper act. Lord Ballec sent me on a journey of penance to understand the truth within the chaos of my action. Praise Hagontha."

"Enough," the guard said. "We seek a killer, not a spewer of holies." He motioned his men forward before looking directly down at Percho's father. "If you were to see a stranger or two, you *would* let me know. Yes?"

"Of course," the old man said, and held his head down to avoid eye contact, but hoped it would be seen as respect.

"And you, priest," the guard said as he rode away. "You should hurry to finalize your penance so you can find if you truly have a temple and reason for penance. Rumor says Ballec has fled and Hagontha has created her doom within her chaos."

"I shall," Jopab said. "Safe journey." He watched the remaining guards trample through the garden, plucking fresh vegetables ready for the harvest.

"Stop! Please," Percho's father pleaded. "Don't ruin our garden. It is all we have to make it through the long winter."

One guard pushed the old man away, forcing him to fall to the ground.

Jewyl tightened in preparation to take that guard's life when she felt another guard tromp down on her foot, twisting her small ankle.

Mersayn jumped up and out of the pile that had covered them. The old woman grabbed Mersayn and held her close; all the while inconspicuously pushing debris to cover Jewyl.

"Please," the old woman said, cowering from the guard's pointed spear. "She is my granddaughter. I hid her to protect her. She is all we have left of our son and his wife – they were lost at sea."

"Tenja!" the old man yelled.

"That's close enough, old man," the guard shouted, noting the rest of his companions were well ahead of him.. "I kill neither children, nor the aged." The guard made a gesture in the air before turning to look at the garden. "Nice. Very nice. You could hide a body in there, and most would be none the wiser.

"Go in Hagontha's chaos and the peace it offers," Jopab said. He pulled the old man against him, and smiled at the old woman and Mersayn.

The guard hastened off to join the rest of his contingent. They quickly followed their leader and disappeared beyond the trees.

"Stay where you are," Jopab said. "The guard on the horse didn't believe us and he is only beyond the trees and will be watching us. Tenja and Mersayn, continue to work in the garden. Inform Jewyl to stay hidden."

"I think Jewyl is hurt," Tenja whispered.

"She is a warrior," Jopab said. "She will nurse her wounds as best she can. Now where is Percho and Chardo?"

"They are inside the hut, probably hidden under the floor," the old man said.

"Oh, fine," Jewyl said. "They are probably – oh, never mind. I hope my ankle isn't broken. Don't worry about me, I'm a warrior. Right?"

"Fine," Jopab said. "Go inside and tell those two to remain hidden until needed. Bring out a platter or something so we can appear to be working on the boar. All of us need to act as nothing has happened and we're returning to a normal day."

"How do you know all this?" the old man asked.

"That guard gave me a hidden signal," Jopab replied. "Remember him? The one you were going to attack? He is a hidden follower of Hagontha and informed me to be very careful and watch."

"How ironic," Jewyl said. "The guard who hurt me also protected me." She shifted around in the debris. "Not the most comfortable, you know."

"We play hide game again?" Mersayn asked and grabbed some leaves to put on her head. "I like hide game. Atchel played game with Mersayn. We hide many times." The leaves cascaded down over her face and back.

"Yes," Tenja replied. "The hide game is a good game, and you played it well, but you don't have to play it now. Only Jewyl gets to play." Tenja brushed a few crumbled leaves from the girl's hair and softly pushed back the loose locks.

"Me play," Mersayn said and pouted. "Me play."

"How about a red ball?" Jewyl whispered.

"Me like red balls," Mersayn squealed and grabbed a few from the plants. She bit into one, juices flowing down her chin. The game forgotten.

Tenja pulled a couple of stray weeds and kept an eye on the men. "I don't know how long you're going to be in there," she whispered. "I'll have Mersayn help me with a few more vegetables before she eats all the red balls."

"Oh, I think I'll just linger here," Jewyl replied. "It's not really all that uncomfortable. Just be sure Jopab remembers me."

"Mersayn?" Tenja called. "Do you like carrots, too?" She ambled over to Mersayn and continued her mundane garden actions for the hidden audience. She wanted to glance over at the edge of trees, to shade her eyes and see if she could find the guards, but she held back.

CHAPTER EIGHTEEN
Back On Track

"I certainly hope there is still some food left," Chardo said as he slipped into the house. "I didn't think the guards were ever going to leave." He glanced about the room. "Has anyone let Jewyl know?"

"Not yet," Percho replied. "Since you didn't return immediately we thought there was a problem."

"Well, there is and there isn't," Chardo said, grabbed another dark blanket and bent down to the floor. "They've left but there is still one out there watching, when he thinks of it. I'll sneak out there, get her, and we'll soon have to be on our way. I heard what the leader had to say." He smiled proudly. "I could have petted his horse," Chardo said and swelled with pride. "You don't get into the Thieves Guild with just a pretty face and cute smile."

"You have to leave?" Tenja asked, ignoring Chardo's last words and glancing over to Mersayn.

"Me go, too?" the small girl asked.

"Not yet, dear," Tenja replied and stroked the girl's long locks. "You can stay with us a few days – help me in the garden to collect the red balls."

"Two... may... toes," Mersayn said slowly and deliberately. "Red balls called tomatoes."

"That's right," the old woman answered and hugged the girl close to her.

"Here," Jopab said, and handed the old man a sheet of parchment.

Percho's father glanced at the scribblings then rolled the parchment and stuck it on a shelf.

"Did you understand what you read, father?" Percho asked.

The old man shook his head negatively. "Should I?" He shrugged. "If somebody comes looking for Jopab, I figure this will answer any questions." He glanced over at Jopab for assurance.

"Very astute," Jopab said. "It states I had to leave, and that

170

the sign necessary for me was obviously the arrival of the guards reminding me of my station within the chaos of Hagontha."

"Oh?" the old man said quietly. "I thought it said something like these people didn't know me and only gave me a place to sleep and eat. They are not responsible for any of my actions."

Everyone snickered.

"If you would prefer," Jopab said.

"No," answered the old man. "This should suffice." He patted the parchment on the shelf. "Sometimes being a simple fisherman makes for a full life." He placed an arm around Tenja.

The door opened and a dark shape crawled into the room.

"Jewyl!" Percho said when the shape stood up and dropped the blanket.

"I'm famished," Jewyl said and headed for the table.

"Eat quickly," Chardo said. "I just noticed two torches where there should only be one. We've got more company than we want."

"Torches? The idiot has torches?" Jopab asked.

"I saw the one torch when I headed out for Jewyl," Chardo said. "A second torch just arrived."

"These guards are truly imbeciles," Jewyl mumbled between large bites of boar's meat. "It's a wonder they ever caught me the first time."

Jopab glanced out the window. "We'd best get this group down to the correct size," he said. "A long line of torches approach."

Percho, Chardo and Jewyl squeezed into the small hole.

"Seemed a lot larger earlier," Chardo whispered. "Just how much did you eat, Jewyl?"

Jewyl elbowed him and he let out a small grunt just as the knocking rattled the door.

"This is Lord Azre's guard. Open up in the name of Lord Azre."

"Good evening," the old man said, profusely bowing and stepping back out of the way to allow the visitor entrance.

"Hagontha's blessings on you," Jopab said and bowed.

Tenja moved swiftly to the obligatory head down and then noticed Mersayn still watched. She pushed Mersayn's head so she was looking at the floor.

"Something tells me that what I see isn't really what I see," the guard said. "Tell me, priest, what is wrong?"

"Wrong?" Jopab echoed. "You have come to right the wrong," he said. "I have spent too much time here in thought. I return to the temple tomorrow. You are Hagontha's messenger to me."

"Perhaps," the guard said and strode around the room. "Still, something nags at me. What could it be?" He stomped on the floor and cocked an ear to listen then stared down at the small crack in the floor where Jewyl gazed upward.

"Stomp game. Stomp game," Mersayn yelled grabbing everyone's attention. "Me play." She proceeded to stomp around the room, including the trap door. "This is fun."

"Yes, child," the guard said, and waved his hand for her to stop.

Tenja grabbed Mersayn and put a finger to her lips. "Quiet now."

"There is so much dust here," the guard said and clapped his hands together to create a small cloud of dust billowing from his fingers. "That's better," he said, rubbed his hands together then turned and faced Jopab again.

Jewyl watched the fine white dust settle down through the cracks. It tickled her nose.

"It could be Chaos," Jopab offered with a simple shrug of his shoulders. "She offers much to understand. Blessed Hagontha."

"Curses on your chaos," the guard yelled and tramped to the doorway. "When you see your goddess, thank her for your life."

The guard trudged out the door and mounted his steed. "We return," he said to his men, yanked the reins of the horse to the right and headed off in the direction they had come earlier in the day.

One lingering guard made some small, almost negligible gestures and Jopab barely bowed his head and blinked his eyes in acknowledgment. Jewyl smiled realizing her small peep hole had allowed her to catch the covert conversation between the two. She rubbed her eyes and stifled a cough.

Jopab placed his arms across the door opening to bar anyone from going out into the night. "The guard is still not satisfied. This place will be watched until I depart. Suggestions?"

"Let us out of here," Jewyl said, and again elbowed Chardo. "You're being just a tad too friendly."

"Funny," Percho said. "That's what I told him when we were

in here earlier."

"Out," Jopab said. "They can't see inside the house so we have some safety there. Just be sure to stay away from the window."

"Do you think he has guards all around?" Percho asked. He pulled a chunk of meat from the plate.

"You can bet your last copper piece on that," Jopab said. "It is mandatory that you three get out of here with all the haste possible." He paced the floor, nibbling on his index finger nail.

"I can get us beyond the guards," Chardo said. "That's the easy part."

"Grouping us," Jopab said. "Now that's the hard part. That guard expects me to be alone when I leave here."

"We team up beyond the watchers," Percho quipped and smiled hopefully.

"The guard has us," Jewyl said. "Could you hike the road and we shadow you in the woods?"

"The trees only continue a short distance," the old woman said and shook her head.

"We split up," Jopab said. "For safety and sensibility. We'll meet at the temple."

"Wise decision," Jewyl said. "They're looking for three men and one woman. When we get to Opula, we split up. Percho and I will remain together. Chardo will be on his own." She smiled at her long-time friend. "When we arrive at Zornal, we will once again regroup and further discuss our plans."

"Why can't Percho and I be together?" Chardo whined.

"Simple," Jewyl said. "A single woman entering the city will be scrutinized as to her reason for being there. Two men can be considered thieves or trouble. A couple can easily slip in without even a raised eyebrow. Also, a single man of your immeasurable talents should astound them if they question the purpose of your visit."

"I like that," Chardo said, and clapped his hands together. "Talents I have, indeed."

Percho frowned.

"Is there a problem?" Jopab asked and placed a comforting hand on his shoulder.

"My parents," he replied. "Will they be safe? Mersayn? What of her?"

"When I leave tomorrow, all will return to normal," Jopab said. "Mersayn will stay here with your parents until our return."

"I guess we should start to sneak out of here," Chardo said. He shook the hand of Percho's father, startling him. "A very nice home you have here, sir." He turned to the old woman. "A feast befitting royalty," he said and bowed grandly to her. "Mersayn," he said and lifted the child into the air. "Be extra good for these people or I'll not teach you how to hide properly." He winked at her and a small devilish smile crossed his face. "Promise?"

The girl nodded her head vigorously. "Oh yes, Uncle Chardo." She hugged him.

Jewyl's eyes opened wide. "Uncle?" she whispered in disbelief. "When did you become Uncle Chardo?"

"We've more important things at hand," Jopab said. "Now, get out of here. Wait. Let me go out and walk toward the ocean. Perhaps Mersayn would join me?"

"Ocean?" Mersayn asked. "Me go with you." She smiled at the man and grabbed his hand.

"I think that we'll join you for a small walk," Percho's father said. "With all of us out of the house, the guards will be wanting to keep track of us and their attention will be elsewhere."

"Of course," Jewyl said. "A distraction which should make our escape very easy." She grabbed Jopab's head with her hands, leaned up and plopped a heavy kiss on him. "Thanks."

Jopab stood quietly, lightly stroking his cheek — a puzzled look on his face.

"Get a move on," Jewyl said. "The quicker you're out of here, the quicker we're on the road. Remember, we still have our original agenda." She swatted Jopab on the backside to get him moving.

"Are you okay?" Chardo asked, and scowled at Jewyl.

"Of course," Jewyl replied and smiled at the group. "What's your worry?"

"Mersayn?" Jopab called. "Let's all go to the beach. Perhaps there are some crabs we can collect."

"Crabs?" Mersayn questioned as Jopab ushered her out the front door.

"There should be plenty," Tenja said. "Come, old man," she called to her husband. "We've not done anything this rebellious in over forty years." She smiled broadly at the group. "I feel so young

174

right now." Nodding her head, she hastened out the door, pulling her husband behind while he flailed a farewell to the remaining three.

"Exactly what was all that about?" Chardo demanded. He placed his hands on his hip, struck a stance and glared at Jewyl. "You kiss Jopab... like that?"

"I'm fine," she replied. "In fact, I feel better than I've felt the last few days." She pirouetted twice to the table. "You're cute," Jewyl said to Percho. "Too bad. It might have been fun."

"Why are you doing this?" Percho asked, his face crimson with a blush.

"Jewyl!" Chardo yelled.

"You want a threesome?" Jewyl asked, placing a finger to her lips and smiling innocently at the two men. "It could be fun." She batted her eyes.

"Shades of Hagontha," Chardo said. "She's gotten into something. Or rather, something has gotten into her. Are there any bites? Spirit bites?"

Chardo reached over and pulled Jewyl closer. He examined her arm for anything might explain her actions. Jewyl's other hand rubbed Chardo's chest then traced a path downward to his belt. He attempted to back away but stopped at the wall.

"Ah, Jewyl," Chardo said. "You are so going to be upset when you realize what you're doing."

"Oh I know what I'm doing," she giggled and turned to look at Percho. "Oh, my, Percho," she said, while her hands groped for Chardo behind her. Chardo squirmed in an attempt to avoid her searching hands. "Now, I see what you found so interesting in my friend. She stepped toward the cleric with her right hand outstretched to fondle him, her left hand still massaging Chardo's groin. "Let's see what Chardo found in you, okay?"

Percho stood still, his eyes wide at the prospect of what was about to happen.

"Shy?" Jewyl jibbed. "Trust me," she said and pushed the cloth of his tunic inward. "You won't be for long."

"Jewyl," Chardo yelled. "You're like a wanton whore." He hesitated. "Wanton?" He grabbed Jewyl again and pulled her close to look at her face.

"Yes," Jewyl sighed and slid her body against his, wrapping her arms around his neck and kissing him deeply.

"No," he said and pushed her away. "Look at her," he said to Percho. "Do you see the white powder on her face? Look closely, it's very faint."

Chardo held her face in a lock with his hands. Jewyl moaned and quivered in his grasp.

Percho inched closer yet maintained a safe distance from the promiscuous woman. He gingerly touched her cheek and squeezed the dust between his finger and thumb. He nodded.

"I thought so," Chardo said. "Wanton dust. Damned wizards. That's the only place the guard could have gotten it. That dust turns any woman into a sex hungry fiend."

Chardo leaned in closer. "But why?"

Jewyl reached out and grabbed Percho. "I thought so," Jewyl tittered. "Both of you want me. Who will it be?"

Percho pulled away, prying her hand loose. "I don't think so," he said between deep breaths. "That stuff is pretty powerful." He slowed his breathing.

"I'd only heard of it in backrooms and things like that," Chardo said and grabbed both of Jewyl's arms and held her in a lock in front of him. "I didn't really think the stuff existed."

"Is there an antidote for it?" Percho asked. "We've got to get going."

"At the present time, I'm not sticking my butt in front of her and I don't think we should leave the two of you together or she'll probably rape you. So much for our escape."

"Perhaps we should call Jopab back?" Percho asked.

Jewyl slumped in his arms.

"Good, seems there is a side-effect. This should make it a bit easier for us, and no," Chardo replied. "Don't bother Jopab. I don't think he wants it to be like this. We can handle this. Get me some water. This is going to be interesting."

Percho grabbed the pitcher and handed it to Chardo. Sliding his one hand up to grab Jewyl's chin, he forced her to lean her head back.

"Just what are you going to do?" Percho asked.

"I'm going to dilute the drug," Chardo replied. "Or at least attempt to rinse it from her system."

"She breathed that dust in," Percho said.

"That's correct," Chardo said. "I just hope I don't drown her

176

when the water goes down her nose. Now help me hold her tight. She's going to fight the minute she wakes."

He gently poured the water on her upturned face, forcing it to flow over her face which she tossed back and forth vehemently. Her hair got wet, as well as most of their clothing.

"You are spawns of Rorc," Jewyl spat. "Let go of me." She reached for her sword.

"Seems to be working," Percho said. "She sounds more like herself. Damn! Take her sword away before she uses it on us."

"Of course I'm myself," Jewyl said. "Who else could I be?" She squirmed in his arms.

"One of the horniest sluts on the streets of Bashiwa," Chardo said, laughing. "Good to see you back."

"I should gut the both of you," Jewyl said pulling at her wet blouse. She held still then pushed her long hair back behind her shoulders. "What possessed you to do this?"

"Possessed," Percho said. "Good word."

"Yes, excellent choice of words," Chardo said letting her free. "What is the last thing you remember?"

"I don't," Jewyl said. "It's all muddy. We were under this house and now I'm standing here dripping wet wanting to know why I shouldn't run my blade through the two of you."

"And that is well, I believe," Chardo said. "You were mauling us, groping and fondling like the best whore in the house. Poor Percho," he patted Percho on the shoulder, "hasn't blushed this much in a long time, especially when you grabbed him."

"I what?" Jewyl yelled.

"It's over," Chardo said. "The guard was setting us up for a fall and he failed. Jopab and the rest are down on the beach distracting the guards. We should make our escape. How do you feel?"

"Like a drowned animal," Jewyl replied. "Why water?"

"It was the only thing I could think of I thought might dilute the dust," Chardo said.

"I guess I should thank you," Jewyl said. "Both of you."

She reached up and grabbed Chardo around his neck to pull his head closer to hers. She gave him a peck on the cheek.

"That's the Jewyl I know," Chardo said.

"Thanks, friend," she said then turned to Percho.

"Please," Percho said, "I think you've thanked me enough already."

"Okay, boys," Jewyl said. "We're out of here. Follow me."

Percho cocked his head questioning.

"Hmm?" she said. "I guess I should follow the person who knows where we're going. Percho, if you please?"

He smiled. "Follow me," he said, fell to the floor and crawled out the doorway into the darkness.

CHAPTER NINETEEN
Zornal

Jopab presented a great performance for his departure, hugging, kissing, and waving intermittently as he headed for Opula. Jewyl shook her head at his antics, noticing Percho.

"What's wrong?" she asked.

"In the rush, I never got a chance to say goodbye to my parents," he said. His voice choked a couple of times.

"How thoughtless of us," Jewyl said and noted Percho's welling eyes. "None of us said farewell to your parents. They willingly put their lives at stake for us."

"What?" Chardo asked. "Get down! The guard is already on the move to follow Jopab."

"Are they all accounted for?" Percho whispered and wiped his eyes.

Jewyl could see Chardo's head bobbing as he counted each of the guards. "All present and accounted for," Chardo hissed back. "Why?"

"I wondered if any had stayed with my parents," Percho said. He fidgeted in his position and scowled with a pensive look on his face.

"What are your thoughts?" Jewyl asked.

"I am sure you would advise against what I am thinking," Percho said. "Still, they are my parents, and I fear for their lives."

""You are a wise son, Percho." Jewyl nodded agreement to his plan. "When the guards finally pass us, go back to your parents. Will you join us in the city?"

"As soon as I know they're safe, I will head for Zornal." Percho said with a smile, then frowned. "Of course, that means you will be alone with Chardo when you arrive at Opula." He paused. "I will meet you at the Searay Inn."

"Be sure to thank them for me." She paused. "Let Mersayn know I will return soon."

"Where's he going?" Chardo asked. The guards had passed them and Percho was quickly sneaking back to his parent's hut.

"To check the safety of his parents and to say his farewells," Jewyl said.

Chardo massaged is chin in thought. "Perhaps I should go with him," he said. "Also, I can help get him to the city faster."

"Sounds fair," Jewyl said. "Don't the two of you dally since you must be inside the gates before sundown. Do you understand?"

"Gates aren't the only way into that city," Chardo said. He smiled at Jewyl. "After all, I was a thief long before I teamed up with you."

"Be careful," she whispered to the departing figure. "I'd miss you, dear friend."

# # #

Jewyl watched the guards gather from the woods and arrange themselves into a neat group. In the distance she could see the tallest spires of Zornal. She waited and was relieved to see all of them leave in the direction of the city. She waited in the shadows of the trees, and watched as Jopab slowed in his stride and finally stopped.

"They've left," Jopab said loudly.

Jewyl yanked the blue jerkin and tan breeches from the pouch she carried. She stood up and waved them so Jopab could locate her. "Here," she said.

He ran to her, grabbed the garments and then swung her into the air before embracing her with a kiss.

"Exactly what is that?" she said pulling back from him. She slowly pulled her hand across her lips in an act of revulsion.

"Last night, you–" Jopab started. His eyes were wide and questioning.

"Last night was last night," Jewyl said. "I was drugged. Forget whatever it is you remember, and get changed. We need to get to Zornal."

"There is nothing here you haven't seen before," Jopab said defiantly, pulling the priest's tunic over his head. He turned so she could see his backside only and slipped into the breeches and jerkin.

"Where's Percho and Chardo?" he asked.

"I saw them earlier but didn't see them enter Zornal," Jewyl said and then scanned the horizon where the guards had disappeared. "It matters not, we will meet them at the Red Stone Inn."

"Probably a wise move," Jopab said. "Are you ready to finish this trek to Zornal?"

# # #

"So, this is the city?" Jewyl said stoically staring up the huge walls. "It is here that we will kill the Holy Father, head priest to Hagontha?"

"It is so written," Jopab said.

"Halt," the heavy guard said and lumbered toward them. "What is your purpose?"

"We have journeyed here to visit the shrine," Jopab said. "Is there a problem?"

The guard surveyed them. "Where are you from?" The voice was gritty and the man was definitely winded from the few steps he'd taken.

"We come from beyond Lisbeth Harbor," Jopab said. "We are mere farmers on a journey to praise Hagontha."

"Why not visit the temple at Lizzy?" the guard asked. "It is practically the same."

"My husband talks too much," Jewyl said. "And says very little. We have come to see the Holy Father. They told us at Lisbeth Harbor he would be in attendance here. We seek knowledge of our son who was lost at sea."

The guard stood there nodding his head, yet there was a hesitancy.

"Son?" he asked. "Look at you. A son to be lost at sea? How old was this seaman son of yours?"

"He wasn't a seaman," Jewyl said, sniffed, and wiped a mock tear from her eye. "He was a mere babe, playing at the ocean's edge while we worked our nets."

"There, there," Jopab said and lovingly comforted Jewyl in an embrace.

"A wave," Jewyl said, her voice cracking. "Little Johab was there, then he wasn't. I ran into the waters trying to find him." Jewyl pushed her face into Jopab's chest and covered her face. Her body moved in the sobs of fake crying, trying not to laugh aloud.

"I see," the guard said profoundly. An awkward moment of silence ensued before he swung an arm toward the gate. "Enter," he said. "Hagontha's blessing on you."

Jewyl patted Jopab's hand and together they proceeded through the large gate of the north wall. Jewyl was sure she had seen Percho pass through while they were delayed by the guard. She smiled knowing that the plan had worked, not exactly as planned, but it had worked. She causally glanced about trying to see Chardo. She shrugged. He'd turn up as planned at the Red Stone Inn.

"Would this lovely couple like to buy a jeweled necklace," a hooded and shabbily dressed vendor hawked to them.

"No," Jopab said and cast a distained look at the man before he waved him away. "Probably stolen, no less."

"Probably stolen," the vendor sneered. "It was, not less than mere moments ago." Chardo lifted the hood and smiled at them. "They really are very beautiful jewels," he said and held the piece into the air for the sun to reflect on.

"You are to meet us at the inn," Jopab said. "Put that away."

"My necklace," a woman's voice yelled. "Give it to me."

"Yes, m'lady," Chardo said and bowed low. "I noticed it being kicked about and picked it up." He bowed, offering up his hand with the necklace dangling from it. "I was looking at its beauty in the sunlight."

The young lady pulled the necklace from his hand as he stood.

"Such a lovely item and much too valuable to lose," Chardo said and smiled at the stranger. "Perhaps a reward?"

"Reward?" she echoed and hesitated a few seconds to stare at Chardo. "Yes, of course," she said and produced a coin. "A silver token should suffice?"

Chardo took the coin from her and gently kissed the back of her hand. "A simple kiss from your lovely lips to my cheek would have sufficed," he said and stepped away from her.

"Get on with you now," Jopab said and pushed Chardo away.

"May Hagontha bless you at evening sun," Chardo said, and slipped into the market place's crowd.

"What a strange blessing," the woman said. "How odd." She admired her necklace then stuffed it into a leather pouch. "I don't plan to lose this again," she said and knotted the pouch's strings to her belt. "Do I know you?" she asked and looked at Jewyl.

"I doubt it," Jewyl said. "What is your name?"

"They call me Halia," the woman said and dropped the filmy scarf that covered the lower part of her face. "I am the daughter of Lord Leniv."

"Sorry, I don't recognize you," Jewyl said. "We must be on our way."

"Safe journey and be careful of our thieves," Halia said.

"Thieves?" Jopab asked.

"Like the one who stole my necklace," Halia replied. "I was very lucky to get my necklace back. If he hadn't approached you, I may never have seen it again."

"Thank you," Jewyl said. "We'll be careful."

"Enjoy your visit," Halia said and casually sauntered into the fray of the market.

Jewyl watched her until she was well out of sight and they had moved beyond their location.

"What is it?" Jopab asked when Jewyl, for the third time, innocently stopped and checked where they had been while pretending to shop.

"Nothing," she replied.

Jopab frowned. "Nothing? I think not," he said. "Who is she?"

Flustered, Jewyl threw down the fabric that she'd been fingering. "I'm not sure if Halia will remember me or not. Yes, I know her."

"Let me guess, this is not a good thing," Jopab said.

"I'm really amazed she didn't recognize Chardo," Jewyl said.

She turned and walked aimlessly down the street. Jopab followed quietly. Jewyl looked up at the sign above her. She smiled. Nanzo's Inn.

"Let's get something to drink," she said and walked into the establishment.

Jopab looked up at the sign then shook his head. He didn't know what was going to happen, but hoped that it wouldn't cause a stir.

"Nanzo," Jewyl said to the thin man carrying a tray. "Two, please."

The man's face squinted momentarily then a broad smile

crossed his face.

"Is it truly you?" he asked.

Jewyl nodded agreement and smiled at the innkeeper. "It has been some time since I last saw you," she said. There was a moment of silence as she thought. "Back at Hound's Inn. What brought you to Zornal?"

"A wife," Nanzo said. "My wild days are over. I have three children now. Ah, here's Isa now."

A petite woman breezed into the room from the kitchen. She carried a small child in a sling over her back.

"Isa, dear," Nanzo said. "Please meet a dear friend, Jewyl."

She stopped and cocked an eye toward Jewyl. "A friend?" Her voice was high and piercing. "Another of your cronies come looking for free drinks?"

"There will be no free drinks to me or my friend," Jewyl said. She reached into her pouch and pulled a small blue jewel from it. "This should cover most of our expenses, will it not?"

Isa took the jewel and fingered it before checking the clarity in a sunbeam. "It is a good stone and will cover a night's keep, supper for two and a few drinks, but no more."

"That will be more than adequate," Jewyl replied. "Now Nanzo, tell me how you met your lovely bride."

"Nanzo," Isa snapped. "There is work to be done. Now is not a time for dallying." She jerked her head toward the group of men in the corner. "They need attending."

"We'll take the room," Jewyl said. "Perhaps later we can talk."

"Follow me," Isa said and tromped across the room. "If you want to refresh yourself, there is a tub in the room out back and there is a trough of water to use."

She led them up the stairs. "This is your room. I cleaned it this morning."

Jewyl stepped in and glanced about the room. A bed, a table, two chairs, a well-used oil lantern, one small candle and a closet. "This will do nicely," Jewyl said. "Simple." She sat down on the bed and noted the straw was fairly clean but the sheets had stains and dirt smudges on them.

"You must be kept very busy here," Jewyl said.

"Nanzo is a good man, but tends to allow his friends to cheat him of an honest living," Isa said. "Your meal — would you like that up here, or down in the tavern." She attempted a smile.

"Up here," Jopab said quickly. "We have much to do. How far to Hagontha's temple?"

Isa stepped to the window. "You can see it from here," she said. "Maybe four or five blocks. You're followers of Hagontha?"

Jopab nodded. Isa looked to Jewyl who shrugged in attempt to be noncommittal.

"No business of mine," Isa said. "I'm sure Nanzo needs some help. I'll bring your supper later." She turned and stomped out of the room, closing the door with a loud slam.

Jewyl placed a finger to her lips and waved for Jopab to be silent. She waited, knowing full well in the manner Isa walked, the woman was just outside the door, listening.

"If you are tired," Jewyl finally said. "I can take a short walk in the market."

The sound of Isa's loud steps indicated her departure.

"Would you like some company?" Chardo said from the window and climbed in. "I didn't think that she-devil was ever going to leave. Dainty, isn't she?" Chardo dusted himself off. "I thought we were to meet at the Red Stone Inn."

"Where is Percho?" Jopab asked.

"Here," came the reply as he gingerly clung to the window's edge and pulled himself in. "I am not a thief, and care nothing for climbing into second story windows."

"At least we are all here," Jewyl said. "Jopab wants to make plans."

"How did you do with Halia?" Chardo said. "I thought she looked familiar."

"Of all the people to steal a necklace from," Jewyl said. She slapped him across his chest. "A full market, and you have to pick Halia? You had to steal from her?"

"Ease up," Chardo said. "She had a cloth across her face. How was I to know?"

"Why did you even bother to steal?" Jopab asked.

"Once a thief, always a thief," Chardo replied. "I have to keep up my practice."

"She knew you to be a thief," Jewyl said. She sat down on the chair by the table. "I just hope she doesn't remember you. If she

185

does, she will soon remember me, and the trouble will begin." Jewyl looked around the room. "Like we're not in enough trouble already."

"Soon," Jopab said. "It will be over."

"I was able to find out the Holy Father is here," Percho said.

"Let us make our plans," Jopab said. He sat in the other chair and pulled a parchment from his bag. "I shall sketch the temple and how we will approach our victim."

"What is your plan when Isa comes back with your food?" Chardo asked and smiled at the group. "She is coming back, you know."

"Let me offer her another gem and ask for two more meals," Jewyl said. "I don't think she'll be against the payment."

"I'm sure she won't," Jopab said. "Although, she might be curious as to how two more people got upstairs without her noticing. Somehow, I feel she will be a woman to reckon with. A formidable force, I'm sure."

"Perhaps Nanzo will be able to control her," Chardo said. "Then again, perhaps not."

"Go do what you must," Jopab said and waved Jewyl away. "We'll wait." He stood up and walked over to the bed. "Probably not that comfortable, either," he said and lay down.

CHAPTER TWENTY
Zornal's Temple of Hagontha

Jewyl quietly closed the door behind her.

"It certainly took you long enough," Chardo said. "How long before we eat?"

Jopab sat up on the bed. "She probably was talking with the owner," he said then rolled off the bed. "Correct?"

"No," Jewyl replied and took a seat at the small table. "I had to wait for her to come out of the kitchen."

"So we have food coming?" Chardo asked. He rubbed his hands together in preparation.

"She wasn't happy," Jewyl said. "She wanted to make sure that you two weren't staying the night. I gave her the stone and assured her you would be gone."

Chardo shook his head. "As usual," he said, "back to the stable or worse."

"Actually, no," Jewyl said. She looked at Percho and noticed him starting to perk up. "I was able to find out there is closed off section above us."

"Above?" Percho echoed in a questioning tone.

"I would have thought the next floor up would be the proprietor's rooms," Jopab said.

"They were," Jewyl said. "Seems Isa didn't like climbing all the stairs and new rooms were built over the stable."

"Whoops," Chardo said. "Seems we won't be sleeping with the horses. No roll in the hay tonight."

Percho grinned and a slight blush filled his cheeks.

"Now, back to the problem at hand," Jopab said. "Have you any idea of how you plan to fulfill your obligation?"

"Simple," Jewyl said. "We go into the temple as faithful followers of Hagontha, get close to that bastard, I slit his throat, we leave. Easy in and quick out."

"Are you mocking me?" Jopab asked. He leaned back on the

bed. "It won't be that easy, nor will we just walk up to the Holy Father."

"Remember," Percho said. "We are being sought after. I'm sure the fellowship of the brothers will be looking for another attempt by us on the Holy Father. I doubt anyone other than the closest of his elite corps will be allowed near him."

Jewyl watched out the window, her face wrinkling in frowns.

"What is your problem?" Chardo asked. He rapped on the table. "Hey! We need your attention over here." He stretched to look out the window. "What is it?"

"Guards," Jewyl replied. "A lot of them and they appear to belong to Azre."

Chardo pushed closer as Percho and Jopab leaned against him to see out the small window.

"It wasn't that easy to fit me through the window alone," Chardo said pushing his way back. "But let's face it, four people crammed into and gawking out a window might bring a little suspicion to a wandering guard."

"I think we need more info," Jopab said, once more laying on the bed. "Let's hope Isa brings up some food soon, and we can wander the streets to find out what we can hear."

As if on cue Isa knocked on the door, startling the group. Chardo opened the door and Isa walked in with four ales and was quickly followed by two others with steaming trays of foodstuffs. She glared at Percho and Chardo.

"So these are the two mystics?" she asked and placed the ales on the table. "They certainly don't look very mystical to me." She stepped back and wiped her hands on the dirty apron. She scrutinized the group before waving the two girls out. "There should be enough for the four of you to enjoy. If you need more, let me know." She made a slight wrinkle of the nose and rolled her eyes toward the ceiling.

Jewyl did a quick inventory: 4 bowls and plates, 4 spoons and forks, 1 cutting knife, a tureen of soup, 4 small biscuits, a small slab of butter, a satisfactory size hunk of steaming meat, a bowl of hot, mixed vegetables and 4 ales. *She's right,* Jewyl thought. *Just enough to feed us.*

"Mystics," Isa murmured. "More likely common thieves." She walked to the door, gave one last glance at the group before pulling the door closed behind her.

Jewyl held up her hand for silence and she listened. She was sure Isa was again listening on the other side.

"Chardo? See if you can get Isa," Jewyl said loudly. "I don't see a cutting knife."

Chardo frowned and pointed at the object on the tray.

Jewyl could hear Isa's foot treads as she hustled down the hall and stairs. She smiled at the group.

"Just clearing the walls of unwanted ears," she said. "Let's eat. This should be very satisfying since we didn't have to hunt, kill or in any manner, collect this meal. Enjoy."

"Another ale for each of us would have been nice," Chardo said. "Still, better than nothing."

"She only has two hands, Chardo," Percho chastised. "This is good," he said pointing at the bowl of soup he held.

"Two hands? Not from what I can remember," Chardo replied and smiled. "I've seen this woman before and I think she belongs to the Thieves Guild." Chardo twirled the spoon in his fingers. "Isabelle of the Ten Fingers." He nodded his head. "Yes, that was her name back then."

"Do you plan to elaborate or is that it?" Jewyl rolled her eyes at Chardo.

"Let me say this, guard well any possession of value." Chardo tasted the food. "Guard it very good, indeed."

"Back to the issue at hand, how to accomplish our goal," Jopab said.

"So, I don't just saunter in and kill our Most Holy Father." Jewyl wiped the juices from her chin. "Anyone got a better idea? Hmm? What's this?" She lifted a small object between her fingers into the air.

"Probably a bone," Percho said. He slurped loudly from the soup bowl's edge.

"Bones don't glisten or glitter," Jewyl replied. "This is a diamond. How odd?"

"Meat don't have diamonds," Chardo said and leaned over to take the gem. He wiggled it between his index and thumb. "Definitely a diamond. Wonder who lost this?"

"My gem!" The woman's voice carried throughout the inn. "Somebody has stolen my diamond."

Jewyl froze. The voice she recognized. It was Halia.

"It had to be Chardo. He tried to steal my necklace earlier." Halia's voice vibrated the rafters. "I saw him come in here. He must be staying in a room since I don't see him now. Call Lord Azre's guards! Immediately!"

"I do believe that is my call to exit and disappear," Chardo said and placed his almost finished bowl on the table. He gazed at Jewyl. "Will you be joining me?"

Jewyl placed her bowl on the tray beside Chardo's. "It would be in my best interest. It is obvious Halia recognized you, so I am more than sure she knows who I am."

"For all of us to leave through the window would be awkward and very noticeable." Jopab nodded toward the window. "I can hear somebody coming up the stairs as we talk. I would recommend an exit and very quickly."

"Best hiding place is above," Chardo nodded at the ceiling and dashed to the window and scurried out. He turned and offered a hand to Jewyl.

"I can do this," she said and quickly maneuvered out the window.

Percho quickly joined them as they scrambled up the wall to the floor above which had been the old residence. Chardo carefully opened the window, peeked in and then cautiously entered.

"We'd best hurry," Percho muttered. "Azre's guards should soon be appearing on the street and we'll have some difficulty explaining our presence out here."

"Percho! Give me your hand," Jewyl demanded and reached out to pull the cleric in.

Chardo motioned for silence. Below Halia ranted.

"Where is she?"

"My wife?" Jopab nonchalantly asked. "She has left with the wizards — the mystics who were visiting — to attend to some business. Is there a problem?"

"My diamond is missing." Halia stomped across the floor to stare out the window. "How did they leave? They certainly didn't come down the stairs."

Jopab bowed. "Good woman, they are two mystics. How they travel is unknown to me." He shrugged. "It is magic. They were here." Jopab pointed at a location on the floor. "Then they were gone." He lifted and held his arms apart.

Chardo snickered and quickly covered his mouth.

Isa scurried into the room and quickly took inventory and then nodded approvingly. "If you are finished, I will take these away." Without waiting for a reply, she began to gather the bowls, plates and utensils. She leaned toward the door. "Tell Janesa to come and help me." Isa carefully poured the unused soup back into the tureen.

Halia watched the woman go about her chores. "When do you expect Jewyl to return?"

"Who is Jewyl? If you mean my wife, her name is Mersayn." He shrugged his shoulders. "I don't know. When she is finished, she will come back. We go to the temple tomorrow to visit the Holy Father."

"I want my diamond returned," Halia screamed and stomped her foot. She gazed at Nanzo, the inn keeper. "My father is Lord Leniv."

Nanzo bowed. "Most esteemed lady, I assure you these people are innocent. They came in, paid for their room and other than speaking with my wife, have not bothered anyone at the inn since their arrival. Could you have possibly lost it on the street?"

Halia paled.

"Janesa, where have you been?" Isa pulled the young girl into the room. "Take these dishes to the kitchen. I'll bring down the trays of food later."

Without the diamond, Jopab thought.

"I will have my servants search the street," Halia whispered. "I fear I will never see that gem again."

Nanzo nodded in agreement.

"Now, if you have no problem, I would like to visit the temple," Jopab said. "I understand it is just a few blocks away." He motioned toward the door in hopes the gathered people would depart.

"Who demanded Lord Azre's guards?"

Halia sheepishly looked at the guard. "I did. Earlier today I was robbed by a common pickpocket, but I was able to retrieve the item back. Just a little while ago I noticed my diamond was missing and demanded somebody get me guards."

"We are here to assist," the guard said. "Have you

191

apprehended the thief?"

"It would seem I was mistaken earlier today. I was sure I recognized the pickpocket and this man's wife as Jewyl and Chardo. Is there not a warrant for their arrest?"

"They are here in Zornal?" The guard stepped back and prepared to remove his sword.

"I was wrong," Halia quickly added. "I apologize." She took the guard's arm and headed him toward the door. "Perhaps you could assist my servants as they search for the diamond. It seems I may have lost it in the street before coming into this inn."

Isa smiled as Halia moved out of the room. Nanzo nodded to Jopab, turned, and left, following Isa out the door. Jopab gazed about the room. Suddenly, it was empty, and he was alone.

"It is now time for me to head to the Temple of Hagontha," Jopab said. He listened.

The shuffling of sandals revealed what he expected. Jopab waited before opening the door. Voicing his actions served two purposes: one, to rid the walls of ears, and two, to let the ears above him know his plans.

Jopab strolled the street, waiting, while all the time he slowly worked his way toward the temple. He knew the others would join him quickly, and very discreetly.

The temple came into sight and he enjoyed the view having never seen it before, arriving in a covered litter with the Holy Father. The holy shrine reached skyward, the turrets ascending in impossible angles. *Very similar to the temple in Bashiwa*, he thought. *Bashiwa. How long ago was that?* Jopab admired the colorful tiles of the building which carried no pattern but a chaotic morass of gaudy paints.

"My husband," Jewyl said and moved closer to him. "I thought you'd await my return before leaving for the temple."

Jopab gazed down at Jewyl and frowned at her words.

"I came back through the window and startled Isa as she sorted through our foods." Jewyl kept her voice low and draped a veil across her lower face. "I am being followed. Chardo and Percho are at the market behind us." She grabbed Jopab's arm. "Come. We

192

must buy an offertory gift before we enter the temple."

As Jopab turned he could see the two men absently fingering items at a market table. Near them, two guards stood quietly watching them approach the market area. At another market table he saw Halia.

"Good sir," Jopab called to one of the men at the table. "Could you recommend a suitable gift as an offering?"

Percho's eyes widened in surprise.

Chardo kept his face down and pointed at the collection of trinkets. "Any of these would make a satisfactory offering." He paused. "We, too, are but humble seekers of Hagontha's chaotic grace."

Percho picked up a necklace to display to Jopab.

"That would be an excellent choice," Jopab said and took the necklace from Percho." He nodded to Percho and lowered his voice. "We will enter the temple and slowly walk to the left. The guards will follow us but we will disappear before they even enter the temple. Percho, you know the second entrance. Take it and we'll meet in Exchange Room number three." Jopab lifted the necklace into the air to view in the sunlight.

"You've been here before?" Chardo asked.

"Twice. The temples have very similar hidden tunnels." Jopab turned away from the two men and faced Jewyl. "Now we pay for this and head into the temple." He smiled.

Jewyl dropped the diamond into the merchant's slotted container. "An offering," she said.

"Hagontha accepts all offerings as part of chaos," the merchant muttered with no emphasis or regard. "Blessed chaos."

Jopab lead Jewyl toward the main doors of the temple. "When we get inside, we will need to make haste to the first column on the left side. I will trip the mechanism, help me push the door and we'll disappear before the guards realize what happened." He nonchalantly gazed back and could see the guards moving toward the temple. Very close behind them was Chardo and Percho. Halia still waited by the market table. Jopab shrugged as the shadow of the temple entrance engulfed them.

Jewyl breathed softly as the stone moved back into place. The guards hadn't come into the temple and now they would never know. She smiled and felt Jopab's lips caress her. She kissed him back, leaning into him as the darkness turned to the sickly green she recognized.

"Quickly!" Jopab said. "We must make haste and get to the exchange room before Chardo and Percho."

"Why?"

"Because Percho does not know the combination and there are no pliocas here, but they will be very near that room."

CHAPTER TWENTY-ONE
The Chaos of Hagontha

Jewyl shuddered, feeling the shiver run a course down her spine. Pliocas! She was not about to let Jopab see her fear of the creatures.

"Lead on," she whispered.

Jopab clicked the flint, a spark ignited the torch and Jewyl could see, even if she didn't want to know what could be crawling on the ceiling above.

"Listen, you can hear the stone on the other side being opened. They'll be at the room shortly." Jopab grabbed her hand pulled her down the steps.

Suddenly Jewyl saw another torch coming toward them.

"It is Chardo and Percho," Jopab whispered. "The four of can enter the room at once." He reached above the center of the door and then pushed on the center of the stone.

Click.

Percho and Jopab pushed together and the stone quickly moved. The four rushed into the chamber before any young pliocas could enter.

"Drop your weapons," the guard ordered. His sword drawn and mere inches from Jewyl's neck. "All of you."

Jewyl glanced around the room at the three other guards with their swords drawn. Four of Lord Azre's men held them at bay. She gently dropped her sword and dagger. Jewyl could hear the others as they released their weapons and they clanked to the floor.

"How is this possible?" Percho asked.

The guard grinned. "Simple. Ballec bargained his life for yours. Make sure those knots are well tied." He turned to the lone cleric who stood in the corner. "Open the other door and we shall see what Lord Azre has to say of our bounty." He leered at Jewyl. "He hasn't forgotten your escape from Dianiya." The guard reached up and slowly massaged an area of his rib. "I've not forgotten your escape, either." His lip curled in a sneer. "My ankle has healed but my side remains to heal. Still, I am capable of serving my lord." The guard played the tip of his sword down the front of Jewyl's body, lingering a moment near the breasts and then continuing to match where she'd driven the dagger into his side. "I still remember your look as I crawled away. Perhaps you'd like the return of a favor?" The guard pulled back the sword in a mock move to plunge it into Jewyl's side. He stopped, laughed and placed his sword in its scabbard. He leaned in and pushed the guard who was tying the ropes around Jewyl's wrists. "I will personally make sure this bitch doesn't get free." He tightened the knot and Jewyl attempted not to show any pain.

"Are we ready?" the cleric asked.

"Get that door open," the guard yelled. "Move it."

He pushed Jewyl and she saw him winced in pain. Jewyl tried not to smile at his discomfort.

The group moved into the dark tunnel.

"It would be best to move quickly," Jopab said. "There are too many of us."

"Yes," the cleric whispered. "This way."

He led the group along the passage and finally stopped. His fingers fumbled along the wall as he attempted to find the release mechanism.

"If my hands were free, I could open the door," Jopab muttered.

"None of that," Jewyl's guard snarled.

"What was that?" A voice from the rear was loud and emphatically scared.

"Untie my hands," Jopab demanded. "If not, we'll all die in the passageway."

The scream was blood-curdling.

"Now!" screamed Jopab.

Suddenly the door outlined in light. The young cleric stumbled into the room, followed by Jewyl, her guard, Jopab, Chardo, Percho and another guard.

Another scream gurgled to an abrupt stop.

Jopab and Percho immediately leaned against the door and shoved it shut. Jopab glanced at the skittering ball as it dashed across the floor.

Jewyl cringed and slammed her foot down on it. A small squeak was followed by a squishing sound. Jewyl trembled under the shiver coursing through her body.

"I don't want to do that again," she whispered.

"What happened to Harco and Menlen? Where are they?" Jewyl's guard looked about the room for the two men.

"For your information, the screams you heard in the tunnel was their last sounds. The pliocas are enjoying their bodies as we speak." Jopab stared at the guard with disdain. "I tried to warn you."

"They have never approached this close before," the young cleric mumbled. His face was as white as his garment. "I've walked that tunnel many times." The tremble in his voice was obvious.

"Only the Holy Father is safe from the pliocas," Percho added.

"Ah-hem." The new voice was loud.

Everyone turned to stare at the man who made the sound.

"Holy Father." The young cleric bowed.

"Why have you all come to my private quarters?" He gazed at the group. "Ah, Jopab. And Percho. I see the traitors to Hagontha have been captured." Ballec allowed himself a few extra moments to take in Jewyl. "So you're the one who thought she could assassinate me in my holiest temple? Jewyl, is it not?" He turned to Chardo. "And you must be her servant friend. Chardo, right?"

"He is not my servant," Jewyl said. She took a deep breath. "He is my friend, though."

"It matters not to me," Ballec replied and waved his hand to dismiss the conversation. "Tonight my goddess will see chaos rule." He grinned. "A sacrifice."

"My goddess, Hagontha, does not need a sacrifice," Jopab said and stepped defiantly toward Ballec.

The Holy Father wavered and stepped back.

Jopab stood straight and glared at the man before him. "If you mean to sacrifice us to Yendisa, then state that. Do not befoul my goddess."

"Chaos be," Percho whispered.

"Who is to be sacrificed?"

Lord Azre stepped into the room. The guards immediately bowed, as did the priests of Hagontha. Chardo gave a nod of his head. Ballec acknowledged his brother. Jewyl stood defiant, glaring

197

at the man she despised.

"So good to see you again, my love." Azre strode across the room to her. "Our last tryst was abruptly, and rudely interrupted by swordplay."

"What brings my brother to my chambers?" Ballec asked.

"I may ask the same question, my brother. It seems you have gathered together those who I wish to arrest." He turned to his guard. "Take them to the main hall." Azre turned back to Ballec. "You did intend to give them over to me, am I not correct?"

"Of course, brother. Why would I do otherwise?"

Azre smiled and sauntered to the door. "A wise answer. Now, about this sacrifice. Once more I ask, who is being sacrificed."

"To honor my goddess, Hagontha, and to begin the deification of Lord Azre." Ballec bowed respectfully to his brother. "I felt a sacrifice of those who were traitors to you would be worthy of the ceremony."

Azre's lips curled in a smile. "Yes, Holy Father. I can understand how you would want to prepare such a grand exhibition, but you have forgotten one little detail."

Ballec faltered. "What detail?"

"One of those you planned to sacrifice is to be my bride. You may make me a god, but it is with my marriage to her I will assure my position as rightful king." Azre strutted to the doorway. "Think about what I have said, and you will realize your folly."

"As you wish, brother." Ballec turned away from Azre, but gave him a sly sideway glance. "As Yendisa demands," he whispered, stepped to the hidden passageway entrance, pushed the release lever, and disappeared.

Azre shook his head and continued his saunter of the hallway toward the main hall. *Finally, my dreams are within my grasp. Jewyl is once more my captive.* He stepped into the main hall and once more surveyed the group.

"Who spoke of Yendisa? Speak now or all of you will lose your tongues." He glanced at Jewyl. "Except her. It was man's voice."

"I did, Lord Azre." Jopab stepped forward.

"I am not an unreasonable man." Azre motioned to the guards. "Everyone is to sit while we talk." He turned his attention back to Jopab. "You come with me so we may discuss this matter in private."

Jopab glanced at Jewyl, then Chardo who could only shrug as support.

Azre stopped and turned to Jopab and scrutinized his face.

"I recognize you. One of my guards the day Jewyl escaped."

Jopab hung his head. "A disguise, my lord."

"Is this another?" Azre pointed to a bench. "Sit."

"Nay, my lord. I am truly a priest in the service of Hagontha."

Azre sat on the bench and again motioned to Jopab to join him. "You speak of Yendisa, and I have just learned of the atrocities performed at Bashiwa."

"Yendisa is a goddess to fear. She seeks blood, human blood." Jopab avoided Azre's stare.

"Look into my eyes, priest. Tell me true. Who serves Yendisa?"

Jopab inhaled deeply and slowly exhaled. There was no way to avoid death with the answer he was being forced to give.

"Forgive me, Mother Hagontha. My service has been short." Jopab turned to face Azre. "There is a small group of priests at Bashiwa who I know not only serve Hagontha, but also favor Yendisa."

Azre leaned in close. "How many priests are involved?"

"Only a few, maybe ten. Perhaps fifteen. Less than twenty, I am very sure."

"Which priest leads this group?" Azre's eyes were wide with expectation. "I will make sure this group is removed from this land."

"You would exile them?" Jopab asked.

"I will have them executed. Now speak. Who leads them?"

Once more Jopab inhaled and glanced at his companions in the distance. "Into your bosom, Holy Mother, I now offer my soul. Protect my travels to you."

"Why do you recite the death rites?" Azre placed a hand on Jopab's shoulder. "Whoever is in charge will not be able to kill you."

"My death will be at your hands, Lord Azre. The leader is the Holy Father, your brother."

Azre jerked back his hand, stood and held his sword at the ready at Jopab's neck. "You dare to insinuate my brother leads this dark group against me?"

Jopab closed his eyes and waited.

"Speak, priest." The sword's point pushed against Jopab's skin.

"I discovered the Holy Father performing a rite of sacrifice to Yendisa. With those close to me within the priesthood, we hired The Emerald to dispatch Ballec."

"You'd have my brother killed by an assassin?"

"To protect the priesthood of Hagontha. Yes, the chaos of the goddess must be controlled in it recklessness. If the Holy Father wishes to bring Yendisa to the people, then he must be put to death."

Azre stepped back and sheathed his sword. "What do you know of the deification of me?"

"I don't understand," Jopab said and frowned at Azre.

"My brother said he was preparing the rites necessary for the deification of Lord Azre to assure myself the kingship."

"Proper deification can only be performed if you are a martyr. To be a martyr, you must be deceased, killed by one who is considered a traitor." Jopab glanced once more at Jewyl.

Azre followed Jopab's stare.

"Even in chaos, the pattern emerges." Jopab nodded his head approvingly. "Sacred is the Holy Mother's chaos."

CHAPTER TWENTY-TWO
Ballec

Blinded by power, my brother cannot see the truth about him. Ballec's thoughts swirled with the possibilities before him with Azre's demise.

A creature curled around his shoulders as it slid from the ceiling.

"Ah, my pet," Ballec whispered lovingly and stroked the head of the plioca. "What is this? A gift?" He took the proffered item from the plioca's mouth where the myriad of teeth glistened in the dark shadows of the tunnel and flickering torch light. The bone was still warm with blood. *Probably one of Azre's guards.* "I'll let the little ones enjoy this treasure," Ballec said and gently tossed the bone to ground. The plioca curled into the air and caressed Ballec's cheek before slithering over his shoulder and down his back to the tunnel's floor.

Ballec reached and pushed the release mechanism. The stone door swung quietly on its hinge. The steps curled and led down into the bowels of the earth where the walls of the passageway flickered from the light below.

Suddenly the cavern chamber came into view and he saw the gathered men as they waited for him. The sacred flames of Yendisa danced in the large chasm which opened to the bowels of the earth. Shadows flickered on the reflective cave walls.

"Hail the Holy Father."

Eleven men fell to their knees in veneration, mumbling a repetitious 'Hail Holy Father.'

"Yendisa's design has been revealed to me." Ballec raised his hands in supplication. "Brethren, the true mother, Yendisa has spoken. Through me she reveals her wishes."

"Yendisa, the Mother of the Beginning," the eleven men chanted.

"Above us, the blasphemy of Hagontha is being appeased.

Lord Azre wishes to be deified. Mother Yendisa grants him his desire at the hands of The Emerald. Stand and hear the wishes of Mother Yendisa."

The men stood and gathered about Ballec as he revealed the plan to not only seize the four captured by Lord Azre, but also Lord Azre. All, including the guards, would be disabled during the evening meal.

"Go! Prepare the banquet." Ballec raised his hand and the men bowed for the blessing as the Holy Father performed the half-circle motion followed by the hand moving toward them.

"In the name of Mother Yendisa, go in her blessing."

The men lifted their arms outward with palms up. "We accept Mother Yendisa's blessing."

Ballec smiled and his eyes narrowed to hide his delight. *Mother Yendisa will have her fill tonight with five sacrifices.* He turned and slowly trudged up the stairs. *As the only surviving sibling of Lord Azre when he is deified, it is my right to take rule of Dianiya, and guide the people to the true mother, Yendisa.* He rubbed his hands together. *Abriela and Meisa will fall and come under my rule. I will bring them to Yendisa.*

# # #

Ballec strolled into the main hall and immediately noticed only Jewyl and Chardo were now in chains. He glanced about. Azre sat on a bench, waiting.

"Where are the priests?" Ballec asked.

"In your absence, I had a chance to speak with these two and discovered the priests were forced to do what they have done." Azre stood. "I sent them to your chambers to await you and receive their absolution."

Ballec stepped back. "In my chamber?" He hesitated and finally looked at one the guards. "Bring them here to the main hall where I can hear their confessions."

The guard looked to Azre who nodded approval. The guard immediately went to get Jopab and Percho.

# # #

The guard entered the Holy Father's chamber where he found Jopab and Percho on their knees, waiting.

"You can quit your prayers, priests. The Holy Father commands your presence in the main hall. Come with me."

He turned and stood by the doorway, waiting.

Jopab and Percho stood, straightened their robes and casually strolled out the door and down the hallway to the main hall. The guard followed behind.

"This is a quicker way," Jopab said and walked through the kitchen where the cooks prepared the evening meal.

"I wish to get a drink," Percho said and stalled by the urn where he poured water to refresh himself.

Jopab glanced at the preparations being made and frowned at the two priests who hovered over the soup, adding a substance he didn't recognize as a spice. He was sure it was Sleeper's Dream, a substance made from certain mushrooms and berries. It was then he noticed the filled bowl, the Holy Father's bowl of soup, sitting to the side and the other bowls yet to be filled. He nudged Percho and nodded in the direction of the two priests. Percho barely nodded his head in acknowledgement.

"Get a move on," the guard snarled. "Lord Azre has better things to do than wait for you." He pushed Percho.

The two priests entered the main hall and immediately noticed Ballec sitting with his brother on the bench. They scurried to stand before Ballec. Both knelt quickly in obeisance.

"I humbly beg the Holy Father's forgiveness for us," Jopab began. "Our transgressions appear serious, but were coerced into a situation. I felt perhaps I could foil the attempt, and continued with the charade."

Jopab and Percho remained kneeling, their foreheads mere inches from the floor. They stretched out their arms, palms up, in supplication to the Holy Father.

"I beg the Holy Father's forgiveness," Percho mumbled.

Ballec stood, retrieved the staff beside him and slowly approached the two men.

"Attempts to kill the Holy Father can only be absolved through proper veneration," Ballec said. "You will need time in solitude to reflect upon the act. But, the final result is death when Truth has been realized. Mother Hagontha only rules if chaos can continue." He spun the staff with the curled dragon wrapped around the top. Its face resembled that of a human female. Ballec stopped before Jopab.

"Kneel to the floor and place your hands on the floor," he demanded.

Jopab did as commanded and waited.

Ballec stepped on the fingers, pushing them to the floor under his sandals. "I absolve you of your sin." He lifted the staff into the air and let it slam downward to pierce Jopab's palm.

Jopab gritted his teeth and using the arts of chaos, turned the pain away. Tears welled and dripped to the marble floor where a slow stream of blood pulsed toward them.

Ballec turned on his toes, grinding his feet into Jopab's fingers.

Percho's hands and forehead were already in position. He waited.

Once more Ballec moved forward, stepped on Percho's fingers, grinding them to the floor. "I absolve you of your sin."

Percho waited. The pain was excruciating as the staff drove through his palm. Percho's eyes blinded white and he wanted to jerk away and cry out, but he held silent.

Again, Ballec turned on his toes, grinding his sandals into Percho's fingers.

"To fulfill Mother Hagontha's rule of chaos, you will not be killed. You have suffered her anger and trial in silence. You may now depart in peace. Go!"

Jopab and Percho pulled back onto their heels and placed a hand over the hole in their palms, sealing the blood flow as best they could with thumb and fingers.

"Thank you, Holy Father," they said in unison. Bowed and headed for the exit where they could get bandaged.

Before they were out of the room, Ballec clanked the metal staff on the marble floor.

"There is to be a banquet tonight in honor of my brother's attendance here in Zornal. All," he waved his hand to include Jewyl, Chardo and the guards. "All shall be included in the feast and sit at my table tonight."

Jopab and Percho gazed at each other in surprise.

"To honor you, Jopab and Percho, who helped to capture my

attempted assassins, I offer you both a place at my table." He waved a hand to dismiss Jopab and Percho. "Go. Repair your hands. Mother Hagontha smiles on you."

Jewyl stepped forward. "It is indeed a great honor to dine with you, Holy Father, but you seem to have forgotten." She twisted so Ballec could see her chains.

"Fear not, Jewyl," Ballec said, his voice sweeter than dripping honey. "During the meal you will find your bonds released." He lifted a finger into the air. "Fear not, brother, I will assign my personal guards to watch over the meal and none shall escape." He paused. "I assure you, Azre, not one soul will leave the room without my permission."

He gazed at Azre. "I can put your prisoners in a room under the auspices of your guards."

"That would suffice, Ballec." Azre stroked his chin, questioning the actions of his brother. *Does he even realize I am here to see his fall as Holy Father?*

CHAPTER TWENTY-THREE
The Sacrificial Dinner

"Come. Hurry." Jopab wrapped the last of the bandage around his hand. "This will make things difficult until it is healed, but better to have a damaged right hand than be dead."

"I agree," Percho said while tying of the ends of his bandage.

"We must get some oil and cinnamon. It is the only thing I know to repel or lessen the effect of Sleeper's Dream." Jopab pulled the cork on the vat of oil and filled the flagon. Another he held ready to assure they had enough.

"This is the cinnamon." Percho held up the dried sticks. "I have a knife." He quickly scraped the cinnamon into a saucer.

Jopab looked up from his work to see if any noticed them in the storage room. *The Holy Father may have absolved us, but he hasn't exonerated us*, Jopab thought.

"Work in haste, Percho," Jopab said. "If we are caught, Mother Hagontha will not be able to save us and all will be lost."

Percho nodded silently and continued to scrape the cinnamon.

#

"Drink this," Jopab commanded and handed the leather flagon to Jewyl. "It will save you at meal time." He handed a second flagon to Chardo. "You, too." He stood back. "Coat your stomach with the cinnamon oil. Drink at least half the contents."

Jewyl grabbed the leather bag and gazed cautiously at it. "You smell of cinnamon already."

Jopab nodded agreement. "This ointment will disguise most of the cinnamon scent unless you talk. Don't talk too much until after you've had something to eat. The soup has been tainted with Sleeper's Dream to make you groggy. Ballec has a foul plan afoot."

The priest dropped ointment on his fingers and quickly

applied it to Jewyl's neck and lower jaw.

"It smells of onion and vanilla." Jewyl pulled back from the scent.

Jopab smiled. "It blends well with the cinnamon to disguise the scent."

Chardo swallowed and wrinkled his nose at the taste of the heavy oil. "How did you get in here?"

Percho smiled. "We informed the guards we were bringing you scented water to curb your thirst before the meal." He pushed the flagon to Chardo's lips again. "The guards were a little concerned and I finally confided it would fill your stomachs and you'd drink less of the Holy Father's ale and wine. The fools agreed and let us in."

"What of Azre?" Jewyl began another guzzle of the oil.

"He is next on our visits." Jopab scrutinized the flagon in Jewyl's hands. "I will ask him which guard he wants to include. One more good gulp and you should have enough." He gazed at Chardo's vessel. "You, too, drink a little more. This will not completely stop Sleeper's Dream, but it will help to keep you in control of your mind. Now drink."

The door opened. A guard leaned in. "Better hurry. They don't need that much to drink."

"As you wish," Jopab said, and nodded to the guard. "Come, Percho. We must be about our business." He took the flagon from Jewyl's hands. "Watch me at the meal for what you must do."

# # #

"Lord Azre," the guard began. "The priests, Jopab and Percho, are here to seek a short audience with you."

Azre absently motioned for them to be allowed in, but continued to read the parchment, gently tugging and pulling on his dark beard. Jopab and Percho quickly approached the man at the small table. They knelt before him.

"Lord Azre," Jopab said. "May we discuss an important matter in private with you?" He gazed at the three guards standing about in the room.

Azre gazed up from the parchment and examined Jopab. He pointed at two guards. "Leave us."

"Jopab, I will not be left alone with a possible traitor. One guard will remain. He is my most trusted and loyal."

"Thank you, my lord," Jopab said. "You have answered the one question I would ask." Jopab stood. "My Lord Azre, I fear there is a threat on your life during the meal. When I was in the kitchen earlier I noticed what appeared to be Sleeper's Dream being added to the soup."

Azre stood, pushing the stool away, allowing it to fall on the floor. "Who would dare to poison me?"

"Excuse me, but as I stated earlier, for you to be deified, you must die. I fear your brother, the Holy Father, is planning to sacrifice all of us to Yendisa tonight."

Azre gazed down at Percho. "Is this true?"

Percho nodded.

"I'll have my brother brought here immediately."

The guard turned and walked to the door.

"No! Wait!" Jopab yelled. "I have brought an antidote to Sleeper's Dream. I only have enough for you and the one guard you trust." Jopab nodded at the guard who waited at the door. "Please, Lord Azre, drink the flavored oil. It will coat your stomach. It won't stop the drug, but it will lessen and delay the reaction."

"Why do you tell me this?" Azre walked to Jopab and stared him in the face. He reached down and fingered the flagon. "What do you gain?"

"I serve Lord Azre. By you setting Percho and I free today, we have been able to move freely about the temple and learn what the Holy Father plans to some extent. Also, anything I can do to stop Yendisa from usurping the powerful chaos of Mother Hagontha, I will attempt to accomplish that which is necessary until my death." He offered the flagon to Azre who took it, pulled the cork, smelled, and then tasted the contents.

"It is oil! And cinnamon!"

"The oil will coat your stomach. The cinnamon will help to make it taste better, and also counter the berries in Sleeper's Dream."

"How do I disguise this strong cinnamon scent?"

"With this, my lord," Jopab said and showed him the vial of ointment. He turned to Percho. "Offer your flagon to the guard."

Azre waved his hand, signaling Percho to move. "Drink!" Azre said to the guard.

The guard nodded and pulled the flagon from Percho's hands. He tipped it to his mouth and guzzled.

Lord Azre waited, watching.

"He still stands," Azre finally said.

The guard wiped his tunic sleeve across his face and smacked his lips. He handed the flagon back to Percho.

Jopab walked to the guard and smeared the ointment on the guard's neck.

Azre lifted the flagon to his lips and drank. Between guzzles, Jopab put the ointment on him.

"Tonight, during the meal, watch me for what to do and don't eat too much of the soup. We will begin to get groggy, but much later. I will be watching your other guards for my queue. They will not have this protection."

"I must keep a close eye on you, Jopab," Azre said while placing a hand on the priest's shoulder. "You are observant." He smiled. "And sneaky."

"As I have said, Lord Azre, I only wish to serve Mother Hagontha." Jopab smiled at the ruler of Dianiya. "May Mother Hagontha smile on us tonight and continue the chaos which is needed to complete tonight's performance."

# # #

Ten priests stood about the great dining hall, five on each of the long walls. Their faces stoic as they held a sword in their fisted hands with the gleaming blade tips leaned against their foreheads.

Lord Azre entered with his guards and stood at the table's edge, waiting. Two large throne-like chairs with small tables in front them sat on a raised dais. Four large chairs, two on each side, were at the closest end to the dais.

The Holy Father arrived with one priest at his side. They entered from the opposite end where Lord Azre had entered.

"Please, dear brother, join me here." He pointed to the dais. "Your guards may sit anywhere at the table except the four chairs of honor nearest us." Ballec twirled his robe in the air and sauntered up the four steps to the top of the dais. He pointed at the chair next to him. "Come, Lord Azre." A moment's hesitation. "My brother."

Jopab and Percho entered, using the same entrance as Ballec.

At the other end, Jewyl and Chardo entered with two guards.

Ballec brought his hands together. "Jopab and Percho. You will sit at my right hand." He pointed to the large chairs on the right side of the table. "Jewyl and Chardo." He smiled. "You will sit on my left side." Ballec sat.

Azre climbed the four steps and sat in the very large cushioned chair.

"I will bring your soup," the priest said and disappeared.

"Ah, a very special soup, my brother." Ballec softy clapped his hands together at the delight. "The flavors are most intriguing. I do hope you enjoy it. I had it made special for tonight."

A flurry of priests entered the room with trays filled with bowls of hot soup. Within moments everyone had a bowl in front of them.

"Eat," Ballec commanded. "Mother Hagontha blesses this food as we partake." He grabbed his spoon and slurped the soup through his lips. "Excellent, as always." Ballec kept watch as the guests spooned the soup into their mouths. He smiled.

CHAPTER TWENTY-FOUR
Yendisa's Sacrifice

Lord Azre smiled and dipped his spoon into the soup and tasted it. "Interesting flavor," he said. "Perhaps I should have my cooks come to take lessons on how to make this."

"It is an old recipe of the temple," Ballec responded. "Tonight is about honor and destiny." He pointed at Jopab and Percho. "We honor these priests who helped to capture those who would attempt to end our lives." Ballec once more turned an innocent look to his brother. "I have been informed she attempted to kill you in your own throne room. Is that true?"

"I offered her marriage, Ballec." Azre frowned. "She refused and wanted freedom. I never once considered my life in jeopardy." He spread his arm to encompass the men at the table. "I surround myself with guards and am protected at all times. Even now you offer me guards to protect me."

Ballec sat back in his chair, surprised by Azre's words. "Why, yes. Yes, I have offered guards to protect you."

Azre took another small sip of the soup to give the impression he was eating. He watched his guards who unknowingly ate the soup with great gusto. It was then he noticed the guards now seemed less excited and moved sluggishly. Azre glanced at Jopab who smiled absently and let his head loll slightly to the left. He let his shoulders slump and he turned a fake gaze at Ballec.

"Have you finished your soup?" Ballec asked.

Azre nodded and let his eyelids flutter, pretending to be sleepy.

"Perhaps I should have the cooks bring in the next course," Ballec offered. He stood and watched Azre's guards.

One guard slumped forward, his face spilling the almost empty bowl of soup. His head hit the table soundly. Another guard repeated the action. Jewyl turned her head away from Ballec, smiled and finally let her head sink to the table as she had seen the guards do.

"Gather them together and bring them to the chamber," Ballec commanded. "I will prepare for the ceremony." He stepped from the throne-like chair and pulled his robe about him as he stepped downward. "Be quick before they are so soundly asleep you will need to carry them."

# # #

Ballec moved ceremoniously down the steps to the grotto where he knew his eleven acolytes would be waiting, ready to move forward with the ceremony. The human gifts would be bound and properly attired for their service to Yendisa during the sacrifice. Ballec smiled. The first to go would be the six simpleton guards.

The firelight of the chasm flared and Ballec hesitated on the last step before making his entrance.

Yendisa smiles on her sacrifices, Ballec thought as the flames of chasm dwindled. He cast a glance at the open chasm and smiled. *Perfect!* The carved arches of the holy chamber glittered in the light.

"Bring me the first offering," Ballec yelled.

Two of the priests grabbed one of Azre's guard and lifted him into the air, just inches off the floor. The drugged guard, now wide-eyed, struggled, jerking and screaming behind the gag in his mouth. He fought to be set free.

"How dare you," Azre screamed.

Ballec turned, knife in hand, to face Azre who stood against the distant wall.

"Careful, Lord Azre," Ballec called, his voice sickening sweet. "As the one most honored and being deified, you will watch the full ceremony until it is your time." Ballec paused, fingering the knife, letting the blade flicker in the firelight. "If I cannot count on your offered silence, it can be arranged to make you silent." Ballec tittered, twisting the knife's blade in the fire's light. "I'm sure you understand."

Ballec strolled to the guard who now stood at the edge of the chasm. The two priests held him tightly.

"Even the slightest flinch, I will push you into the flames," the priest on the left whispered. "Be a man."

Ballec held the knife high above him. "Mother Yendisa. I call you to witness your beginning with the end." Ballec took the knife and pulled it quickly across the guard's neck.

The shocked guard didn't have a chance to even react as the blood pulsed from the gash.

The priests released their grips, letting the guard spiral to face the chasm of flames. They pushed the guard forward. He fell silently into the pit of flames. A large flame leaped from the chasm to play against the cavern's ceiling.

"Mother Yendisa accepts our first offering." Ballec raised his arms, his billowy sleeves sliding down to reveal his strong arms and leather armor beneath.

#

Jewyl watched the crazed man at the fiery chasm. His eyes told her what she needed to know. Ballec was delirious. She was in no way in the same stupor as the poor guards, but she still felt the effects of the drug.

Suddenly Chardo was nudging at her. "Turn," he whispered. "I have a knife. Let me cut your ropes."

Jewyl stretched her arms toward Chardo and turned ever slightly. She didn't want to appear obvious.

"Where did you get a knife?" she asked.

"Percho." Chardo worked furiously to work through the bindings of the priests. "He took one from the kitchen and hid it where the guards wouldn't look — just in case." He smiled. "I told him I could perhaps help retrieve it, but he assured me it wouldn't be necessary."

"Is that all you think about?" Jewyl shook her head.

"No. Right now I'm trying to figure out how we are going to escape. Our number is greater than theirs, but Ballec is quickly changing those odds as we speak."

Jewyl glanced up to see the priests push another guard into the fiery chasm. She turned to face Azre. He held his head down, defeated. She felt her wrists suddenly loose of their ropes.

"Lord Azre," she called. "Give me your wrists. I have a knife to cut the ropes."

"How many of us are free?" He glanced at those beside him.

"All of us except you and a couple of your guards at the far end. For sure, the six of us when I cut your bonds."

"I wasn't that drugged not to notice the Holy Father's guards did not remove my weapons when they bound me." Azre nodded toward his hip to his sword and dagger.

"Done," Jewyl said. She continued to hold onto the knife.

"Ballec," Azre yelled as he stood, drawing his sword. "You have no right to offer my guards as sacrifices to Yendisa." He stepped forward toward the two priests and a sacrificial guard.

Ballec, just beyond, turned to face Azre, his eyes wide with surprise. "I am the Holy Father."

The guard stood wobbling at the chasm's edge between the two priests. The man was completely engulfed in a state of grogginess, unaware of the situation — a silly grin on his lips, barely opened eyes gazed at the open space before him.

"Behold my power!" Ballec grabbed the guard's arm and yanked him forward, casting him over the edge, and into the flames below.

Azre leaped forward. The priests, surprised by his action, immediately stepped back. They wore no armor or weapons.

Behind Azre, Jewyl and Chardo also moved forward to help in the attack.

Jewyl forced her way forward, slashing and cutting with her sword. Suddenly she realized she was on the tongue of the sacrifice altar and the fires of Yendisa flared upward to lick the stone pedestal where she was. Time held as she stared into the abyss, seeing a swirling morass of flames with a dark center. A priest charged. She moved. The priest continued into the chasm, flailing as he fell. The black center turned into lips of a mouth and swallowed the priest. A face emerged from the flames and moved upwards. The beauty of the face encased in a dragon skull helmet mesmerized Jewyl.

Yendisa, Jewyl thought and moved away from the edge and around the guard who was nearest her.

The flaming goddess continued to gain in size, consuming the air above them. Her dragon head skull helmet couldn't contain the hate in the eyes of Yendisa as her image wavered in the heat of the fiery furnace below. The goddess snarled, her beauty wavered.

"The Sword of Shiyula is hidden for all time," Yendisa howled. "You will never find it."

Unaware of Jewyl's movement, the priest's eyes widened as Jewyl stepped menacingly closer toward him. He moved back, his foot balancing on the edge. He lost his balance. Jewyl reached to grab his hand, but was too late. The man turned to face the flames of his new-found goddess. A hand of flame reached up from the furnace, grabbing the falling offering and shoved him into the gaping mouth of emergingYendisa.

Jewyl stood there, legs apart, waiting when she felt the presence of Ballec. He moved toward her, sword at the ready. Jewyl could feel his aura even though she still had her back to him. The essence of Yendisa before her now oozed from the man. Jewyl knew the goddess' dark eyes watched them from beneath the dragon's skull.

Jewyl raised her left hand, waiting. Behind, she could hear Ballec's boots as he moved closer and closer. Jewyl lifted her index finger, waiting. She could almost feel his breath on her neck. Jewyl pivoted, turning in a flash while lifting her sword to a swinging attack.

Ballec was caught off guard, his sword still at the ready, but not up to protect or deflect the blow.

Jewyl's sword cut the air, grazing his white leather shoulder pad on its path to the neck.

Ballec smiled at her, waiting for the end. Jewyl held the blade against the pale flesh of his neck. She gazed at the flames of the chasm and the wavering image of Yendisa above them.

"Do you wish to offer yourself to your goddess?" She nodded to the flames.

"Hold." Lord Azre's voice echoed through the chamber.

###

The priests of Yendisa turned to flee. Chardo lurched to follow, but Jopab already had the exit secured. None would leave.

Lord Azre stood firm, the fires of Yendisa glistening on the polished leather.

"You are the Holy Father because I gave you the position." Azre paced toward his brother. "You never earned it."

Ballec stood his ground, a snide grin curling one side of his lips. He shrugged.

"Tonight I have seen with my own eyes the corruption you have wrought." Azre turned to look at the remaining people in the grotto and the hovering image of Yendisa.

All of Ballec's priests huddled together. Jopab, Percho and Azre's personal guard now stood at the entrance, blocking it.

"I owe you nothing," Ballec said. "I am the Holy Father. All bow to me." He inhaled deeply, pulling himself to full height.

"You are correct, brother." Azre lifted the sword above his head. "You owe me nothing. I owe you nothing." The sword came swinging down in an arc.

The cut was clean. Ballec's head poised for a moment before tumbling to one side and falling into the fiery chasm. Ballec's body convulsed then crumbled, leaning toward the waiting fiery gap. It tumbled and fell into the chasm. Flames leaped high. Yendisa reached out to snag the offering.

"Lord Azre!" Jewyl called. "Your brother?"

"Let us attend to what remain of my guards." Azre sheathed his sword. "We shall all go back to the main hall." He gazed at the remaining priests of Yendisa. "They shall remain here with their goddess. The entrance will be sealed." He glanced at the flames of the chasm. "If they so desire, they may offer themselves to their goddess." He sighed and pointed at the flaming chasm. "Otherwise, they will die of starvation. I will not have their diseased minds in the temple of Hagontha." He gazed at the chasm of fire. "The flames cannot be quenched or dampened. Let them burn for eternity, unseen by human eyes." He paused and heaved another sigh as he gazed at the hovering image of the goddess. "Let Yendisa die within them. She is no more."

"I am the Void," Yendisa howled. "I am forever. I cannot die. I am Yendisa. I was before you. I shall be after you."

"You are nothing," a voice called from above as the ghostly image slowly descended into the open area above. "I am Hagontha. Chaos reigns. Be gone, you foulness of evil." A spectral hand grabbed Yendisa's dragon skull helmet, pulling it away. The beauty Jewyl had seen within the helmet now wrinkled with putrescence.

Yendisa screeched and dropped toward the churning flames of turmoil within the chasm.

"Leave the room, now," Hagontha commanded. "It shall be no more."

Above, the myriad arches creating the secret chamber darkened and crumbled as the flames faded in the crumbling dust. Two priests ran to the edge, paused, and finally leapt to their deaths.

"Hurry," Jopab said and hustled the group out the entrance, blocking it against the remaining Yendisan priests.

Jopab stepped through the doorway and Chardo closed the heavy door and placed a beam to hold it shut against anyone pushing on it from the other side.

Only the slightest sounds of the crumbling pillars and falling stones could be heard.

"Let us clean the temple of those who followed Ballec," Azre said and led the group up the winding stairs. "We will also seal the door above so none may use it."

CHAPTER TWENTY-FIVE
The Holy Father

Lord Azre sat on the throne-like chair in the main hall. All the priests of Hagontha's Temple stood in attendance. Azre stood.

"Tonight, my brother, Ballec, the Holy Father, was consumed by the flames of Yendisa in a sacrifice to her." He strolled across the room. "There were several priests who covertly praised Mother Yendisa." Azre stopped. "If any are among you, you have two choices. One, to come forward now, or two, be forcibly taken from your ranks when discovered. I shall count to ten. To run will be your death."

Azre stared at the gathered men. He took a deep breath and then began to slowly count.

Three priests moved forward, their heads bowed, ashamed.

Azre gazed at the men before him. "I count only three. There are no others? "

"Pardon, Lord Azre." A priest moved forward. "Huglo and Renz have taken their lives. They were the ones to put Sleeper's Dream into your food, helped the Holy... your brother, Ballec, perform the sacrificial ritual. They imbibed the remainder of Sleeper's Dream."

Azre nodded his head. "If that is true, then you three will be placed under arrest and jailed as traitors. You are stripped of all priestly duties and no longer to live within the chaos of Mother Hagontha. You will be jailed in Dianiya until your last day."

Jopab stepped forward. "My lord, if I may?"

Azre nodded acceptance.

"These men were misled by Ballec. Also, at the temple in Bashiwa, there are those who served your brother in the ways of Mother Yendisa. At the other temples we may discover more. May I ask humbly for your forgiveness of them. I agree, allow these men to be stripped of their priestly duties, but instead of being imprisoned, may I suggest they become servants and confined within the prison's

218

chambers. The same treatment for those at Bashiwa, and elsewhere."

Azre moved to the throne and sat. He tugged at his beard as he thought.

"I will allow the new Holy Father to decide their fates." He gazed at Jopab. "Do you feel that to be fair?"

"Most fair, my lord," Jopab said. "Do you wish the priests to decide on the new Holy Father, or will you deign who you feel to be a proper choice?"

Lord Azre smiled. "I will not assign a Holy Father." He hesitated. "I will suggest a candidate who I feel will serve Mother Hagontha. It will be a final decision by the priests."

Jopab nodded and stepped back.

"Do not shrink back so easily, Jopab." Azre lifted his hand and indicated Jopab should come forward. "I feel my choice should be one who knows me. Also, it should be a priest who is strong in his faith to Mother Hagontha, and be understanding of her chaos. I hereby suggest to the gathered priests of Zornal the priest I know as Jopab to be the next Holy Father."

"A decision well made, Lord Azre." The voice was old and weathered. "As a Holy Father, I highly recommend Jopab to be the new Holy Father."

"Who speaks?" Azre searched the area where the voice emanated.

"Lord Azre," the old man said and bowed. "I am Harsborz, Holy Father before you assigned your brother Ballec." Harsborz turned to face Jopab. "If any man is true to his faith, it is Jopab. When he learned of the blasphemy by Ballec regarding Yendisa, he went in search of a solution."

"Do you wish to be Holy Father again?" Azre leaned forward.

"I was Holy Father. I will remain a Holy Father until my demise. Today, I see Jopab as the new Holy Father." He turned to the collected priests. "Is there any who contest Lord Azre's suggestion?" He paused. "Speak now."

A murmur spread through the group of priests. Finally Percho stepped forward.

"Lord Azre, we accept your suggestion. Jopab will be installed as the new Holy Father."

Azre gazed down at the humbled man. "Congratulations,

Jopab. You will indeed make a very good Holy Father. As you have taught me, even in the chaos, there is a plan. Mother Hagontha now reveals this to me."

"I thank you, my lord." Jopab once more stepped back into the shadows.

"The priests are now dismissed." Azre waved his hand.

Jewyl stood beside Chardo, before her sat Lord Azre, once again, staring at her.

"What shall I do with you, Jewyl?" Azre shook his head. "I offer you marriage, and you deny me the pleasure." He glanced at her companion. "And Chardo. You can't dance and look terrible in a dress."

Chardo shrugged.

Azre placed his elbow on the chair's arm and rested his chin in the palm of his hand.

"You saved my life today." Azre shrugged. "That cannot be dismissed, or forgotten."

"You killed your brother," Jewyl stated. "Is there no remorse?"

"I executed Ballec," Azre said. "He was my brother, true, but he was also a person of treason. The law is not above any."

Chardo leaned over. "Don't get him mad. Remember the last time?"

"But, Ballec was your brother." Jewyl wasn't about to quit.

"Yes, he was my brother. He was the bastard son of my father with a servant." Azre slammed back into the chair. "He was never full royal blood. He was a half-brother, at best."

Jewyl folded her arms before her. "Half-brother. Royal blood. All of it is nonsense. He was your brother."

"No, he wasn't my brother," Azre snarled. "He never acknowledged me as a brother until this very day. Did you not hear his voice? He mocked our relationship."

Jewyl eased back. "My apologies."

"No, you don't understand. He never accepted his position. At my coronation, after the death of our father, he had the nerve to call my mother a 'princess whore' tricking our father." Azre stood. "It

220

was his last chance. Our father had promised him the position of Holy Father, I gave it to him, and wanted nothing more to do with him." He paused. "And, so it was until you escaped."

"So are you going to put us in prison?" Jewyl watched him, waiting.

Azre stepped toward them, directly in front of Jewyl.

"No, Jewyl. I am not placing you under arrest." He glanced at Chardo. "Nor you." He strutted to his personal guard who held weapons. "I return your swords and daggers. You won't have to dance for them, Chardo."

"You feel safe to allow me a sword?" Jewyl played the sword before her.

"If you wish to kill me, so be it. I give you both your freedom. Even though I know you to be The Emerald, I cannot bring myself to arrest you. Today, you both showed me loyalty in defending my life. I know Jopab did most of the covert work, but he was only making sure his plans were coming to fruition. Ballec had to be stopped." Azre took a deep breath. "You are free."

Jewyl sheathed her sword. "I thank you, Lord Azre, but you are still a descendant of a traitor to my grandfather. I could never marry you." She smiled. "But when the time comes and I decide to take a husband, I might consider a traitor."

"With you by my side as my wife, Jewyl, we could reunite the three lands and bring your Shiyula into existence." He leaned forward and kissed her on the cheek.

Jewyl stepped back, but didn't wipe the kiss away.

"You're blushing, m'dear." Chardo eased her away, heading out of the temple where the world, a broken Shiyula, and a hidden sword awaited.

<<<< THE END >>>>

This page left blank

About the Author

My name is Robert S. Nailor but most people call me Bob.

I'm retired from the federal government. I was a computer geek and still do some programming yet today. One would think I should have plenty of time to write but I actually seem to have less now. So, to make sure that things work out correctly, I force myself to sit down and write. That doesn't always work. Today, writing is fun and I find it relaxing. I get to visit those fantastic and strange places within my mind and well, if I don't come back right away, there is no longer somebody behind me writing on a pink sheet of paper.

I live with my wife, Violet, in a ranch home snuggled into a small wooded acre in NW Ohio. I was born in Sioux City, Iowa but my parents moved to Ohio in 1953. I have four sons and currently have ten grandchildren - 7 granddaughters and 3 grandsons. Plus, I have great-grandchildren – 2 great-granddaughters and 3 great-grandsons.

My interests are camping (have RV, will travel), gardening, music, cooking and reading. So where do I travel? I've been in 46 of the 50 states and strangely, Hawaii is one of the states I've visited. I have also visited two of our territories - Puerto Rico and the Virgin Islands. Traveling allows me to add the ambiance to my stories and to some of the characters, also. Gardening is a bit gamey since we live in the country and have the wildlife visiting us constantly — deer, rabbits, raccoons, birds, squirrels and many others. So vegetables don't always make it to harvest but what does is more than tasty. There are flowers, sometimes too many, to keep me busy. Music? I love New Age music and my favorite group is Mannheim Steamroller... and not just because of their fabulous Christmas albums; I was hooked on them before that. I also have created some of my own electronic music which I've been told is pretty good. Should I mention cooking? I love to cook and do gourmet cooking. Having worked with Boy Scouts for several years, I have taught many boys the basics of cooking beyond hotdogs and beans. I have won quite a few contests. As to what I read; well, obviously a lot of science fiction, fantasy and some Christian. Horror, romance, adventure and other genres are also great reads when they catch my attention with an intriguing tag line or cover.

Bibliography

Novels:

The Secret Voice ~ Book 1 in the Amish Singer series
The New York Voice ~ Book 2 in the Amish Singer series
At Death's Door ~ a collection of "light" horror stories about death
Eternal Blood ~ a Barry Hargrove detective mystery
Pangaea, Eden Lost ~ a Barclay Havens, relic hunter misadventure
Three Steps: The Journeys of Ayrold ~ a Celtic fantasy for today
2012 Timeline Apocalypse ~ the Mayan calendar comes to an end

Coming Soon...

The Amish Voice ~ Book 3 in the Amish Singer series
The Vietnam Quilt ~ war and peace, Englische and Amish, in love
The Englische Heart ~ does Love really conquer all, learning Amish?
Circle of Stone ~ when more than one Stonehenge isn't enough
I'htha ~ a Native American vampire/werewolf tale
The Pearl ~ Book 2 of the Shiyula series

Anthologies:

52 Weeks of Writing Tips ~ tips to improve one's writing ability
Cracked: The Writing Mystique ~ writing secrets de-mystified
Telling Tales of Terror ~ essays on how to write horror and dark fiction
Mother Goose Is Dead ~ a collection of favorite fairy tales, fractured
Dead Set: A Zombie Anthology ~ a collection of unusual zombie tales
The Complete Guide to Writing Paranormal-Vol 1 ~ various essays
Nights of Blood 2 ~ different takes on the vampire theme
Guide to Writing Science Fiction ~ essays on writing science fiction
Firestorm of Dragons ~ an eclectic collection of dragon stories
Fantasy Writer's Companion ~ essays on writing fantasy
13 Night of Blood ~ 13 amazing vampire tales
Spirits of Blue & Gray ~ a collection of Civil War ghost stories

PLUS more at www.bobnailor.com

www.ingramcontent.com/pod-product-compliance
Lightning Source LLC
Chambersburg PA
CBHW071151260626
47162CB00003B/1008